Phaedra,
One voice can change the world!

Breaking Eselda

A Kingdom of Fraun Novel

Tabatha Shipley

ISBN: 978-1-4834-8329-0 (sc)
ISBN: 978-1-4834-8331-3 (hc)
ISBN: 978-1-4834-8330-6 (e)

Library of Congress Control Number: 2018903711

Lulu Publishing Services rev. date: 04/09/2018

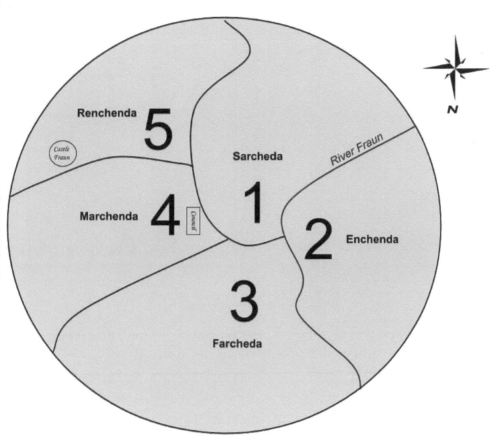

The Kingdom of Fraun

Chapter

1

"BUT MEN DO NOT LIVE forever." My voice echoes off the stone walls and back to me, lifeless and flat. That's wrong. I missed a word again. The school visit is tomorrow. I must be ready today. One would assume, after annuals of delivering this speech, that I would have it down. But no, I keep messing up the lines.

I close my eyes and tip my head back to the ceiling. I can feel my hair swishing along the back of my dress. Hair is such a status symbol in Fraun. I was so worried that my hair would be thin, making me look like a peasant. The thick ropes with their reddish hue leave no doubt I am royalty. I can do this.

I return to the practiced stance and adopt my best speech voice. "But men, even great men, do not live forever. Oberian died, passing the rule of Fraun to his son." I stomp my foot. "Damn it. I missed another one." The angry words echo off the chamber back to me. Not very regal sounding, Princess. Deep breath. Try again.

"But men, even great men, do not live forever. Oberian died, passing the rule of Fraun to his only son." There. The one extra word my father and his council cannot live without. Apparently, this single word explains we're discussing the king who only had one son instead of the guy with many.

"Good morning, Princess."

I recognize the voice but startle at the arrival. I did not hear Tutor walking the hallways. I spin to find my ears have not deceived me. Tutor has arrived. I can only smile at the classic I-don't-care-about-my-appearance look my personal tutor has thrown together. My heart softens as his smile dances across his lips and then his brown eyes, hiding behind the lenses he has manufactured to improve his vision. "Tutor, I'm glad you are here. I'm having difficulty with the speech. I'm sure I'm overthinking it. Can we practice?"

"Actually, Princess, we have something we should discuss. You are approaching an age where you will no longer be in need of my services." He shifts on his feet and wrings his hands.

"You're nervous. Why are you nervous?" The question halts his shifting, telling me I'm on the right track. "We have been at this training for many annuals knowing that I am one day to take the throne of Enchenda. What more could we possibly have to discuss?"

"I was speaking with the king this morning and new information has reached me. There are things we have not yet discussed about mannerisms and royal blood. I thought--" He shakes his head. "It doesn't matter what I thought. The point is we have much to cover."

"Am I unprepared to serve the second realm?" I feel a fluttering in my chest. I change my mind, deciding I don't want to hear his answer.

"I fear you may be unprepared for the men you serve Fraun with," he answers.

What does that mean? "Tutor, you're being strange. Explain yourself."

"Let's just begin the training for the day, please."

I fold my legs under me as I flop to the cold, stone floor. Maybe if I play along, he'll give me more information.

"Let's review your basics. A queen must know the basics better than she knows her own name. Name the five virtues in order of the realms they represent," Tutor prompts.

I sit up straight. First would be Sarcheda. "Strength." Then us. "Humility." Third would be Farcheda. "Speed." Fourth is Marchenda.

"Mirth." Fifth is Renchenda. What is Renchenda known for? Oh no. I can't remember. If only I were a little smarter.

Oh. "Wisdom."

"You hesitate. A queen cannot hesitate. If you are being introduced to some underling from the third realm, you must instantly know to compliment his speed and not his humility." Tutor leans down toward me. "You must focus. The council is going to be waiting for you to err, Eselda. Do not give them that."

"You make the council sound positively wicked."

Tutor throws his hands up. "Eselda, I cannot think of another way to explain it to you. The men on the council will not be trusting of you because of your age alone. You will have to be flawless."

"I have time. Has something changed?" I try to match his frustrated pitch. I hate when he gets cross with me and treats me like a child. I contemplate teasing him again about his name--what did his parents expect him to do with his life after giving him a name like that?--but decide I'll see where this goes instead. He is obviously sitting on something important.

"That is not my place to discuss with you." He sighs. "Let's just focus on getting this all right, please. Name the leaders of the realms in ascending order."

"King Tin of Sarcheda, King Gregario of Enchenda, King Mick of Farcheda, King Larecio of Marchenda, and King Jordyn of Renchenda."

Tutor drops to the floor in front of me, adopting my cross-legged stance. "That was better. Now think, Eselda. Tell me what you know of the ages of these kings."

Ages? What an odd question. "I don't know much. I know Tin and Jordyn are young, closer to my age than my father's. The others are older. I'm not sure how many have grayed."

"Two of the three. King Mick's hair remains dark," Tutor says.

"Why are we speaking of age?"

"You are royal blood. If you knew the full ramifications of that we would speak of nothing else."

I rise, glaring down at him. "Tell me."

"I had hoped your father would tell you before you came of age."

"I have already passed fifteen annuals, Tutor. If he was going to tell me before that, he has missed his timing. I suggest you spit it out." I stretch myself tall, showing off the two marks I reach on the medicine tent display, and fix him with what I can hope is a stern look. I'm trying to remind him that I am a princess in this house and it would be unwise to defy me. In truth, he runs these tutoring sessions, but I hope he won't remember that right now.

"Tell me the age markers that affect all in Fraun."

"At five a person is capable of full speech." I know all these markers; I would usually balk at having to deliver them. Today, I can tell Tutor is building to something, leading me to an understanding. I will not argue today. "At ten, they are full height and fully mature. At fifteen the hair becomes silken and soft but ceases to grow. Citizens are considered adults once this stage has passed. Finally, at forty, the hair will whiten or gray and the citizen will die."

"There are age markers the council keeps silent," Tutor whispers. "Markers that only affect those born of the royal blood." Tutor's voice is low and light like summer breeze blowing through the room. I sit back down opposite him; I don't want to miss a word of this.

"At twenty annuals, citizens with the blood of Oberian in their veins will become dark and malicious. They will want power above all else and will stop at nothing to get it. This age marker will bring out the worst in the royal."

I recoil from the words, sliding back a little on the floor. "How have I never heard this before? Is it exactly twenty annuals? Tutor, I haven't been tracking how long it's been since I passed the fifteenth."

"I haven't either, but it's been at least three annuals, Princess. I was hoping he would tell you."

"This will happen to me? We are sure of it?" Fear begins to build in my belly, hot and strong.

"It will. There is more. Should I go on?"

"Well, yes. Get it all out there now. No point in delaying again."

"At twenty-five annuals, a citizen with the blood of Oberian will replace that longing for power with one for flesh. They will be consumed

4

by their desire to procreate and satiate their lust." A blush rises in Tutor's cheeks. "This age marker helps to ensure the bloodline continues."

"Are you kidding me?" I stand up from the floor and begin pacing. "When do these fantastic little bombs you've brought me end?"

"I'm told they each last five annuals."

"Let me summarize here. In less than two annuals, I will become mad with power. That will last five annuals and end only when I suddenly begin lusting after any warm-bodied man. That will also last five annuals. I shudder to think how many men I will chase in that time. If my math is correct, that leaves me with ten annuals to be a level-headed ruler of Enchenda before my hair grays and I die. Sound about right?" I hit him with a cold stare.

He sits silently on the floor, watching me. He continues to look like a smart child with a book, studious. It angers me further. I wish he would show an emotion. "With all of this affecting everyone who has ever ruled the people of Fraun continue to believe that those of us with royal blood are better rulers. Would you care to explain that to me? It seems as though Fraun would be better off with someone who isn't affected in this way," I point out.

"Royal blood has served us for over a century, Princess."

"Yet it has also been making rulers crazy for over a century, apparently."

"It is your cross to bear, Eselda, not mine." He removes his glasses and rubs the bridge of his nose. "It is my job to prepare you to bear it. I understand the shock of this knowledge and I had anticipated your anger. You must learn to control that before you are twenty annuals. You cannot sit on the council and let that anger out. It is what they will fear the most."

"But they all went through it. They all experienced it."

"Experience," he corrects.

"What?" I stop pacing and look back down at Tutor.

He sighs. "Kings Jordyn and Tin are both inside the malicious age marker."

"Two of the five rulers at the table are driven by a desire for power? How is that best for Fraun?"

"I have never sat at that table nor been invited to that room, Eselda. All I can tell you is that it would be in your best interest to not show them anger and remind them how close you come to being a third."

I draw a deep breath. "Now I'm scared," I admit. Tutor is one of my oldest friends in the world, always at my side to help me learn. I see him daily. He is the person I can confide in. Suddenly I'm glad he was the one to tell me about the age markers. I drop back to the floor and take his hands. "Honestly I haven't been counting the annuals since my hair turned. Are you sure it's been at least three? How long do I have?"

"You father may know better than me but I think this will be the third school visit you've conducted since it turned. I kept hoping that he would tell you when you met about the visits. Twice I've been disappointed but not had the gumption to tell you myself."

"I appreciate that you told me today. I can't believe this secret was kept from me for so long."

"I should let you think on this. You're prepared for the visit tomorrow; your practice was well done. I'm going to let you have the rest of the day and I will see you tomorrow." Tutor stands. "Eselda, you handled the knowledge well. I'm proud of you."

The complement swells in my chest like a balloon. It doesn't completely lift my spirits out of the fear they've rooted themselves, but it helps. I nod.

When he leaves and I'm alone the fear overwhelms me. Craving power above all else? What will that feel like? I'm the person who will turn from something bad or dangerous, I'm a coward. This leaves me with a whole new problem. After all, I can't run from my own blood.

I will have to face this, one way or another.

Chapter

2

"PRINCESS ESELDA?"

The voice floats through the oaken door that blocks me from the rest of my house. My ancestors built this house to be a good quality, but the door doesn't quite fit into the frame. It leaves little gaps so the sound travels right to my sleeping ear. "Yes?" I bellow.

"The school visit is today. The king would like to speak with you before you depart."

Squeaky voice, slow speed. This is a common roach. "Thank you, Eee." I wait for the sound of the scurrying feet on the brick floor before throwing off the warm blankets and rising. My first stop is the reflection wall. I'm not a person who spends time standing at this wall. I'm a representative of the house of humility in Fraun, how would that look?

But today I want to see if any obvious physical signs of the fear brewing under my skin are present. Can you tell I'm afraid of what will happen to me in a few annuals? My green eyes look the same, my pale face looks the same. There are no new wrinkles or taught stretches of skin. There is no new fear anywhere on the outside.

I cross the room again, this time headed to the cabinet holding my clothing. I pull the heavy wooden door open and begin running my fingers along each garment. The clothes are all tailored to fit me, repurposed from the clothing left behind by the giants. There are so many fabrics and colors here, I don't know how to choose today.

I linger a little longer on a purple silken dress. "This will do," I say to the empty room. "After all, I'm spending the day with school children."

My feet move quickly through the empty hallways. The entrance hall with its tall ceilings is bustling today with roaches and the footmen preparing to take me to the school visit. "I need only a single roach, no carriage. That formality is not befitting of the house's humble image," I call the order as I continue my fast pace to the room.

Turning left I enter my favorite room, the dining room. Across the room from me a fire burns, warming the air and sending off a pleasant smell. Seated at the head of the table in the center of the room is the king of Enchenda, looking completely annoyed that I have arrived after him. "Good Morning father," I greet him. I bend down and kiss his forehead through the lock of white hair that is perpetually falling there.

"You are late."

I restrain the sigh that wants to escape. "Yes, sir. My apologies. I forgot this was the morning of the school visit."

"The school visit is one of the single most important acts of a princess."

I start eating my bowl of berries and grains. This speech could take a while, I have time.

"Our people should know of the greatness of our ancestry. The five brothers created Fraun, but each gave something different to our realms. The children of Enchenda cannot hope to live up to our ideals if the princess does not speak the ideals to them," his booming voice commands authority. It is impressive.

However, I could give this speech myself after the number of times I have heard it. I can feel my frustration brewing, just under my skin. This speech you repeat but you never thought to sneak in a tidbit about my blood?

"It's bad enough," father continues, "we have such a young council. Your generation has not married and given birth to many. What will become of Fraun when there are no princes or princesses to speak this truth? I fear for our future."

I turn my head enough to hide the rolling of my eyes behind the ropes of my hair. My father and his council bring up two things more than anything else. My age, which makes sense now that I am fully informed, and my lack of children. I have had all my reproductive parts since I was ten, like everyone else around here. I have been considered an adult since I was fifteen. Why do I not have a spouse or children?

Actually, their problem goes deeper than that. Two of the five rulers, Jordyn and Tin, also have no spouses or heirs. Another two, my father and Larecio, each have only a single heir and have lost their spouse. That leaves one realm, Farcheda, who they believe is fully prepared to continue to serve Fraun in the future. Farcheda is run by both a king and a queen, they have children, and some of their children are even married with children of their own. The council of people I rarely see wishes me to be more like this realm and less like theirs.

"If some disaster strikes Tin or Jordyn, what will become of Fraun?" Father asks.

"What would be the disaster if someone not of the brother's blood were running a realm?" The look of frustration and disdain that crosses the king's eyes makes me wish I had the sense to refrain from asking the question. My hand freezes midway to my mouth from the bowl.

"The brothers personified important ideals that the people of Fraun need to emulate. It is only when all five ideals are balanced that we are our strongest as a people. The royal blood of the brother's flows in your veins. Do you not feel the power of that blood within you?"

My anger brews. I drop the spoon back into the bowl where it splats against the berries. "The power of the blood? You mean the blood that will make me a vehicle for violence in less than five annuals?" The sentence is out before I remember that, despite this comfortable setting, I am speaking to my king in that tone of voice. My hand slaps over my own mouth too late to stop the anger that shows in his narrowed eyes.

There's only one way I fix this. I throw my shoulders back, toss my hair over my shoulder, and plaster the royal smile on my face. "On second thought, I know what you mean. Our blood is our lineage and our lineage has served Fraun well. I am the product of the brothers who brought Fraun to greatness."

Father's angry eyes never leave my face, but he reaches for his spoon and begins eating. I follow his lead but I know this isn't over. He is not happy.

Chapter

3

I N THE CENTER OF EACH realm, a small area is designated for the education of the young. Children attend the facility from five annuals until fifteen annuals. They learn all about Fraun. They are taught basic rules of speaking; a few exceptional ones are taught to write. They are taught numbers and gardening. Each is taught the ideal of their realm. Once an annual the children are visited by the royal family of their realm to hear the history of Fraun and have their questions answered.

The realm of Enchenda is bordered on all sides by the River Fraun, which curves around and disappears into the thick forest marking the end of Fraun territory. Enchenda houses hundreds of families, all living in homes made of materials the giants of legend abandoned. Enchenda, like all other realms of Fraun, makes no materials of their own save food.

As I disembark from the roach who has carried me to the school, whispers spread through the assembled crowd of children. There are many of them today. The teacher, who rushes over to shake my hand and welcome me to the school, is taller than I remember and stands probably two clicks above my head. I straighten my posture. Height is a big deal to us here. The older children, the ones who have heard this speech before, are seated to the back of the crowd. Younger children, eager to hear what I have to say, are in the front. Some smile, others stare with reverence. Either way, I'm known here.

"Good morning, children," I greet as I take my place on the log at the front of the clearing.

"Good morning Princess Eselda." The line has been rehearsed. It was said as one. Equally as rehearsed, the students flop to seated positions on the floor silently. The teacher, beaming with pride, settles herself in a standing position behind me.

I take a deep breath, settle my hands in my lap, and launch into my speech. "The world we inhabit now was once a land of Giants. The giants built massive cities of all materials they could find. No material was sacred. No land was spared. The Giants created much and used more than they needed. Even their production levels, legendary as they were, could not provide enough for their endless needs.

"During the time of the giants, our people lived quiet lives. Hidden among the houses of the giants, repurposing items the giants forgot, our people survived. It was a lonely existence, never knowing if others lived on. All that changed with the war.

"The giants declared war on each other. For years blasts and fighting were the sounds that filled the world. Our people stayed holed up in the homes, hidden from the battle we didn't understand. Then came the explosions, which rocked those homes. When the silence began, we waited. After a time, our scouts went out to find the giants all dead or gone." A quick check of the faces in the crowd shows me I have their attention. "One man, Oberian, began to organize our people."

Some of the younger children in front begin excitedly twisting and whispering. "That's Fraun," the whisper floats to my ear. I can appreciate the innocent interruption, a child too excited to realize they know this story. The teacher does not share my appreciation; she slams her finger to her lips in a shushing gesture.

"Bonded together by our mutual fear of an outcome similar to the giants we organized cities from the ruins of the giant villages. Fraun became our name, and Oberian our king. Oberian proved himself a good man and an honest ruler. He established many laws to keep us safe. We learned to use only what we needed and waste not, to rectify the wrongs of the giants who had died for this error. Under the rule of Oberian, Fraun became strong.

"But men, even great men, do not live forever. Oberian died, passing the rule of Fraun to his only son. Oberian the Second believed it was his right, and our duty, to amass his own wealth and power. The people of Fraun were commissioned to build a palace for their king, which stands in Fraun to this day. The king took three wives in his time, having five boys born to him before his death. He was a greedy man, but he was not all bad.

"In the wake of the giants we were not the only race who rose up. During the time of Second, we learned of large bugs who had survived and created the society of Roach. Second ordered scouts to travel to Roach and speak with them. No treaty could be reached. Instead, Second ordered a war. Frightened of this word, our people hesitated. Second was an insistent man, and war ensued.

"Our people were triumphant, and the inhabitants of Roach became a part of Fraun. Many of them took jobs as servants in exchange for food and homes. Their people are small to the ground, many-legged, and fast. They are excellent warriors and they mind not being ridden into battle. Earning their partnership was the legacy of Second.

"After the death of this king, the sons wanted to avoid a fight over the throne. They requested two sun paths of bereavement for their father as they devised a plan for his replacement. At the end of that time, the brothers had agreed upon a plan to divide power. Absolute power, they claimed, was dangerous to Fraun. Their father had abused that power to earn a castle, they did not want to fall to similar temptations.

"Their plan was five realms. Each realm would have a royal family to rule them. In the realm, your king would be the final word. The Five realms would be numbered. The royal family of the first realm would lead the council of rulers. The council would vote on all decisions affecting Fraun as a whole. No decision would be carried forth without a majority vote of the council.

"Over the next century, the numbering of the realms changed often with leaders. The council would choose to renumber in favor of a strong king, or to overthrow one corrupt or weak. Rule of a realm was passed through families, all descendants of the great brothers who named our realms. As Fraun grew in number and power we remembered our past.

"Today you have heard the tale like your parents heard before you. Someday we will tell the tale to your offspring as well, it is our legacy."

A few children clap even as one tiny hand shoots up from among the crowd. I point to the young child, who likely doesn't even reach the first mark on the measurement chart. She rises and squeaks out her question, "How were they numbered, Majesty?"

"Good question." I rise and approach the child, placing my right finger lightly on the girl's forehead. As the children watch with rapt attention, I trace a circle to the right repeatedly around the girl's face. "The realms are always numbered along this same circle. The first realm is chosen by the council and the rest fall into place." I know, even with my back turned as I return to the log, that the children will pull her excitedly back into their midst. When I seat myself again I see a few children tracing the same line along her face, like I have left something there for them to gather at their own fingertips.

My eyes travel the faces of the audience as I begin to speak again. "The realms were named after the five brothers. Let us name them." I know the children will name the realms in the order they now fall in, and I recite with them. "Sarcheda, Enchenda, Farcheda, Marchenda, and Renchenda."

My eyes fall upon an older student at the back. Yellow hair brushes near his eyes and his clothes look hand altered to fit him. He is handsome, he looks familiar, and yet I cannot place his face among the many in my memory. He is too old for schooling, I think. What is he doing here?

Without removing my eyes from the familiar stranger, I continue my rehearsed story. "The eldest brother being the oldest, had the first choice of realms. Not all the realms are equal in size or in power, my children. But the eldest brother did not choose the most powerful or the largest for himself. Does anyone know why he didn't want the first realm?"

Hands from the back shoot skyward. Of course, the older students have heard this tale. They have heard it repeated every annual since they began their education. I nod in acknowledgment and make a gesture that forces their hands to fall back to laps as I answer my own question. "He was scared."

The younger students gasp. Immediately a small boy raises his hand and waits to be acknowledged by his princess. "Princes no have afears," he says.

"I assure you, child, they fear just as you fear." I gesture for the child to sit before continuing. "The eldest prince feared *himself.* You see, when his father was alive a castle was erected. The prince loved the status the castle gave him. The prince recognized that his love of the castle was truly a love of power." Was that prince perhaps twenty annuals? Has this secret been before me my entire life, waiting for me to notice?

The handsome man catches my eye again. This time it's the tilt of his head that draws my attention. The man is nodding at my statement. Who is this man who believes I crave his support?

"The prince knew," I push on through the speech, "that if he accepted the power of the first realm, and with it the castle of Fraun, he would abuse it. Can anyone tell me where the eldest son chose to reside?" I choose a girl from the middle of the room.

"Enchenda." The girl drops quickly back down after speaking her answer.

"Very good maiden. Because the eldest son chose our kingdom, farthest from the castle, for the sake of the good of Fraun we are blessed to be humble. Our humility, as your teacher has doubtless taught you, allows us to guide the council to decisions which benefit all of Fraun."

A hand from the middle precedes another question. "Enchenda was always second realm?"

"Perhaps an older student will respond to that good question in my place." I smile at the back of the room.

The handsome boy speaks without rising. "Enchenda has been every number except fifth. For Enchenda to be fifth, Farcheda would need to be first. The youngest son, Farcheda, bestowed his speed upon his people. They are quick to do many things, including react. They are quick of temper. This quality bodes negatively for a position of power." The boy's voice is strong and captivating. It fills the clearing like sunlight, warming me in the same way.

Despite my frustration at his rudeness, I am impressed. "Correct good sir, but why rise you not for your princess?" I ask.

"My apologies, Majesty. My legs are injured." The man smiles.

"Fair enough. Thank you for your intelligent and thorough answer." His eyes stay fixed on my face as his mouth turns up in a smile. I feel my face flush and move my eyes quickly to focus on something else. "What further questions have my people?"

"Why you ride roaches?" a boy asks.

I grit my teeth to hide my impatience. "As I explained, inhabitants of the land once known as Roach became part of Fraun after the second war. They hold jobs here, including transportation. They have real names. In fact, the one who brought me here is called Zee. However, many citizens of Fraun call the species Roaches, after the town they once ran."

"What really happens at a council meeting?" The question is posed by a boy near the back of the crowd and I have to choke back the groan that begs to escape. This has long been a question I want to be answered.

Although a princess by rights, I am not ruling at this time. That means I am not allowed to attend the council meetings. Council meetings are for kings or queens alone. A princess would not be permitted attendance unless the king was absent for whatever reason. Exceptions are never made.

Still, I am familiar with the answer Tutor would expect me to give. "Council meetings are run by the king of the first realm. They are a place for the leaders of Fraun to discuss important issues and make decisions for the betterment of Fraun. At a council meeting strength, humility, speed, mirth, and wisdom are truly balanced."

A strange noise comes from the back of the room. I look around only to discover the handsome intelligent man with the face I cannot place is trying to wipe the small laugh from his face. "Excuse me, sir. Did you have a comment?" My face is burning; did he laugh at me?

"Pardon me, your Majesty. It was a cough." The excuse is feeble, as he chuckles amidst the words.

I choose to push on, although my building irritation is making it difficult. "See the medicine tent for that cough, good sir, and for your legs as well. Are there further questions?"

Another child is recognized and rises. "Why don't we make nice things here?" The question is rehearsed, likely fed to the child by a parent eager for answers.

I stand and sweep my hand delicately down the front of the long purple dress I selected. This morning I completed the outfit with a gray overskirt, wrapping it around my backside but not fully attaching it to the front. In this way, it protects the fabric of the dress when the I sit on this rough log. My feet are bare, but I wear a thin chain around my right ankle, a gift that had once belonged to my mother. I have tied the top of my hair up in a purple ribbon but left the curlier underlayer to flow down my back. "Do I not wear nice things?"

A few older children in the back snicker, laughing lightly at the corner I have backed the poor boy into. "You look nice, Princess," he answers, bowing. "But our homes have broken things. Why not we make more?"

"Enchenda follows the laws of Fraun young lad. We build not from a desire to show power, but from necessity. Why build anew when the giants left behind so many ruins we can use? We waste less time, energy, and resources this way." I return to my seat, and the small boy follows my lead and takes his as well. This time when I smile at him, the young boy returns the gesture.

I finish the question session without further incident, the school visit has gone well. I shake a few hands, mostly older students who will not be attending next annual. One such girl asks me to consider taking her on as a lady-in-waiting, which doesn't actually seem like a bad idea. It is during this exchange that I notice the man who laughed at me leaving on his own accord, on his apparently fine set of legs, his head towering over the other students as he makes his retreat.

Chapter

4

"**W**ELCOME HOME, PRINCESS," THE ROYAL attendee, my father's hire, greets me at the wall bordering my family's home. "How went the school visit?"

"Well, thank you." I let the man take the reins of Zee's harness and reach for the doorknob. Before I can even wrap my hand around the cold metal, the thin wooden door is whipped open.

"Child, we need a meeting," father barks. His expression is grim, his eyes dark.

"Is something amiss Majesty?"

"Nothing to worry you, just a thing or two to discuss. We shall meet in one hour. That leaves you enough time for eating and chores, I believe."

"It does, Majesty. Shall we meet in one hour in your study?"

"That is a plan."

Father turns on his heel and returns down the dim hallway he came from as I enter the house. Across the room my eye spies a lady-in-waiting. The servants in this house see and hear all. A plan forms in my brain. "I require some lunch, good lady. I do not like to dine alone. Would you care to join me?" The lady needn't look so surprised. The servants here spread rumors around like butter. If anyone would know of the agenda for the meeting with the king, I intend to find it.

"It would be my pleasure, Princess."

"Excellent." I clap with joy. "Follow me to the garden."

The garden of the royal family of Enchenda houses bushes marked with ripe berries, tomatoes the size of my body, and cabbage that have to be picked before they are full size. The cucumbers are so long; I notice it will take both of us to get it onto the table. I select a cucumber and the woman helps me hoist it up on the table in the center of the garden. The servant girl brandishes a sword and begins making cuts in the vegetable.

"I realize," I begin, "that I do not know your name." I cross the garden and start gathering leaves from a nearby tree. I bend up the fabric of my overskirt to make a basket to deposit them into.

"Linchanta is my name, Majesty."

"Well, Linchanta, you are cutting beautiful chunks of that cucumber. Would you be so kind as to chop a tomato next?"

"Yes, Majesty. Of course."

The woman is loosening up, responding to the simple tasks and reveling in the ability to complete them to my liking. I drop the leaves into a glass container and begin grinding them with a long stick. "I think, Linchanta, that we should have some tea with our lunch as well. What say you?" I am already adding water hot from the sun pitcher as I ask this.

"Majesty that is not necessary. Such a big meal for two people," Linchanta answers.

This answer is expected. The people of Enchenda have rather small appetites. This much food would fit to serve us both for quite some time. However, I notice that Linchanta doesn't hesitate in her chopping. It is possible the woman is hungrier than she plays at being.

"Well you and I shall eat our full," I declare, "then you can take the rest among the people of Enchenda while I meet with father." The line is delivered masterfully. I can tell by her smile that she is pleased by my answer.

I, on the other hand, am watching for signs that the woman knows of the meeting with the king. There. The eyes flashed quickly toward the house. The woman knows something.

I sweep the cucumbers, now chopped into tiny pieces, into a large pot and drop a tomato on the table. "I wish I knew what the king desires to speak with me about. He scares me," I whisper.

The servant's eyes steal a glance at my face. I have time to look suitably scared, it's not really an act. "The feeling is worse if I am unprepared," I admit.

"I may know something of his agenda, Princess." The voice is merely a whisper carried on the breeze.

I allow myself a smile before squealing with girlish glee. "Oh, you must tell me what you've heard."

Linchanta takes her time adding the tomatoes to the bowl. "I shouldn't, Majesty. I am sworn to silence."

"I understand." I smile. "Let us enjoy our lunch." I set glasses of fresh tea on the table and we eat in silence for a few minutes. How long do I have to pretend to let the matter rest before asking again? What is polite? "Please consider telling me, Linchanta. I won't speak of it to anyone." I place my right palm over my heart, a symbol of promise.

Linchanta leans conspiratorially toward me. "Repeat nothing." I notice the servant has dropped the formality of my title, this is a good sign. "I hear your father wishes to take your ideas before the council."

I could not have been more surprised if a magic fairy had risen from my tea and turned me into a giant. For a moment, my surprise is such that I forget the details of my plan. "He what?" I yell. "My father thinks my ideas are ludicrous daydreams. There is no way in Fraun that my father would care for my opinion in front of his council."

The servant jumps and immediately drops her eyes downward. "My apologies, Princess, perhaps I heard wrong," Linchanta says.

I feel horrid. The bad information doesn't warrant being yelled at by your princess. "I am sorry. My shock seems like anger, but it is with the news and not with you, maiden." I reach for the woman's hand but she moves it too quickly from the table, leaving me grasping at air. "Linchanta, would you be so kind as to distribute these leftover plates to the people?" I ask, rising.

"My pleasure, your Majesty, and your people thank you." The servant's formality has returned; her voice is controlled.

I feel a second of sadness, but only a second. For the good of my cause, I have learned the secret I came for. I will spend what is left of my allotted hour pacing the floors of my home and thinking.

I am familiar with father's opinion of me being over fifteen annuals and not yet engaged. Perhaps he wants to discuss betrothal. It certainly wouldn't be out of character for him to bang his fists on the table and demand I marry...who would he demand I marry? Well, someone, anyway. It is within his right to choose a mate for me.

Upon the second tumble through my nervous brain, I conclude he would never do that. Gregario prides himself on being humble, as do all from Enchenda. He will never pretend to know who is better for me than I do. If I cannot think of a suitable mate, surely he will not push one on me either.

That arrangement, of course, only works in my favor so long as my union is not a burden on the greater good. My father is many things, but selfish is not one of them. King Gregario serves Fraun above himself at all costs.

A knock at the door pulls me from my reverie. "Yes?"

"Princess, it is time for your audience with the king." Slow speech, soft clicking of feet.

"Thank you, Eee. I will be along presently." The walk to the study is torture. Each step brings with it a new worry about the topic of our conversation. We speak at breakfast, hardly any other time.

When the door opens my fears are not abated. On the contrary, they double. My father, recently gray hairs catching the firelight and reminding me of his age, is sitting straight-backed in the chair and has fixed his cold eyes on the door frame. He does not look happy to see me. I bow low. "Good afternoon, father."

"My daughter, I have something I must tell you. But first, how was the school visit?" He gestures to the seat opposite him, commanding me to sit with only the flick of his wrist.

The ease with which he orders this as well as the booming voice reminds me of the strange man from school. "It was well, father. There was, however, an odd person in attendance who didn't rise for me."

Father chuckles. "He was a child, my dear. Children can be trying, but don't let it vex you. His teacher will likely sort that out."

"I am not convinced he was a child, Majesty. He was probably three marks once he rose."

At this, the king startles. "Three marks is impressive indeed. What did he say when he spoke but didn't rise?"

"He merely answered the question asked by a younger child. But the answer was eloquent and informed."

"He was well spoken?"

"Indeed."

"Well dressed?"

"Certainly so, father."

Something in the king's expression clouds. His voice drops in sudden anger. "Talk no more of this man."

"But father--"

"No." He cuts me off with a wave of his regal hand. "We have more important issues to discuss. This man will be tabled for a later time. I have learned some news that affects your life, Princess."

"Good news, my king?" Hope sparkles in my chest, please let it be good news.

"I believe so, yes. It has become necessary for you to attend council meetings beginning in a fortnight's time." Father delivers this blow casually, not at all like one should deliver such news.

The excitement begins a slow simmer, the thought of finally seeing what happens in council meetings makes me giddy. To be seated with other kings, even for only a short time, is intoxicating. "I do not understand, Majesty. Why would I attend?"

"I have fallen ill. The medicine man confirms it. It is my age. I have not long left in this world, I am sure. Enchenda requires an educated queen."

As fast as it began, the excitement is gone. In its stead, there is only consuming sadness. I want to sit at the table, but not at the expense of my father. "Surely something can be done. You are the king. Who deserves miracles if not the king?"

Father's voice is low as he answers, an acknowledgment of the pain likely written on my face. "The lowliest of our people deserve miracles if it serves Fraun. Always remember that. I have you to follow me, miracles need not be wasted here. I must prepare you for the council, there is much you have yet to learn."

"Father, another time. I want to process this new situation."

His voice rises. "There is no more time. We talk now."

Despite my opinion, I nod at my king. I have always been taught to put my own feelings aside for the sake of my people. I will swallow this sadness.

"Things have been heating up between the first and third realms, Daughter. Mick, King of Farcheda, believes the last eight kings of Sarcheda to be corrupt."

"What reason has he?"

"They have been building much. It has been done quietly and always in the name of growth, but it makes the council nervous. Once or twice we can turn a blind eye. But when your realm nearly doubles in buildings, the council needs to ask questions. So claims Mick."

"Does this include King Tin?" I know little of Tin, King of Sarcheda. Tin is not much my senior, and he rules alone. He was crowned king of the first realm when his parents fell to their deaths down a ravine.

"Growth has continued during his reign, yes. Mick has taken these claims seriously, Daughter. He calls for a dramatic solution. Be prepared for all options to be presented in turn."

"I will think on this before council, father. You have my word." I start to push myself off the chair.

"One more thing, Eselda."

I'm not sure I can handle one more thing. Yet I know I cannot stop the king of my realm or my powerful father from explaining whatever he desires. I hesitantly nod my head.

"The council knows of my illness. That man today may have been sent to see how your education progresses. The council may well be nervous about your pending rule."

Tabatha Shipley

I swallow the rush of anger at hearing my father's precious council knew of his demise before his only daughter. It must have benefit Fraun if that is the decision he made. "Who could that man have been, that the council would see fit to send him?"

"That I do not know. Perhaps you should ask at your council meeting. That is all for today, Daughter. I must rest. You may go."

Outside the door, alone in the hallway, I try out the words. "I'm sitting on the council in a fortnight." I almost cannot contain the squeal of joy.

Chapter

5

Council of Kings of Fraun,

As you likely are aware my health begins to fail me. Forty annuals have come and gone, marked by the silver now atop my head. My only daughter, Eselda, will join me at our council meeting next, preparing herself to take the throne of Enchenda in my demise. Please welcome her as you would me.

Respectfully,
King Gregario
Enchenda

T HE PARCHMENT IS ROLLED BACK up and dropped onto the heavy wooden desk. In the dark room, under the light of the small fire, the smile that stretches eerily across the face of the young king is barely visible.

The elderly king is preparing for death; this is good news. I have been waiting for the tables to turn in my favor. The council is old, weak, and useless. I cannot hope to change Fraun if I first do not change the council. I need young blood at the table if I am to make the changes. Eselda is young herself if memory serves correctly. The young queen can be swayed to my side.

The king turns his attention to the young chambermaid cleaning in the corner. "I am a nice enough looking young man, am I not?"

The young maiden blushes fiercely but looks his direction anyway. Her eyes quickly return to her feet before she allows herself to answer. "Of course, Majesty."

The king crosses the room in two strides. He drops to a single knee in front of the chambermaid, who is scrubbing the floor on her own bruised knees. When the woman raises her eyes to him he holds her chin in his right hand to keep her eyes on his. "Look properly, maiden," he commands.

Intentionally he softens his tone to that of a potential lover, "What do you see in me?"

The blush on the young woman deepens but a coy smile touches her lips. "You are markedly handsome, Majesty. Any woman would be weak in the knees at your touch."

The king returns the smile and stands abruptly. "Thank you, that is what I hoped you would say."

Yes, if this chambermaid can be lead to believe in the touch of the king then Eselda can be just as easily swayed. After all, for a king in Fraun, anything is possible. Eselda can be brought to my side.

Fraun is about to change.

Chapter

6

I T IS DARK, NOT YET dawn. The house is full of the shadows of my greatest fears. Sounds carry an echo in every direction. I have woken early and seated myself on the study room floor. If I am to sit before the council Tutor has warned me about, I am going to need to face my fears. I close my eyes, take a deep breath, and extinguish the torch.

The room plunges into total darkness.

The darkness is briefly broken by the slice of light surrounding the door. Tutor slowly walks the outer edge of the room, using a candle to light the torches on the wall. He turns to face the center of the room and he throws himself backward at the sight of me sitting there, my lithe legs curled underneath me in the darkness.

I hold my hand up, stopping any words Tutor had been prepared to hurl. "Before you speak I have something to say. I have accepted my fate, as have my ancestors before me. I am strong and I believe I can rise above my instincts as I mature. If Fraun desires me to rule, then rule I shall. Speak no more of it, but prepare me to accept my birthright."

"Name the five virtues in order of the realms they embody," he prompts.

"Strength, humility, speed, mirth, and wisdom." I dare you to find something amiss with that, old friend.

"Name the rulers of the realms of Fraun."

"King Tin of Sarcheda, King Gregario of Enchenda, King Mick and Queen Salicia of Farcheda, King Larecio of Marchenda, and King Jordyn of Renchenda." I do not drop my chin or hesitate.

"Soon many of our kings may approach death. Tell me, Princess, what would become of each realm if the king were to expire?"

"I will answer as best I can, good sir, although the topic brings me personal sadness. The first realm would crumble, causing other realms to absorb the land because King Tin has no heir to speak of. Second realm command would fall to Princess Eselda. The third realm would fall to the reign of Prince Hector, the eldest prince. Queen Salicia, regal though she may be, has not a drop of royal blood. The fourth realm would be run by Prince Carsen. The fifth realm would fall the way of the first, to be absorbed for lack of an heir," I answer.

Realization drags its icy fingers down my spine. This is what the council fears. Two of their realms are but one tragic death away from being absorbed and leaving Fraun with only three realms to rule.

"Why was Fraun set to be run by five realms?" Tutor leads.

Because there were five sons. No, that can't be the answer he seeks. That would be too simple, something anyone could answer. Tutor seeks the solution of a queen. Tutor seeks the thinking of one who runs a realm. "Five council members means there will never be an issue that results in a tie. There are enough people to keep balance in the kingdom, but not enough to throw us into chaos. Five is the same as the fingers on your hand." I hold up my own hand for emphasis. "When they all work together they keep your hand balanced. With five realms there is always someone to hold the kingdom together."

I take my time closing my hand into a fist, one finger at a time. "With five realms, someone is always strong enough to protect Fraun even if the others are vulnerable." I close the fist by placing the thumb gently on the other fingers.

There are no words of encouragement from Tutor, merely a nod.

The round door to the room bursts open, shattering the approving quiet and catching us off guard. A small squat man holds out a scroll, his head bowed low to the floor. "Princess, excuse me, I bring a message from King Tin of Sarcheda," he says.

I snatch the scroll away, angry at being shocked after the careful display of my own readiness to rule. The man is gone, retreated out of my sight, before I can even begin to think of how best to chastise him for his interruption. Instead, I angrily slice the waxen seal of strength with my fingernail.

Dearest Princess Eselda,

News travels through Fraun faster than, perhaps, it should. I hear talk that you will join us at the council meeting in a fortnight. I should not be writing to you, as you're gracing us with your presence is a secret at this time. I trust two outcast young rulers, such as we, can keep that secret. My messenger can be trusted. Besides, he cannot read.

I look forward to seeing you again, it has been too long.

Faithfully Yours,
Tin

I read the short message quickly. The last time I saw Tin I had just turned ten annuals. Tin, recently fifteen annuals, visited Enchenda. Slightly taller than I, he is a gorgeous dark-haired boy. He was on a visit, his last before the accident befell his parents, to see what lies beyond the River Fraun. Never in his life, he explained, had he visited the realm across its border. I remember the boy well. The pull of my first crush tugs warmly at my center. I allow the fantasy to spread its sunshine across my chest briefly before forcing myself to remember the reality.

Tin is now a king. A king who has lost both parents and has been thrown to rule earlier than planned. A king accused of being harsh. A king I don't really know at all.

"Princess, should I continue to wait?"

I startle a little at the voice, having forgotten Tutor was in the room.

"No." I roll the scroll again and slip it beneath my green robe. "I can continue."

"What says King Tin?" Tutor inquires. Irritation and distrust are apparent in his tone.

"He merely wanted to express well wishes for the health of our king."

"I feared he may have been discussing council politics in an attempt to sway you."

"Fear not, sir." I hold my face in my most honest smile, hoping my lie is not showing through. This letter was merely an innocent letter between two young people, more like flirtation than outward disrespect of council protocol.

"Well. I am sure he breached trusts with good intentions. However, a breach must be dealt with milady. I shall report it to your Father, yes?"

"Allow me to deal with the matter myself, Tutor. Put a little trust in your future queen. I will speak with both Father and Tin when the timing is right." I sweep to the door, turning my head over my shoulder just before my exit. "I must away, good Tutor. I will see you tomorrow and we can continue this lesson then."

"Yes, Majesty. Thank you."

In the hallway, I pause to read the letter through once again. This time, when the flame of the crush ignites I don't have the desire to extinguish it.

Chapter

7

THE COUNCIL MEETS IN A small building toward the center of
Fraun. As you are riding up to it the building almost looks like a
rock, round and gray. It is not until you draw closer that you see
there is a single door. This door brings you to an antechamber, lit and
warmed by torches. There is another door, directly across from that one,
which leads to the council room. This is the room I find myself in this
morning, nervously awaiting the men who rule Fraun.

The table in the center of the room is a large circle. Around the circle
are six chairs. The chairs are very close together, probably due to the
fact that there are customarily only five chairs at this particular table. At
my left sits father, in all his regal glory. For the meeting, Father insisted
upon us both wearing Green, the color of Enchenda.

A very small, very round man enters the room. Despite his unusual
shape, the man has a commanding presence. His hair is white and his
eyes have a sad look about them. He is wearing yellow, identifying
himself as King Larecio of Marchenda. "Gregario," Larecio's voice
booms throughout the room, echoing off the bare walls. He wears the
largest smile I have ever known. Father effortlessly rises and I have to
scramble to get my feet underneath myself. I watch as father's hand
envelopes the smaller man's and shakes vigorously.

"Good morning Larecio, how are things in the fourth realm?"

"Well, as usual. We are a happy lot. How are things in Enchenda?" As he asks, Larecio frees his hand from Gregario's grip and lets it fall to his side.

"Things are well with us. Larecio this is my daughter, Princess Eselda."

Beside him, I curtsy politely and dip my head. "Pleasure to meet you, your Highness."

"I have a son about your age, and we've met before." The tone holds no negativity whatsoever. In fact, it rings with a clear sound, not unlike a bell.

They really are the embodiment of happiness over in Marchenda. I wonder if he ever gets mad. "That's right, I had almost forgotten. How is Carsen?" I ask politely. In truth, the fact had not escaped my mind at all, I had almost hoped to meet the young prince.

Larecio smiles. "He is well; I cannot wait to tell him you joined us at the council meeting. He will hold a high interest in the beautiful princess."

Another man enters the room, this one loud and boisterous. My gaze turns to the doorway and falls upon a tall, thin man with light hair. I guess the man to be just under three clicks tall, impressive. His eyes are darting around the room, taking in all who are present and making me feel like a specimen he is examining. The man is wearing Blue, the color of Farcheda. The speed at which he moves to his council seat, on the left of my father, confirms that he is indeed from the third realm.

"Gregario, Larecio, Eselda." The man nods at each of us in turn. "Welcome. I know I am not tardy, so I acknowledge your earliness. I hope I did not offend. We will begin shortly, I am sure."

I notice he even speaks quickly. I blink my eyes in surprise.

"King Mick, I have never known you to be later than I. Welcome." Father returns to his seat as he greets the king of the third realm.

Looking around I notice Larecio is already sitting as well. I need to pay more attention. I hastily plop back into my chair, embarrassed. Before I can worry about what to say to the assembled men, another enters the room. This one is even taller than the last, standing proudly at three marks. He is very thin and his blonde hair falls almost to his bright blue eyes. He is startlingly beautiful, standing in the doorway in his orange shirt. But it is not his hair or eyes that draw my breath from my body in a gasp.

This is the man who refused to rise for me at the school.

He moves calmly around the table, shaking hands with each person in turn. I can see his mouth moving, but my brain is not processing the words. What would be the reason for Renchenda, the kingdom of wisdom, to spy upon my speech?

The man reaches my seat and holds out his hand to shake. "Greetings, Princess Eselda. We are glad you could join us." There is a twinkle in his eyes.

Is he daring me to mention the school visit? I don't think I have the nerve to do so in a room full of kings. "Greetings, King Jordyn." I bow my head slightly and the man moves on.

Only once Jordyn is seated at the table do I take my eyes from him. I may have let him off the hook in front of the council, but I plan to find out what he was doing in Enchenda unannounced.

I move my eyes around the table again, cataloging the behavior of the kings. Father, Jordyn, and Larecio sit comfortably in their chairs. Mick, however, is tapping his fingers on the table unnaturally loud. My eyes fall on the empty chair to my right. Of course, he is waiting for King Tin to arrive and begin the meeting.

Since the beginning of Fraun, the numbering system has been in place. There is always one realm who is given the task of leading the council. This member is expected to run the meeting and uphold the norms at all costs. I have been studying those norms for ten moons, in preparation for this night. The king from the first realm, presently Tin of Sarcheda, ensures all meetings begin and end on time. That king can call for a vote on any issue being presented at any time, but they have no sway on its outcome. All present must vote and all votes are a simple majority. Disagreements are accepted, neigh encouraged; but words are your only weapon in Council Hall. At any time, a member of the council may call for a renumbering of realms if they feel as though the first realm royalty is not leading the council well, but again a majority vote must back that up. The council historically does not like to dishonor a current first realm without a very good reason. In fact, Sarcheda has ruled the Fraun for the last twenty-five annuals without question or call to vote.

My ruminating on the rules of the council is interrupted by the entrance of a muscular man dressed in red and black. Probably half a mark taller than I, he is not the tallest in the room, but his bulk is the most impressive. Arms, legs, chest, and shoulders show muscles I have rarely seen. He is dark of hair and eyes and carries himself as a living embodiment of strength. This must be King Tin.

"Good Afternoon gentlemen," his gaze falls upon my face, "and lady." He winks one eye in my direction before dropping into the seat beside me. "Let's begin without further ado. What issues have we to discuss?"

Up close I notice even more muscles than I first saw. Tin is a stark contrast to Jordyn, seated to his right. Jordyn is lanky and thin everywhere Tin is filled out and strong. Jordyn is light skinned, light haired, and bright-eyed. They are opposites in every way I can measure with my eyes.

Beside my father, King Mick raises his hand up and begins speaking in a clear, loud, but rapid voice. "We need to discuss the safety of Fraun."

He gestures to the table, pulling my eyes down toward it. Painted on the table is a map of the Fraun. Each king sits proudly within his territory. Father and I share the space that is Enchenda. The border lines look carved into the table, as do the names of the five realms. The borders enclosing Enchenda have been painted a blue color.

The River Fraun. My eyes trace the beautiful painting, taking in the colors the artist has used. In addition to the faint traces of the realms colors; Red, Green, Blue, Yellow, and Orange, the artist has added touches that indicate the type of flora one may find in the realm. There are green spots that look like tree groves, brown patches that may be sand, and even a black spot which I have heard is uncharted territory toward the border of the fourth realm.

A circle in the fifth realm shows the Castle Fraun. At the beginning of our history, that castle was inside the first realm. I have been to the castle one other time in my history, for the announcement of King Mick's youngest child, Margina. Each royal baby in the history of Fraun is presented to the other royals at a ball held in Castle Fraun. In fact, any special occasion that would call for all royals of Fraun to be together would be held there. It is the way of the Fraun.

I jump slightly when I feel the weight of my father's hand upon my own. "Pay attention, child," he whispers.

I hope I was the only one who heard that. I force myself to focus on King Mick's rapid speech. "The kingdom of Fraun needs this for the safety of our people. We must secure the borders against what lies beyond. My son, Hector, discovered the body of a large flying bird in the outskirts of our realm. What brought about the death of such a large animal? I desire not to encounter that villain alone."

"What do you propose we do about it?" King Larecio asks. He is sitting upright, actively listening to Mick's speech. Father is equally attentive.

King Jordyn, however, looks as though he is listening, but there is a cloud to his expression. Does he not agree with the stance of the third realm?

King Tin is the only one communicating obvious disgust with his body language. I have never seen a king look so uninterested in a conversation. Certainly, my father would never sit so relaxed. Tin is turned a little in his chair, leaning toward Jordyn. His knees are drawn up to the arm nearest my chair, and he is leaning his head back. In this manner, he is now focused not on King Mick, but on the ceiling above. I turn my eyes back toward Mick, not wanting to be caught searching other faces.

"I propose that we enlist a guard of young Fraunians to patrol the borders of each realm. The guard can be trained up together, a guard of Fraun, and report to the realms after training. I am willing to conduct the training myself," says Mick.

"Now there I must stop you, sir." Tin's voice accompanies a shuffle. I turn to see he is now seated in a more proper position, leaning on the table. His eyes, dark and dangerous, are now glaring full at King Mick.

Bubbles of nerves tickle up my throat. "You are asking this council to assume an awful lot, sir." Tin growls the words.

"I am doing no such thing. Jordyn can tell you that I am being logical here. I have presented only facts."

"No, you have presented a hearsay account of a dead bird. Birds are living creatures, Mick. They die."

My heartbeat quickens in fear. It is impressive to be able to call emotions from listeners simply with your speech. This is a skill I must learn, as queen.

Tin continues, "Let's assume, for a moment, that you are correct. Let's assume that something killed that bird, something large. I see no reason at all why the entire kingdom of Fraun should have to put together a patrol. It seems to me the problem lies in the third realm. Should you desire to train up a guard of your men to waste their days patrolling, I'm sure the council will see fit to allow you such." King Tin relaxes his posture again but does not pull his knee up. The gesture clearly communicates his belief that this conversation is finished.

"Now see here, Tin. I want all of Fraun to be safe. One kingdom, one goal," Mick says.

This is a mantra I have heard before. Each generation seems to let this concept become less and less spoken of, to the point where my generation doesn't hear it much at all. It's hard to stand behind such a concept when you can go most of your life never meeting someone from another realm. Even I, a royal princess, have only met these people on a few occasions.

There are nods of assent around the room, however. "I must agree with Mick," Larecio states.

"There's a surprise," mutters Tin.

I turn to him, shocked at the informal outburst. Instead of pretending to ignore me, as I would probably do after such an error, he meets my eyes and winks. I force my eyes down to the table again, even as the fiery blush fills my cheeks.

"If the people of our realms are to remain carefree and happy," Larecio continues, "then we must provide them some security. If word of this patrol in the third realm spreads, then our people will want one as well."

"Enchenda would be in favor of a patrol as well," father's voice booms from beside me.

I jump. Would we? Father's task on this council is to put the safety of Fraun above all else. All of Fraun. It makes sense that he backs this concept. I smile in agreement.

"Well then..." Tin lets his eyes travel slowly around the room. "Far be it for me to keep you from something the majority agree on. We can have a vote on this issue at the meeting's end. I do have one more point to clear up, however. If we are in favor of a patrol, why in the name of Fraun would we have this man," he gestures to Mick, "train up our patrol?"

Mick slams his fist down on the table, but the sturdy wood gives nothing. Instead, I feel vibrations in the floor where my feet rest. "What are you implying, Tin?"

"I imply nothing. I accept that you would be the fittest to train them for speed, but I am the most fit to train them for strength."

"I am not giving you a personal army to raise how you would like," Mick spits.

"I am not giving that to you, either, with all due respect."

Somehow Tin makes it sound as though no respect were due. His words drip with irony. The room crackles with tension.

"I have a comment," Jordyn says.

All eyes in the room turn toward Jordyn, who has been silent up to this point. I have heard, from Tutor, that in Renchenda this is often the case. People there, known for their wisdom, often do more listening than talking. Because of this, they are able to draw more logical conclusions without interjecting their own personal feelings.

"If a patrol is to be started and trained as one, which is what I am hearing," he pauses and waits for the council to nod. I notice they all do, including Tin. "I believe the idea of training them with the king of strength," he gestures to Tin, "makes logical sense."

Mick rises. "Now, of course, you believe that. These two, both of a malicious age, are ready to organize an army. What would stop them from declaring war on the rest of us, with their army to back them up?" Mick's eyes are locked on Larecio's face as he speaks and gestures wildly with his arms.

I have never in my life heard someone speak like this. I'm suddenly glad my father is still beside me to bear the brunt of this anger.

"Mick, sit down," Tin says. "I would like the council to recall, before this ridiculous accusation, it was Mick's idea to begin a patrol. Neither Jordyn nor myself made that suggestion. Surely if we desired to...what did you call it...organize an army? Surely we would've suggested it ourselves."

"That is true, I hold no such desire," Jordyn says. "I was merely saying that if our goal is to have a strong patrol that can battle whatever large being may be beyond our borders then strength would be a desirable characteristic of this patrol. If I was mistaken in the goal, and we are instead desiring someone who can warn us fast enough to take action, then yes they should be trained for speed in the third realm." Jordyn's voice has a calming effect on the men. It's not hard to understand why, as I feel calm washing over myself as well.

Listening to him talk, I cannot believe I didn't realize Jordyn was royalty when he visited the school. It seems so clear to me now, he is obviously educated and confident. How did I miss this?

Mick drops back into his seat. "If this is what the council chooses to vote on, I will have no part of it," he states. His anger sounds dispersed.

"It was your idea, Mick. But I see no reason to call a vote if you are no longer in favor," Tin smiles at the room as he speaks.

"Then call it not, Tin. What else have we to discuss?" Mick drops his hands, resignedly, to his lap. The room falls silent.

I look around the room again. Everyone looks beaten. These men have been called together to make decisions for the sake of Fraun, but they accomplished nothing but arguments in their time. It is a frustrating way of conducting business. I am aware that many meetings, in the past, have been more fruitful. Many meetings have stretched endlessly, with no party willing to concede until a decision of some kind has been made. In this case, however, it appears as though they have reached an impasse. I don't really understand why. Can Mick truly fear Tin's nature that much?

It makes sense to train a patrol in strength. Why would they oppose that? I remember what Tutor told me, at twenty annuals those with royal blood can become dark. Tin is that age. Perhaps this is all about age markers. Does the council fear Tin could not control himself with an army at his command?

Wait, could he?

Cold fingers of fear enclose my heart. I swallow the building fears with an audible gulp. What is coming my way?

"If there is no further business, I call this meeting to a close," Tin states.

"I second," Larecio croons with a smile.

"Meeting adjourned. See you fine people in one lunar cycle." Around the table, everyone rises. Tin leans in toward me, "I am glad you could join us, it brought beauty and grace to the table. I look forward to the day when you can speak your mind freely here. I'd love to hear your thoughts on this issue, I'll contact you regarding a meeting if you have no objections."

This close to him, I feel flutters in my stomach. The man before me is truly remarkable in his strength. He reaches to touch my arm, and his exposed muscles flex. "I object not, your Majesty," my voice cracks, embarrassingly. I resist the urge to groan at my own youth. "Thank you."

Tin smiles warmly. "Thank you," he practically purrs. He winks at me, again, as he turns to leave.

I feel warm all over. That man has a decidedly commanding presence. I shake myself back to reality and hustle to catch up with father. In the antechamber, my father waves to me. "Daughter, I must chat with King Mick. Stay here until I am finished and call for you," he calls this over his shoulder as he disappears out the front door.

I can see daylight is waning as the exterior door slips closed behind him. I am alone in the dark antechamber. I walk to the side of the chamber, turn my back toward it, and rest my foot up against the cold wall. I prepare myself for a long wait.

I feel the presence of another person in the room before I hear anything. When I turn my head I find King Jordyn standing in the doorway to the council chambers. "Good Afternoon, Princess," he smiles but doesn't step any closer.

"Hello again Majesty."

"Again?" he asks. His eyes give away his amusement; he is enjoying this.

"Were you not witness to the school visit I conducted in Enchenda recently?" I try to mirror his mock amusement in my own expression.

"Oh that. Yes, I was there. Fine job you did, Princess." Jordyn chuckles. "Did I offend you?"

"Why was the king of Renchenda spying on my school visit?" I take one aggressive step toward him, dropping my foot from the wall.

"Spying?" His face falls. "I was not spying. I am sorry you thought that." Something in his expression tells me he is serious.

"Why, then, were you there?"

"I have no heirs, Princess. I conduct my own school visit annually. I wanted to witness another realm and see how the visit is conducted there. I was hoping to learn something, and I did. You demonstrated remarkable confidence and preparedness. I was thoroughly impressed."

"Thank you." My resulting blush is deep. I can even feel my chest redden. "I am proud to have impressed the king of wisdom."

"Can I ask you something?" Jordyn takes another step.

He is now close enough that I could reach out and lay my hand on his chest if I so desired. "You may ask me something, yes."

"What is your opinion on the issue the council discussed?" his blue eyes hold steady to my green ones.

Do I deserve this focused attention? "I am but a princess, Majesty. My opinion is not as important as that of my king."

"We are not at a council meeting; you can speak freely. I did not ask you to put your opinion on the table in front of the kings. I merely asked for you to give it to me. It will go no further."

"Very well. I believe it would be in the best interest of Fraun to have a patrol. I see no harm in it being one of strength. Your logic appears sound to me. I don't understand the problem with it."

"Rest assured, there was no problem with the logic." Jordyn's eyes flash with a sudden anger; giving a rare glimpse of what may be brewing under the surface.

"I didn't mean to offend. I only meant I agreed with you," I quickly explain.

Jordyn's gaze softens. "Of course. Thank you." He leans back on his left foot, pulling away from me.

"Does that answer not please you?"

"I fear the council would see it as though you were siding with the young kings. How many annuals are you?"

The question fired quickly, catches me off guard. It is probably for this reason alone that I answer such a personal question. "Past fifteen."

"Not yet to twenty?"

"Not that I'm aware, Majesty." How do I admit I have not been counting my own age? Is that a normal thing? Don't most Fraunians know their own ages? A question has pounded my brain for days. A question I was too afraid to ask anyone else. Pulling together my courage I quietly ask, "Would I be aware of it?"

"You would." Jordyn sounds so certain, almost sad.

I wish he would elaborate. Time ticks by in silence.

Finally, Jordyn speaks again. "Have you thought about what you will do when your father betroths you?"

I sigh at the sudden change in topic. I don't want to talk about this. I want to talk about what is coming my way. "What makes you think he will?" I throw my chin out in a show of regal strength I don't really feel.

"You are aware he will die soon, yes?" Jordyn's tone is not confrontational. He delivers the line like someone merely stating scientific results of a test.

I am mildly affronted by his attitude. This is my father's death he speaks of. On the other hand, I am finding I quite like the way he seems to always speak with logic and reason on his side. How can one not trust a king backed by such high morals? "I am aware of that, yes."

"That would leave three of us ruling our realms during a malicious age without heirs to speak of. Avoiding a war between the three of us would be..." he turns his eyes upward as he thinks of the perfect word, "...difficult".

"You think we would war with each other?" I watch Jordyn's face carefully as he thinks. It is as impressive as watching a machine move, each movement of his eyes is so controlled. He looks down again, locking eyes with me.

"I think that when you reach twenty annuals you will truly understand how much Tin and I are holding ourselves together for the sake of Fraun. It is harder than I imagined it would be." His honest answer is touching.

I have an urge to comfort him but talk myself out of it. I feel as though my arms wouldn't really move anyway. "Is it scary?"

"It can be. Sometimes I find myself in a situation where I know my instinct is not right. It is hard to fight your own instincts. If it weren't for my wisdom, I'm not sure I'd be able to stop myself."

My heart races. This is the closest I've been to another person who has experienced the feeling I have feared since I learned of it. I have so many questions to ask of him.

Jordyn interrupts before I can ask another. "So that is why I think your father, one of the men on our council who have grayed, will be sure to marry you to someone who has passed this state before his death. Have you considered that?" Jordyn asks.

"I have not."

"There are a few I would see as good options, I wonder if your father has already spotted that." Jordyn's eyes focus on something over my shoulder. I turn my head and see nothing but the cold stone wall behind me. I am about to ask him what he is looking at when the outside door opens, letting in a cool breeze. Immediately, Jordyn steps back, putting respectable space between us.

"Eselda, we can away," father calls. His voice leaves no room for questions. I nod my assent and begin to follow my father, who has already turned away from the building.

"It was a pleasure meeting you, Your Majesty."

"Please, call me Jordyn." His smile makes his slim face even more handsome.

Instincts kick in and I feel my own smile tugging at my cheeks. "Goodbye, Jordyn."

"Until we meet again, Eselda."

I am aware my thoughts should be on betrothal, patrols, and policies. Instead, they fall on the two young kings who have captured my attention today. I spend the ride home childishly daydreaming about them in turn.

Chapter

8

THE NIGHT BRINGS AIR THICK with humidity and dark clouds which threaten to bring rain. Out the window of his home, the king watches. The only noises around are related to the weather and the night. Everyone in the realm is asleep.

Asleep or dead.

At the king's back lies the body of the young chambermaid who drew her last agonizing breath tonight. The young chambermaid who helped to bring confidence to the king, the same chambermaid who occupied his bed in secret for the last twelve moons. The chambermaid who overstayed her welcome when she chose to call him by his given name, instead of calling him her king. *The chambermaid who would've surely ruined my reputation by telling someone about the affair when she had the chance.*

She won't have the chance now. The thought makes him chuckle.

In the morning he will have to have his men remove her body from the house silently. Surely people will not miss such a girl, he had never known her to take time to spend with a family. He will either have to choose men who can be trusted with a secret or men he can kill after the job is done. *No one can know of this affair. Least of all the young princess.*

The king has a plan now and Fraun help anyone who tries to stop the plan. "You're next, Princess," he whispers into the night.

Any Fraunian on the grass of his lawn, were any present, would only have heard the laugh that followed; high and dangerous.

It is a laugh that promises terrible changes for Fraun.

Chapter

I HAVE NO IDEA WHY I'M awake. The bed is warm and comfortable, it's silent in my house, and yet I find myself staring up at the ceiling with thoughts of the council meeting yesterday running through my head.

"Princess Eselda." The voice carries through the door.

I jump out of bed and close the space quickly. I send the door swinging on the hinges as I whip it open. "You are losing your touch, Eee. I woke on my own this morning," I tease, smiling down at her.

"My apologies, Majesty. I will arrive earlier in the morning."

Roaches are notoriously bad at understanding jokes. "Eee, I was only kidding. Please relax." I will have to resign myself to waking earlier now, roaches can be so difficult.

"As you wish, Majesty." Eee hurries out of sight.

I dress quickly and hustle through the hallways to the dining room, well aware that being late for breakfast with my father would cause the old man grief. Lately, father has been acting strangely. At first, when we arrived home from the council, I assumed it was because of the tensions at the meeting. Now a fortnight later I am concerned it may be another sign of his failing health. Though I put on a brave face it isn't easy to accept the fact that my father and king is not long for this world.

"Good morning your Majesty." I bend to kiss him on the cheek before taking my customary chair across the large table. "How are you feeling this morning?"

"I am well, Daughter. How are you fairing?"

"Well, thank you. Is there business to discuss this morning?" Traditionally we will talk of schedules in the morning. Lately, we have been discussing policies around Fraun, grooming me for the inevitable takeover of Enchenda.

"Not really. I have a short meeting with a few leaders from the realm this afternoon, it will be boring and is not necessary for you to attend. Two of the gentlemen are simply requesting permission to increase the amount of food grown on their land. As you know our population has been growing lately, I will grant this request when they make it. Is there anything on your schedule, daughter?" the king asks.

I think through my scant itinerary. "I believe Tutor is scheduled to come by this morning. Otherwise, I have nothing planned."

"Perhaps you can do a favor for an old man since you are free this evening."

"Anything father."

"It has been requested that I meet with King Tin this evening for dinner to discuss in further detail his idea for the patrol, which you heard suggested at the council meeting. I grow weary in the evening and although I made the arrangement I fear I will be too tired to hold up my end. Would you consider traveling by roach to the meeting in my stead? I am sure King Tin will be more than willing to hear your side of the issue."

Father's speech sounds strained, leaving me no doubt that he speaks the truth when he talks of his fatigue. The man has tired already and it is only morning. "I could do that for you, Majesty. King Tin mentioned a desire to hear my opinions on the issue after the meeting, actually."

His hand halts partway to his mouth. His eyes leave his plate and land on my face. "When was this exactly?" he asks.

"Directly after the meeting, before I even left the table in the council chambers. It was nothing serious, father." I can't even begin to fathom what the king's problem could be. He is about to send me to the king's house for dinner with him, alone in his home. Surely a quiet conversation in a room full of other kings is no concern.

After a beat, the king resumes eating with vigor. Assuming this means all is forgiven, I follow his lead and devour my meal as well. When the plates are cleared away by a lady in waiting, I rise. "I should be off to meet Tutor, your Majesty." I bow, respectfully. "I shall meet Eee as the sun begins to fall to travel across the River Fraun."

"Thank you, Daughter. Please remember to keep your discussion with the king to that of policy."

I scrunch my face, "What else would we speak of, Majesty?"

"I know not, Daughter. I was speaking without thinking."

My father doesn't speak without thinking. I decide not to challenge this and, instead, head for the garden.

Chapter

10

G REGARIO REMAINS IN HIS CHAIR, looking every minute of his forty-four annuals. Although he prefers not to remember his age, he has always counted. Few Fraunians actually count the annuals as they pass, but Gregario has always enjoyed numbers. For example, he remembers that exact moment eighteen annuals back when Eselda was first placed into his arms. Any father can tell you that when you look at a child, regardless of age, you still see shades of the baby they were.

He can still recall little Eselda wrapping her whole hand delicately around his pointer finger and cooing gently at him. *When,* he wonders, *did that baby become the beautiful woman I just dined with?* Some days the old king worries that he is not preparing her for ruling in Fraun. Some days he worries that she is not the right queen for the job.

But what choice do I have?

A small roach enters the room. This is the new baby born to Eee. Gregario knew the baby would be a good addition to his household, Eee was irreplaceable in raising his stubborn daughter. He is pleased to be returning the favor by working with this baby. "Majesty." The voice from the roach is high pitched, different from that of an adult roach.

"Yes, young Ekk."

"King Mick is here, sir."

"Very well, show him in." Gregario feels mildly guilty for not mentioning this meeting to Eselda. He knew Mick would likely be early to the meeting, being king of speed and all, but he neglected to mention it in hopes that Eselda would be gone when Mick arrived. The old king of Farcheda is often controversial and does not look favorably on the princess.

This way is easier for everyone.

"Gregario, how goes things?"

Mick, Gregario knows, is younger than himself. Although he knows not how many annuals the king has walked the Fraun, he knows they entered the world within five annuals of each other. By all accounts, Mick should look worn and tired like Gregario himself, but that is not the case. Perhaps because Mick has always been faster. *If you slow a race roach down, can it still not beat a common roach?* "It is well, Mick. Welcome to Enchenda."

"Thank you. Let's get down to business, shall we?"

"We shall. You called this meeting, what say you?"

"We need to talk about war." Mick's voice booms clearly in the room.

Gregario's eyebrows raise, as do the small hairs on the backs of his arms. "War?" *The concept is scary to all from Fraun, certainly not in the best interest of the kingdom.*

"Yes." Mick sits forward, his elbows on the table. "I believe we could declare war on Sarcheda. If we win, Sarcheda would be absorbed into the Fraun and we would need to redraw the realm lines. Each realm would increase in size, but we would be able to rebuild without the fear of Sarcheda beginning a war." Mick's voice, although he is not yelling, carries across the room.

Neither man notices the small observer hiding in the shadows of the mostly closed door, listening to every word.

Gregario pauses to give the impression that he is thinking over the ludicrous idea. When he speaks, he chooses his words carefully to avoid offending the guest. "I am not in favor of starting a war to avoid one, Mick. Besides, what chance have we against the realm of strength?" Gregario wishes for Jordyn to be at the meeting. He would even settle for any representative from the realm of wisdom. He cannot seem to think of words that will convince, but not offend, the visitor. *I cannot simply tell a king he is being an imbecile.*

"The fear of war is only effective if those in power can remember what war causes. If we bring a new war to the forefront, it will keep them in line for a lot longer. Longer than you and I will be ruling, that is for sure," Mick answers.

Gregario rubs his face, fatigue clouding his emotions. "Mick, I fear war," he answers, honestly. "I wish to avoid it at all costs. Let us discuss other options."

"Gregario, do you believe that King Tin should be allowed to lead Fraun?" Mick delivers a loaded question.

The king of Enchenda has thought of this often, as is his duty. *True, Tin harbors an obvious hatred for the king of Farcheda. But is that feeling not returned? It seems unfair to punish one without punishing the other. In his time as king, Tin has stopped the vote on many things that the rest of the council would like a word on. But renumbering the realms is always controversial.* Gregario feels every moment of his age pile upon him. He rubs his hand along his face. "I don't know what I think, honestly."

"Let's think this through. If I called for a renumbering at the next meeting, what would happen? Assuming you sided with me..."

Gregario looks abashed. *Did Mick not hear me just now?*

"...which I realize is still left to be decided."

Gregario smiles. *Good, he got that message.*

"Assuming though, for just a second, that you did side with me in favor of renumbering, we are still not guaranteed for it to be approved. We know that realm five would side with Tin in voting to keep the numbers as they are, those boys agree on everything. We cannot be sure which way Larecio will fall, the man is inconsistent. So, even if you do agree with me today and we call for a renumbering at the next council meeting there is still a chance it could be ineffective," Mick says. Suddenly he adopts the deflated look that Gregario knows means he has convinced himself of the flaws in his own plan.

"What has you so convinced that King Tin cannot rule the Fraun, besides his age?" Gregario's voice is cautious, hesitant.

"What if I told you I believe the man killed his parents?" Mick asks.

Chapter

11

I HAVE NEVER KNOWN TUTOR TO be late. Today, I sit in my favorite garden and cannot enjoy the place at all. I mindlessly work my fingers through my long hair and watch the sun move up the sky slowly. "What if I had somewhere to be today?" No, that's ridiculous. Tutor would know my scheduling conflicts better than I do. In fact, having spent ten annuals as a boy living in Farcheda, Tutor is never tardy.

Cold fingers of worry start inching their way up my spine. What if something has happened to the man? The longer I sit with this thought in my head, the more it becomes a real fear. I rise, intending to find my father and express my concerns to him. He will know how best to proceed.

I race back to the dining room, holding my long black skirt bunched up in my hand. As I approach the door, which is unlatched and not quite flush with the frame, I slow to a walk and catch my breath. I am in the act of reaching for the door handle when a voice reaches my ears and turns me to ice. Interested, I lean my ear to the door frame.

"Then we agree on the need to remove power but it seems we cannot agree on the best solution." It is King Mick, speaking in a booming voice.

"Not war, Mick. I will not abide war. I've told you already I do not think we have a chance in a war against that realm," father answers. I know that tone of voice. It is the tone father takes with me when I am being argumentative and he is annoyed. I have never heard it taken with another, especially another king. I wince for Mick, that is a tone of voice I never like hearing. Poor guy.

"Then we shall need a renumbering," Mick says.

Renumbering? What are they talking about? Why would we need a renumbering? I really wish I had shown up at this door a little earlier. Why did I wait so long?

"It appears so," says father.

"We will need Larecio's vote to fall with us."

"How do you propose we ensure the vote of the king of mirth?"

"There is a way--"

"No," father's voice cuts through the room like a blade. I wince again at the power. "That decision is not ours to make," he softens his tone with this new sentence. My shoulders relax, slightly.

"As you wish, Gregario."

"If we only need one vote, must it be Larecio's?"

"I suppose not, what are you proposing?"

"Perhaps we can get to Jordyn?" Father's voice rises at the end, turning it into a question.

Outside the door, I am perfectly shocked. Two kings of Fraun are behind closed doors discussing ways to sway council votes. I don't understand what is happening, but it is giving me a terrible feeling.

I shift nervously and the voices halt. I must have made noise and betrayed my position. I inhale deeply and swing the door open. On my face is a careful smile belonging to someone showing up to the conversation and not one who has overheard. For a beat, I panic because I cannot remember why I came to the room. I hope that comes across as shock at seeing a guest in the room. "Oh, King Mick, what a pleasant surprise." I bow low to the king. "Pardon my interruption, Majesties, but I wanted to inform you that my tutor is mysteriously absent. I have chosen to head to town and mingle with the people. If Tutor should happen to show up, please handle it accordingly in my stead." I am shocked at the words which leave my mouth. I had intended to ask father's opinion on the absence. Perhaps my brain rightfully thinks overthrowing kings of Fraun is more pressing than a missing tutor.

The door clicks softly behind my retreating back as I dash from the room before questions can be asked. I freeze just outside the room, wondering if the conversation will continue.

"What did she overhear?" King Mick asks, in a quieter tone.

"I trust my daughter, she heard nothing."

I take that as permission to run out of the building entirely, although I wait until I'm outside to allow myself to breathe deeply.

What did I just witness?

Chapter

12

I HAVE ALWAYS FOUND THE REALM to be calming. Enchenda is filled with small houses, lined up neatly in rows along dirt streets for roaches and feet to travel. Many people have gardens in front of their homes. Some grow food, others grow flowers, few grow both. In this land, it is normal and expected that if you are one to grow food you will share with one who does not. The same is true for flowers.

The day is shaping up to be beautiful. The sun is radiating warmth down on Enchenda, making me glad I wore a sleeveless dress this morning. The black ensemble is one I often wear with a traveling cloak. Obviously, I left in a rush. The heat on my shoulders makes me smile. The silver lining to the secret meeting I overheard may just be this excuse to walk in the warmth.

I use my walking time to think through the overheard conversation. Why would the kings want a renumbering? I remember how they spoke to each other at the council meeting; Kings Mick and Tin are obviously not friends. Surely that is why Mick wants Tin out of the first seat. But father? What reason would he have to want the realms renumbered? Who are they numbering in favor of?

I slow as I approach a busy area of the realm. I am out of the tree-lined area surrounding my home and fast approaching the center of town, where the school and a few shops are located. There are kids playing in the road here, kicking a mini watermelon around and running. There are women working in their gardens at two homes by the end of the road. There are a few men working on a cart, one that will attach behind a roach. They look as though they are fixing broken parts underneath the cart, one is trying to hold it up high for the other. "Is there anything I can do to help?" I ask.

The man underneath the cart slides out and looks at me, not able to hide the shock on his face. "Do you know how to work on a cart, Princess?" he asks.

"Not truly. However, I do believe I have a better solution to holding that thing off the ground than using your friend here." I gesture to the smaller man, who is dripping sweat from his head onto the ground as he lowers the cart back into the dirt. I look around the street, searching for something. The men watch in disbelief as I collect a long, strong stick and three rather large rocks. I bring the items to the men one at a time.

"Now, please hoist that cart up one more time for me. Be sure it's as high as you can, please. I'm going to prop this stick underneath it," I instruct the younger man.

He nods his agreement, cracks his knuckles, and raises the cart.

I hurry, nervous as I watch the man's arms quake from the exertion. I push the stick underneath the cart, keeping it at an angle with the ground. Then, while he is still holding the cart high, I gather the rocks around the base of the stick. I test the contraption, trying to wiggle it from side to side. It holds firm.

"Okay, you can start to put the weight on the stick. Please lower it slowly, I'd like to be sure it isn't going to slide." The man begins to comply. At first, the stick holds and pride swells within my chest.

As if to remind me to practice humility, the stick begins to slip. "Wait, please."

The man halts, taking the weight of the cart again with a loud grunt.

Feeling guilty, I push the stick firmly into the soil before gathering the rocks closer. "Try again, please." This time, the stick holds the full weight of the cart.

The older man leans onto the cart, which continues to hold. "Princess, this is brilliant. Is it safe for me to crawl under?"

"It should be, although I'd advise against hitting the stick with anything. I also wouldn't stay under there for a very long time."

"What should we call this?" the young man asks, excitement showing on his face now.

"My tutor calls it a lift. You two gentlemen have a good day." When I leave the two men are hugging. It feels good to be helpful. I feel as though the day's warmth is now matched in my soul.

I continue on my path to the center of the realm, pleased to see so many people out in the main area of town this morning looking happy and alert. There have been times in the history of Fraun when people could not mingle like this; times that weren't this happy. I should be glad to be taking over the rule now, as opposed to then.

A woman nearby, arms loaded with vegetables, is calling to her children behind her. The woman silently offers me a carrot stick, which I delight in accepting. This is the beauty of Enchenda. This walk has been exactly what I needed to raise my spirits and my mood out of their funk. I close my eyes and breathe in the smells of food cooking somewhere, feeling the last of my stress leave my body.

A noise startles me. Eyes now open, I find a rock has landed on the ground a little way in front of me. A look around finds a group of sheepish looking young boys, one of whom is holding a stick. "Sorry, Majesty. We didn't see you there when we hit it," he nervously calls.

I pick up the rock and toss it back to them, smiling.

"Thanks, Majesty. You're the best," calls the tallest boy. The boys turn their backs to me, resuming their game.

"Your Majesty?" The quiet voice comes from a woman, seated on some stairs in the shadows to my right. The woman is gray, tired looking, with wrinkles cascading down her face.

"Good morning madam."

"I thought that was you." The woman smiles, yellowing teeth filling her mouth. The gray hair of the woman falls in two even parts down her front, carefully and lovingly braided by someone. It is still beautiful and glistening, despite its coloring. Someone cares for this woman.

"What can I do for you this morning?" I ask.

"You can tell that old father of yours that his time is near," she croaks.

"Excuse me?" What a rude thing to say.

"Your father is graying. He may have doctors who help him hide his age well, but some of us remember. I know as well as he that his time draws to an end. It shall be a race which of us perishes first like it was once a race for our mothers to birth."

"You know my father?" It is the first thing out of my mouth, and yet I silently chastise myself for the stupid comment. Everyone knows my father. He is the king. "I mean; you personally have met my father?"

The woman laughs cordially. "Our mothers were childhood friends. The king, your grandfather, could've had either wife. He chose your grandmother because her baby was born first."

My shock must be evident on my face because the woman laughs again. "I take it your father never told you he was born before your parents were wed? You better come inside, Princess. I have a tale to tell you."

I turn to look at the sky. Judging by the position of the sun I have enough time for this before I am supposed to head to Sarcheda. Then again, after an introduction like that to set a match to my curiosity, I would make time even if there was none. I follow her inside.

The house is smaller than I am used to and made of wood instead of the warm stone of my family home. The pieces have been borrowed from ruins of the Giants, so they are not even in length. Because of this, the roof tilts a little to the right. The room we have entered into must be a kitchen. There are three chairs around a wooden table, a small cooking stove made of stone, and a chimney reaching to the heavens through an opening in the wooden planks that make the roof. There is a bucket in the corner, underneath another small opening in the roof. A length of fabric is draped along the left side of the room, blocking my view of anything further. "Is that hiding your sleeping space?" I ask, pointing at the curtain.

The woman follows my gaze. "Yes, my bed is beyond there." She bustles to the small stove and sets a kettle down on the wood. She then leans in and blows softly on the wood, causing flames to stir up from the embers. She sits at the table and gestures for me to do the same.

"My name is Charlotte. My mother's name was Devon. You should remember those names; your father will confirm that he knew us well. Before your years, when King Kris and his wife Laurina ruled the realm, my mother and your grandmother lived next door to each other in matching houses. They were beautiful girls, and they did everything together. Kris and Laurina had a son, Stefan, your grandfather. Stefan was a young prince who didn't like to be cooped up in his father's home. He often ran through the village, playing with the townsfolk and hiding in plain clothes. Of course, like you, they knew who he was. But he enjoyed pretending to blend in."

Haven't I been playing the same game? The long-buried tie to my grandfather pulls me into the story, I lean across the table on my forearms.

"One day when Stefan was out in the village he came across two beautiful girls playing in the River Fraun. At first, he chastised them; the River wasn't safe for playing. Technically, he told them, the River is not part of Enchenda. The girls laughed at him and invited him to play in the river. When he refused, they pulled him in. After that, I'm told, the three got along swimmingly." The old woman chuckles at her own pun. "Stefan would often leave the home of his father to seek out Angeliq and Devon."

Behind the woman, the kettle whistles. She rises and slowly pours water into two mugs. I watch the woman add mint sprigs and tea leaves, crushing them with a spoon. Angeliq and Stefan were my father's parents. The rest of this story I have never heard. I hold my doubts in my throat, where they have balled up. The woman cannot answer my questions, I will let her tell her story. The king will fill in the details. The thought of bringing this topic to my father, fuel for an epic fight, makes me impatient for the woman to finish the tale. My leg begins to bounce under the table, making a noise as my bare foot strikes the ground.

Setting the teacups on the table in front of us, Charlotte continues. "Where was I? Stefan had met the women of his dreams, yes? Well, the problem was the girls were always together. My mother, Devon, and your grandmother, Angeliq, were often mistaken for sisters. I'm told they loved this mistake. When the girls were fifteen annuals they were invited to a party at the home of King Kris. Stefan took each one away from the party, alone, and professed his love. He told each girl that she was the one he had decided to court, but that she must keep it a secret because she had no royal blood. He let each woman believe that it was not worth the heartache it would cause her friend to know the truth. He explained to each that he would personally tell the other when it came time. In this way, he was able to court both women, in secret, without the other knowing.

"It drove a wedge between them. Devon and Angeliq would no longer see each other. They were either sneaking out with Stefan or hiding in fear that their friend would ask where they were. It was no fun for anyone." Charlotte pauses, sips her tea. "Well I suppose it was fun for Stefan," she laughs.

I don't know what to say. Instead, I wrap my hands around the mug of tea and take a sip. It is delicious and warm, comforting.

Charlotte continues, "It wasn't long before both Devon and Angeliq were with child."

"Excuse me," I interrupt. "This is all fine, except how can we be sure that he managed to impregnate both women at the same time? Are we sure there was not another man?"

Charlotte laughs again. "They were twenty annuals before they were pregnant, Princess. This means your grandfather had reached his twenty-fifth annual. Let's say that this meant they spent a lot of time in bed, not..." she clears her throat "...sleeping." She winks at me.

Is this woman speaking of the age markers? My cheeks flush with embarrassment at what she is implying. Who wants to think of their grandparents like that?

"Anyway, they were both with child together. This is what actually drove the women back together. Now they were about to be unwed mothers, people who are shunned even in Enchenda. They fell to each other for comfort. In tears, the women told each other everything. In this way, they came to be angrily standing on Stefan's doorstep. Stefan would need a queen. His father had died recently. His mother was graying. The women proposed that Stefan choose one of them to be his wife. It was decided that he would save the other from banishment by claiming that child belonged to his foot soldier, a man named Shawn. Stefan would provide money to Shawn and his bride for as long as he lived. The problem was that Stefan loved both women and couldn't choose.

"It was decided that he would take the first to deliver the baby. Greg was born three suns before I was, so he became a prince and I became a commoner. Our parents were actually wed on the same day." Charlotte leans back a little. The smile is gone from her face. "Stefan was true to his word about providing for my family, and Greg has helped since Stefan's death, but I expect that will stop with you."

I look again around the shabby home with the leaking roof. "My father continues to provide?"

"Your father provides much. That tea you drink comes from your family gardens."

There is no sign in the small house of another being. Yet the woman appears cared for. I decide to push the issue, see if I can gain more information. "If you have never married and you claim you aren't long for this world; who do you wish I provide for?"

Charlotte swallows and drops her eyes to the teacup, turning it in her hands. "I want my story to live on. Stefan was as much my father as Greg's, you owe me that."

I swallow hard. My foot ceases its tapping as the truth of this conversation slaps me in the face. *There is royal blood in Enchenda that the council knows not of.* "You are my aunt."

"I am."

"It seems so strange, I have never met you. I have never heard of you."

"That is what I wish you to fix." For the first time since beginning her story, Charlotte looks tired again. Telling of her heritage had given her energy.

"I will speak to my father of this." I rise from the chair. "You have my word."

"Thank you, Princess. That is all I could ask. Please see yourself out, I feel I must rest now." Charlotte says, her voice barely a sigh.

I show myself to the door and march straight back to my father's home. Once there, I am greeted by a chambermaid of my father's. "Excuse me, ma'am. Can you please tell my father that I wish to meet with him tonight after I have met with King Tin? I will meet him in the garden upon my return, we have important issues to discuss." I deliver the speech with my chin raised high, completely at odds with the flutter under my skin.

Technically I do not have the right to summon my king, but this woman does not have the right to question her princess. The chambermaid nods and scurries from the room. I rush off to my own chambers. I must push aside the thoughts of Enchenda and royal blood.

I have a king to meet with.

Chapter

13

THE RIDE TO TIN'S HOME near the Southern border of Sarcheda is brisk. I have decided to keep the same dress, for lack of time, but dress it up for the occasion. Feeling it is appropriate to represent the colors of Enchenda, I have gone with a dark green overcoat. Around my neck, I have looped something long and silver with touches of a beautiful stone that glitters the color of blood. I hope to please him by wearing a shade of red, the color of Sarcheda, when I meet with the king.

The roach, Gee, was chosen by the stable hand. It is the largest roach in our employ, making him able to withstand such a journey. He is pleasant, normally, but cannot talk on this ride because of the weight he is carrying and the distance he is traveling. This leaves me alone with my thoughts, again.

The news this afternoon, upon meeting my "Aunt" Charlotte for the first time, is leaving me with much to consider. I try to recall my family tree into my memory. The family lineage is painted along one wall in the dining room. On the tree, those with royal blood are circled. I can effortlessly recall my father's name, painted in the eloquent scroll, Gregario. His name appears next to that of my mother, Rubina, and is connected to her by a faint line. Underneath, and connected to both, is my own name, Eselda. Both father's name and my name are faintly circled. Mother's is not. Those details are easy to recall.

It's recalling further up the chain, to the parts of the lineage we have never discussed, that is proving challenging. Stefan and Angeliq appear above my father, that memory is hazy but present. Obviously, Stefan's name must be the one circled; but I cannot really remember that detail. Is there a faint line trailing off from Stefan's name in an unknown direction? Is there any mention of Charlotte's existence at all? Surely my family must be aware that another with royal blood exists? Aren't there implications of that?

Beyond that, Charlotte knew of the age markers. She commented on my grandfather spending a lot of his time in bed. I have only recently learned of those age markers myself. Someone must have explained them to Charlotte. There must be another person tutoring this woman in the ways of the royal blood.

Armed with this new realization, I can hardly wait to get my conversation with father underway, I am clenched by a strong desire to turn the roach around and head back to confront him straight away.

My humble training kicks in, guilting me into continuing my ride. What would happen to relationships between our realms if a meeting like this were canceled? Surely it wouldn't be good. Besides, if I'm being honest, it cannot hurt to see King Tin again. I feel the flare of my crush again and I allow my mind to wander toward those muscles of his. I can picture the shape of his arms, wildly different than the tubes of everyone else. I certainly can admit to myself that I am partially traveling all this way just to see him again.

I arrive at King Tin's home just as darkness consumes it. A foot soldier is waiting to take the Roach from me and bring him to food and water. A lady-in-waiting, whom I assume was hired for the occasion since no women live in Tin's home, is ready to lead me to the dining room. Tin is seated at one end of a long table. His home, like my own, is made of rocks and stones. It is warm, owing to the fact that a large fire burns brightly behind Tin. He is illuminated completely, both by the fire at his back and the candles on his table. The table has only one other place setting, to Tin's right. I sit in it and smile at my host.

"Good Evening, your Majesty," I greet, bowing my head as much as the heavy wooden table will allow. It is hard to show regal respect to one my own age, even if he is a king. Tin's face breaks into a smile, and my crush burns full force. How can someone this handsome be talking to me?

He has dressed in all black again, although more casually than he was for the council meeting. There are touches of red in the shirt, straining against the muscles underneath. I hope the lighting is such that he cannot see the blush that I can feel taking up residence along my cheeks.

"Good Evening, Eselda." Tin reaches out his hand, and I place mine lightly in his. He bends, placing his lips upon the back of my hand. His dark eyes never leave my face. I feel my heart flutter. "You look lovely in red beads," he says, straightening in his chair.

"Thank you. I thought it fitting for a meeting in Sarcheda." The thought of pleasing this man warms me more than the fire could.

"Shall we dine? You must be hungry from your travel." Tin waves his arm and a chambermaid flees from the shadows through a door in the wall. When she returns seconds later she is leading another woman and both are carrying trays of food. Each woman steps behind a royal party and begins placing identical dishes in front of them. I lean back to allow them access to the table.

The soup sends swirls of steam into the air above the bowl, it smells faintly like zucchini, one of my favorite vegetables. A small plate of bread lands next, dark in color and shining as though butter has recently been spread. There are not many in Enchenda who make bread, I am excited to eat it again. Next is a smaller plate, this one holding slices of large strawberries. Finally, there are glasses of water placed in front of each guest. When the women depart, I follow Tin's lead as he grabs a spoon and begins eating the soup.

"So, Eselda, tell me your opinion on the matter of a patrol," Tin prompts between spoonfuls of the hot stew.

My opinion. What should I tell this king? Should I mention my initial reaction, which was to agree with him and Jordyn? Perhaps that is not the best answer. My father must know more than I if he is willing to entertain the idea of a renumbering to overthrow Tin from his given position of authority. "I feel as though I am not learned enough to have a true opinion yet, Majesty. I was shocked to even learn we were in need of safety." The answer is honest but incomplete. It will have to do for tonight.

Beside me, Tin nods. His dark hair shines almost blue in the firelight, I have never seen hair that color. It looks soft and supple, as it should since he is past fifteen annuals. I am distracted by my sudden desire to reach out and touch it. Tin glances my way and finds my eyes on him. I drop my eyes to the table, where they find the basket of bread. In an attempt to cover my embarrassing stare, I reach for a slice and take a large bite. It is warm and sweet, a pleased sound escapes my lips and my eyes slip closed as I savor it.

"The bread brings you pleasure, milady?"

My eyes snap open again to find the king smirking at me. "We don't have many bakers in Enchenda."

"I expect that's because it takes some strength to form the loaves. I'll have to send you home with a few for your father. Tell me more about life in Enchenda, since you obviously intend to shy away from political conversations tonight." Tin reaches for a slice of strawberry as he leans on one elbow toward me.

"Enchenda is a beautiful land. Warm and bright, happy and delightful." I recall my walk through the town today, before meeting Charlotte. The memories flood me and I find this is exactly what I need to talk about to forget all my recent concerns. "The people are so friendly. Everyone is willing to drop what they are doing and help another person. Just today I helped someone learn a new way to get a job done efficiently. The men were so gracious and accepting of the help. They spoke kind words they must have known I needed to hear. I knew immediately the men would take what I had taught them and pass it onto more people, as I had done. It is truly a great place to live."

"An embodiment of the humility you learn."

The complement feels awkward. "We try Majesty. Thank you for noticing."

"I didn't mean your town. I meant you, Princess. You speak of your adventures today, but talk of the men you helped instead of yourself. You say 'we' as if to ensure you include all the people of your land, lest I think it is only of your house you speak. You are sure to tell me how nice everyone else is. You are a beautiful example of the humble nature your realm attempts to cultivate. If all around Enchenda were like you, there would be no worries there." As he speaks, his eyes travel my body. I can feel their warmth spread through me as though he had touched my body with his hand. My stomach flutters in a way that has nothing to do with the meal lying on the table between us. When he reaches out his hand and brushes mine, I feel a spark jump between us.

"You are too kind, Majesty." I choke on the words leaving my mouth as a whisper. "Tell me about Sarcheda." I need to hear more of your voice.

"Sarcheda is a solid place. Everyone here is an excellent builder, so we make good use of what the Giants have left behind." I can tell this is true, the table I sit at is a much better quality than the one in my own home. "We have repurposed many tools to allow us to make bread and other foods. We have annual competitions for strength, and the people enjoy this time to show their skills. We are a tenacious people here and we have a lot of pride."

His voice washes over me like water, relaxing me. I can imagine the people he speaks of, built strong like himself. I can imagine groups of people, not unlike those I saw around Enchenda today, gathered together baking. Gathered together throwing large stones as far as they can. Cheering one another on.

The men in Tin's realm must have no need for contraptions that lift for them. They could easily heft that weight without thinking. My eyes fall to Tin's arms, thick and muscular. I feel the blush creep slowly back along my face. What is wrong with me today? I reach for a strawberry slice to hide my sudden desire to reach for Tin.

"Your soup is gone. Let us begin the next course."

Before I can object, Tin raises his hand to alert the chambermaid that the next course can be delivered. The women return with laden trays. This time they are following two women carrying empty trays. The empty trays are loaded with the plates from the soup course as the next course is laid before us. A single plate hits the table in front of me. The smell is amazing, but the food is not one I recognize.

As if reading my mind Tin explains, "Ant and rice, Princess. I hope you'll find it to your liking." He reaches for his spoon and slips it below the creamy surface in the bowl.

In Enchenda we often eat ants. Many of the scouts who patrol the land beyond Fraun bring back the bodies of ants they have killed for safety. I know our kitchen staff is well skilled in preparing the meat, although I have never observed the process. I take the spoon and try a taste of the mixture. It slips down my throat. The taste is magnificent. "I have never had ant cooked like this, it's wonderful. What did you call this?" I pick up a single white grain, holding it in my fist.

"Rice, princess. It is harvested from along the Eastern border. The people of Renchenda have taught us how to prepare it. It's a remarkable treat." Tin gives me the impression he is amused by my naiveté. I'm not sure whether to be offended he think I am sheltered or happy he is broadening my horizons.

"It's delightful." I smile and return to the bowl.

Between the two of us, we probably have two ant legs steamed up and chopped. This is mixed with a few grains of rice and a creamy sauce. The kitchen staff has likely used the entire ant, hopefully parceling out the remaining meat amongst the staff.

We consume the dish without more conversation, I simply cannot get enough. When I finally finish and push the plate away, my stomach is more full than it has been in a long time. I am not one to go hungry, but I have also never eaten to excess before. I assume this spread was put together to impress me. I must ensure that he knows it has been a success. I adopt the smile I associate with tasks of the princess, one that is regal and yet feels awkward at the corners. "This meal was simply divine, Majesty. Thank you for inviting me."

"We are not finished yet, Princess. Allow me to share my favorite dessert with you, please."

I am not sure I can fit more food into my stomach, but Tin has already gestured for it to be brought to the table. The women clear the dishes and place a single silver dish between the two of us. Inside is a brown, sweet smelling dish. There are two spoons resting alongside. Tin smiles at me and takes one spoon, indicating I should take the other. "This is called a cookie. My chefs are amazing at preparing it, but it would not be possible without a rather large fire. Try it, please," he explains.

I am surprised to find my spoon slips effortlessly into the food and comes out gooey. I lift the spoon to my mouth and the explosion of flavor sends me leaning back in my chair. "What is this made of?" I ask once I have swallowed the delight.

Tin laughs at my reaction. "Larecio informs me it's called Chocolate. They have a supply of it in Marchenda that the giants left behind. He sent it here, especially for me to treat you with, at my request. Do you like it?"

I can only nod and reach for another spoonful. The flavor is so impressive that I have completely forgotten how full I am as I devour as much as I can.

Tin sits back in his chair and watches me eat the dessert. When I have eaten as much as I can, he leans forward again to rest on his forearms. The women clear the table and fill our cups with more water from the River Fraun.

"Can I ask you a personal question, Eselda?"

A little afraid of what kind of question may be hiding behind the dark eyes which are setting my skin on fire everywhere they land, I merely nod.

"Are you being courted by anyone in Enchenda?" This time I am sure he must notice the blush that creeps up my neck and dots my cheeks. "I don't mean to be forward, milady, but I find myself bewitched by you." He reaches for my hand, closing his own around my fingers, swiping his thumb across my palm as he waits for my response.

"I am not being courted, Majesty." My voice trembles as I consider what he is implying and feel the electricity coursing through my hand.

"It would not be proper for me to request to court you, a princess awaiting a throne, without first speaking with your father. Allow me to ask you to wait, I will speak with him shortly. That I promise." He raises my hand to his lips and kisses it, closing his eyes as though imagining it is my lips he brushes instead.

"I have enjoyed meeting with you more than you can imagine, but I fear I must allow you to return home while it is still possible for me to let you leave. You see, I fear if I keep you here longer I would simply need you to stay forever. I grow fonder of you by the second." Tin rises. "Until we meet again, Eselda." He closes one eye, winking at me in a gesture that makes my heart race and my stomach flutter.

The lady-in-waiting reappears to lead me out of the home. This time I notice intricate details I missed on my rush in. There are decorations around the home I don't quite understand the purpose of. Paintings of Tin himself, paintings of landscapes, and a small reflective wall hung up across from the door. Unlike my own, this one has been trimmed around the edges with a wood that has been ornately carved. As I leave through the front door and mount the waiting roach, I notice that the door fits securely and latches well. In fact, I see no small defects at all in the manufacturing of this home.

I find myself, on the ride home, thinking of the promised courtship. Thinking, despite my earlier woes, that Sarcheda would be a nice place to live.

Chapter

14

THE WIND WHIPS THROUGH THE garden, stirring up the plants and shaking my thin frame. Just pulling up in sight of my house sent the questions I have pushed out of my mind all evening to resume their buzzing in my brain. I practically dove off Gee to race to this garden to see if father has honored my request to meet. *There is so much to discuss.*

The cold soil beneath my feet drops my body temperature. I wrap my arms around myself and jiggle my legs to keep warm. The empty garden speaks volumes. I'm so stupid. Who am I to demand a meeting with the king? I will have to catch him at breakfast.

The thought of breakfast gives me another idea. The family tree is painted on the far wall across from the fireplace in the breakfast hall. Perhaps I can still get answers from the tree. Glad to have a warmer destination, I bolt for the dining hall.

I pause just inside the door to listen for noises. The house is silent. My dinner with Tin was late and the ride home long. It appears that I have stayed awake longer than even the roaches and servants who normally travel the halls at night. I creep along the corridors quietly. After being in Sarcheda I see things in my own home with new eyes. The bricks making up the walls here are scratched, damaged, used.

Were Tin's walls marked this way? Perhaps I will ask him how to clean off such imperfections.

I light the torch at the entryway to the dining hall and free it from its hanger to carry it to the family tree. The tree has been painted in gold, careful script along the stone. At the top of the wall, very near the roof where I would need a ladder to reach I see Oberian's name. The name is circled, indicating royal blood, and starred, indicating he served as king. There is a line connecting Oberian to his wife, Alicia. Underneath that is another line connecting him to his single son, Oberian II.

Oberian II had three wives. Therefore, I can see three lines connecting to him, Suzeth, Ramona, and Rebekah. I know there are descendants of all three women living in the Fraun today. This tree, however, only shows those of Suzeth's single son, Enchenda.

My eyes trace downward, past the scrawls of names that have come before me. Circles and stars decorate the tree, reminding me again of the power royal blood holds over this family. Just beyond halfway down the wall, around my own eye height, I see the names for which I search. Kris and Laurina, my great-grandparents. Laurina's name is circled and starred, Kris' is not. That information, for some reason, startles me. My great-grandmother was royal born and served as queen of Enchenda. Interesting.

Underneath their names I see Stefan, as expected, circled and starred. He is connected to Angeliq, just as I recalled. Of course, my father, Gregario, was their only son. I lovingly run my fingers along my mother's name, Rubina, before tracing the line that connects to me.

Mother was always a warm woman. I remember my mother teaching me the traditional age markers. She would talk to me about the markers and my future while she sat behind me on my bed, brushing my hair. She would fantasize with me of the day when my hair would be shiny and bright, like the sun. It's heartbreaking that Mother never lived to see that day.

I pull my eyes away from mother's name. This is not why I came in here. I trace the line back up to Stefan. Seeing nothing, I trail further up. There is another line jutting from Laurina's parents. Following it, my eyes take in another circled name. Tricia. Apparently, Tricia,

Laurina's sister, married a man named Stu and birthed a child Tometh. This man, this Tometh, has no further lines connecting to him. What happened to him? He has royal blood, but never served as king. Did he die as a child? Is he still alive? He would be Stefan's cousin and my great-uncle.

There is a black spot of coal dirtying the wall near Tometh's name. Absent-mindedly I begin to rub the spot as I think. Pulling my finger away to clean the soot, I notice there is none on my finger. I lean closer to the blemish and scratch it with my nail. From this angle, with my nose practically touching the surface, I can see it is actually black paint.

This odd oval is covering something.

I look around it. Sure enough, I find a very thin, very faint black paint line connecting the blemish to Stefan's name.

Did I just find proof of Charlotte?

I grab a nearby chair and stand on it, eagerly poring over every detail of the family. Up near the top of the wall, I notice a spot with only a few descendants. In fact, the ruling stars had jumped from one branch of the tree to the other. There, underneath King Charles and his wife Elena, I find two black ovals. These two are connected to each other and faintly connected to Charles and Elena. I rub my fingers over the circles, and again my finger comes away clean.

What stories are buried here? Why write the names if the children were not to be tracked? What becomes of them after their names have been erased?

If I had come here for answers tonight, I am not going to get them.

Clearly, these blemishes cannot be cleaned away so simply.

Chapter

15

"ESELDA," GREGARIO'S VOICE BOOMS, ECHOING off the walls of the dining hall.

My eyes flutter open and take stock of my surroundings. I am curled up on the floor underneath the family tree. There is a chair beside me and the torch is in a holder beside the painting. I meet my father's angry expression and drop my eyes in shame. "Father, forgive me. I must have fallen asleep after my late meeting with King Tin."

"What were you doing in this room, then?"

"I was only looking at the tree, father. Please, I have many questions. Is this a good time for us to talk?"

"Very well, I suppose I cannot delay our conversations much longer. There is much to discuss. I will have the chambermaid prepare our breakfast. You should make yourself presentable. I will meet you back here shortly."

"Thank you, father." Despite my desire to start this conversation now, I don't wish to anger him. I dash out of the room quickly, before he can change his mind.

I rush through the tasks of scrubbing my face, rinsing out my mouth, and brushing my hair. Then I change into a simple green dress. Satisfied, I race back out of the room. I arrive in the dining room just as a chambermaid is dropping a bowl of fruit into my place. I smile in thanks at her while simultaneously bowing at father.

"Where shall we begin our talk this morning, Daughter. Or do you wish to eat first?"

"I couldn't possibly eat around all these questions in my gullet, father." I struggle to decide which issue, which question, to bring up first. "I think we should begin with your meeting with King Mick. Please, tell me what that was about."

"I suspect you overheard some of what we discussed."

"I did hear some, I didn't mean to eavesdrop." I take a bite of watermelon to stop myself from trying to further explain. Sometimes a simple answer satisfies.

"Mick has concerns about King Tin's loyalties to Fraun," Father says.

"But why?"

"Each realm has a family tree, not unlike the one you slept beneath, painted somewhere in their home. Mick claims to have seen all five trees, something I personally have never done. According to the king of speed, the trees hold evidence of some dirty secrets hiding in Fraun's past. Secrets that prove Tin, and his family, to be breaking council rules."

Rules like hiding royal blood as common folk in their realm? I take a deep breath in, wondering how bad this could truly be. On my exhale I ask, "What rules?"

"The council ruled, many annuals past, that our kings are to take only one wife. Mick claims to have evidence of this rule being broken."

I stop myself from rolling my eyes and take a bite of melon before moving the conversation forward. "How exactly would taking multiple wives prove Tin is unfit to rule? Remember, father, he has not even one wife."

"Eselda, why do you think the rule was put in place?"

Because a man should marry one person whom they truly love and no other? I am used to ruminating over questions like this for Tutor, so I don't answer right away. Questions like these usually require answers that are different than my true opinion. I sit straighter in my chair, hold my head high, and project my answer in my strongest voice. "To ensure our kings are decent people."

Father laughs. My posture deflates and all confidence leaves me with a sigh.

"The kings can be whomever they want, so long as they uphold the quality they are asked to possess. I can murder if I so choose," he explains. My eyebrows fly up. Father picks up on the gesture effortlessly. "You doubt that? I certainly can, so long as it is in the best interest of the Fraun. So long as my doing so isn't for my own pride. So long as I remain humble.

"No, my daughter, the rule was not created to ensure we are good people. The rule was created to keep the royal blood contained. If a king takes many wives, as Second did, there are often many children born. In this day and age, if a current king were to do that, there would be many children who will never be needed to lead producing offspring with royal blood."

What a perfect opportunity to ask about Charlotte. "Father, is that not an issue that exists anyway?" I ask, attempting to flood my voice with innocence.

"I suppose it could be, I know not." Yet his eyes cast downward and he takes a bite of food.

"Then what of Charlotte?" I ask.

Now I have his attention. His eyes snap to my face. I brace myself for a scolding.

"Your curiosity never ceases to amaze me, Daughter." He surprises me with his soft tone. "Charlotte was an accident."

"How can a person be an accident, father?"

"Stefan was a fool. Any man can fall in love, a fool believes he has fallen in love with two. A fool believes that love is for him and not the one he loves. Stefan forgot to be humble, as we are taught, and it was his undoing."

I watch as the king drinks his tea and eats his fruit. Evidently, he expected this conversation to end here. I have no such desire. "Father, are you upset that I know of Charlotte?"

"No, Daughter. I thought that I would be when you found out. My father disgraced our trait by bedding another woman, after all. But I find myself relieved to have someone to share this burden with. I have carried Charlotte's weight on my soul for a long time. It is nice to share it with you." He reaches out and squeezes my hand, briefly.

"Is that her name, blacked out on the wall there?" I ask, gesturing to the first of the three ovals I found.

He doesn't even turn to look at the wall behind him. "It is. I had our tree painter add her to the wall but black her out. I felt terrible knowing that my father didn't even feel she needed to be up there. In gold paint, below the black, you'd find the name Charlotte. I also had him circle it. It remained up, drying, for a full sun before I allowed him to cover it."

"What gave you this idea?" I ask, hoping father knows of the other two similar circles.

"It is tradition to shun a woman and a baby when the baby is born out of wedlock. This is how the kingdom handles that shunning. The names are painted but covered. I knew of this tradition and felt it befit Charlotte."

I hold my new knowledge in a secret hug; the other two ovals must have been an unwed mother and her infant. "What becomes of those women, father?"

"A shunned woman is free to live a normal life among the commoners, but not to speak of her experiences."

"But what if they have families? Are those families not added to the wall?"

"For Fraun we ask them not to have children. Again, royal blood must be contained." Gregario's voice sounds sad, tired.

"That's a terrible fate."

"I agree with you, but it cannot be helped. It is something we do for Fraun," he says. "Now do you understand why it was easier for the rule to be one wife? Those kings were trying to prevent sorrow like this from reaching the offspring."

"I'm beginning to see it, yes. I'm afraid I still do not see what this has to do with King Tin, the bachelor." I emphasize the last word carefully.

"Yes, well. The problem is not exclusively with Tin himself. Mick

77

believes that the kings before him have taken many wives in secret. He claims the evidence is written on the wall, not even blacked out. The wall, however, is hidden in a location none others have ever seen. I am not sure how Mick came to bear it witness. Mick supposes that the wives were taken to help ensure a line of strong, male rulers. Sarcheda is the one realm among us who has always birthed a king to lead, and never a queen. This, combined with the fact that Tin himself often opposes issues the council is in favor of, has led Mick to believe it is time to renumber."

"That hardly seems like solid evidence to remove someone from a seat of power," Eselda answers.

"You must remember, Eselda, we are not talking about stripping him of his title. No one can do that. We all have blood rights at that table. We are merely talking about renumbering. If he were, for example, king of the fourth realm, what would really be different?"

I mentally count out the circle, curious what would make Sarcheda fourth. I bristle as I realize it. "You're talking about making Farcheda first realm?"

"It was an example daughter, calm down."

"Farcheda is not fit to be the first realm." My voice rises of its own accord. "They are too quick of temper." Those are Jordyn's words, I recall. The king of wisdom fed me that information at the school visit.

"They have never been given a chance, Eselda. They are the one realm who has not held the seat. Besides, of the five of us, Mick's house is the most prepared for the future. Surely even you can see that."

My jaw falls open. "We are back to the idea of children, age, and marriage again."

"We are of royal blood. We are always going to be thinking about royal blood. There is never enough of it." The king punctuates each sentence with a slam of his fist on the table. The tea and plates jump.

"Apparently there is often too much of it, or should we ask Charlotte what she thinks?" I yell back. Our little show of mutual respect has completely faded. His anger is evident on his face and, I'm sure, matched by my own.

"That is enough." Father swipes his hand across the table and sends my teacup flying toward the fire. I cower back from him, shrinking into my chair. "You are not thinking clearly. I will leave you time to process this information. Perhaps you will be more insightful when you have more time." This time, it is my father who storms from the room.

I find myself sitting in the room alone with my thoughts. Tin has done nothing wrong. They have no basis to accuse him. This means that for the first time in my life my father is wrong about something important. It's like a perfect bubble wrapping around his image has finally popped. The problem is, I'm not at all sure I like the man I've found inside.

Chapter

16

TUTOR IS AWARE HOW MUCH trouble he could be in today. In the last few suns, he has missed probably a dozen appointments with the princess. Sure, it could not be helped, but the Royals are not exactly known for being understanding.

People have been fired for less than this.

Gingerly, he pushes the door to the small study room open and lights the torch. He shakes his head, finding the room empty. *It was foolish to think, after all my missed meetings, Eselda would still rise to sit in this room and await me. I will check the garden. It is her favorite spot.*

In the garden, the wind is blowing and the sun is rising into the sky. Tutor glances up and allows himself a moment to wonder what else is out there in the world. He has recently had the pleasure of meeting a troop of scouts, who gave him a rather savage lesson in the reality beyond Fraun. They were filled with experience, only some of which Tutor himself was privy too. *They certainly lead an interesting life.*

Tutor snaps himself back to reality. The princess is nowhere to be found. Intending to leave a message for her with a hired hand, Tutor heads for the dining room. Typically, this time of day the help can be found cleaning the room in which the princess and the king have just finished consuming breakfast. He is surprised when he finds the object of his search, instead, occupying the room. "Princess Eselda?"

My attention is pulled from the wall. I squint at the man standing in the doorway. "Tutor?" The feelings churning inside me are mixed. I am happy he is alive and well, for I had feared worse when he failed to turn up for our sessions. That brings with it an anger. Why has he missed sessions? None of that changes the fact that this is my oldest friend and he is here. I don't stop myself from running to him and pulling him into an embrace.

It takes a second before Tutor recovers from his surprise and returns the hug. The second his arms tighten around me I notice their strength. Where did a private tutor gain this strength? The hug is over quickly and I'm staring at the man who has been absent from his position in my home. "Where have you been?"

"I have been ill, Princess. I was not well enough to travel. This prevented me both from getting word to you and from tutoring you."

"Could you not send another to give me word? We worried."

"I have no others, Princess, save for some who are either too old or too young to travel Enchenda alone."

"I searched for you in town, but I know not where to look." I find myself embarrassed at this admission. Why do I know nothing of his family; has he never offered or have I never asked?

"You shouldn't have done that Princess. My home is of no consequence to you. Please forgive me for missing meetings. Can we continue today or have I been let go?"

I take a step back from Tutor, toward the chair in which I had been sitting when he arrived. I wonder if he notices that the chair has been moved to the lineage tree. I wonder if he questions my sanity. "I do not believe a new tutor could adequately prepare me for the role I am to undertake before it is too late. Please stay, but know that another missed meeting like those of late will not be tolerated." I return to the chair, turning my back to Tutor and fully refocusing on my newest obsession.

Tutor takes another chair from the table and drags it to the wall beside me, the noise of the scraping wood along the rock giving away his progress. "What are we studying today, Princess?" he asks.

"Lineage."

"I had gathered such. What is it about lineage we are learning?" Tutor keeps his eyes on me instead of on the wall.

"Truth," I whisper.

"A noble quest, Majesty."

I turn to face him. "Do you know the truth of this wall, Tutor? Do you know of the people who have been blacked out?"

Tutor pulls his eyes from me to look at the wall. He has been in this room before; he has even seen the lineage tree before. Yet he gives it a careful look now, one you would give a puzzle or a challenge.

"I have heard rumors. Rumors that royal families in the Fraun intentionally leave bloodlines off their trees. That there are women who are shunned, babies who are left off the wall, or lines that appear to stop when this is not the case at all. Of course, rumors are never specific. There is no incident I am personally aware of."

I can see the moment when his eyes register the black ovals high up on the wall. He squints in frustration, trying to draw the memory out. "I know not who they are, but I am aware of the reason they have been blacked out."

"Because they were shunned?" I ask.

"Yes, that would be my assumption."

"But why? What would cause the family to shun a child?" I look back to the wall, finding the names above the black ovals. "Why would Elena and Charles shun one child and not the other?" I use my finger to gesture timidly toward the circle around Selena, evidently the sister of the shunned name. This name is circled and starred. "Whomever this shunned person was, their sister was Queen of Enchenda for a time."

Tutor sighs. "It is the belief of the ruling family that the shunned persons become nameless commoners. They are told not to have children. They are asked to live a life devoid of their past. They are asked to speak not of their beginnings. If anyone asks, they are to make something up or avoid the question altogether."

He shakes his head. "Princess, I know not of this tale. I do know people are shunned for many reasons. Royalty here does their best to be practical and humble. If someone here was shunned, causing their name to be removed, there must have been a good reason."

I sigh. He is hiding something. I can see it in the way his eyes cast downward when I ask a question. "I had hoped you were more adept at your history, friend." The final word rings with mockery.

"I fear I have let you down. I would tell you information I was privy to, Princess." He places a hand, lightly, on my arm. When I smile at him, he removes his hand quickly like one would remove it from hot coals.

"Perhaps you are better with more recent events." I rise from my chair, reach out my hand and smack it, hard, over Charlotte's covered name.

Tutor's eyes take in the area surrounding my hand. "What are you covering, Princess?" He leans toward the wall to better see. When I don't immediately move my hand, Tutor reaches out and pries my fingers off. I have drawn his interest. If I can get him interested, he will talk.

As Tutor takes stock of the wall surrounding the oval he mumbles to himself. "It appears to be connected to King Stefan, but no mother is linked. Typically, when one sees a blackened oval on a lineage chart you would expect to see an unwed mother blacked out as well, as is the case on the other spot. This, however, is a strange one. King Stefan must have had another child. But why would that child even be acknowledged on this wall?"

"Do you know what name this blemish hides?" I ask.

Tutor does not remove his eyes from the wall. "No, I honestly do not know."

"So it wasn't a scandal you had heard?" At this, Tutor turns to me. I try to flatten my hair and my disheveled dress under his gaze. Surely he notices I have been spending entirely too much time analyzing this wall.

"I have not heard anything that would make me think of this mark, no," Tutor says.

"I find that hard to believe. You have lived in this town most of your life. You have worked in this house much of your life. Yet you have heard nothing?"

"Eselda, how old do you think I am?" Tutor chuckles. "I have been alive only about five annuals longer than you. Whoever this is..." he places his finger on the spot "...would be a generation older than I. Their tale would have happened before I was born."

I sigh and sit back in my chair. Tutor follows my lead but remains sitting straight as I slump back. I pull my feet carefully underneath me and hide them beneath the folds of my blue dress. We sit in silence for a beat, I have resumed staring at the wall but I can feel Tutor's eyes on me, watching.

"Her name is Charlotte," I whisper.

"Whose name?"

I turn my eyes on him. "The shunned girl, the daughter of Stefan."

Tutor narrows his brown eyes at me, doubtful. "How would you know this?"

"I met her."

"When?"

"When you failed to show up I went looking for you. A woman told me her name was Charlotte and that she was my father's half-sister."

Without warning, Tutor wrenches his eyes from mine and stands. In his rush, he almost topples the chair. "What reason do you have to believe her? It's rather convenient that you wanted this information and she gave it." His arms gesture wildly as his voice raises.

His sudden anger is out of place with his previous calm. I'm not sure how to proceed. He's never been like this in front of me before. I try to speak in a low tone like one would calm an animal. "I actually talked to her first. I found the black spot afterward, confirming her story."

Tutor bristles and takes a step back from me, toward the door. "No. You have something wrong. Something is wrong." His voice is too loud. His face is darkening dangerously.

"My father confirmed it, Tutor. I don't understand why you think it is wrong." I gesture toward the empty chair. "Please, sit and explain it to me."

Tutor shakes his head. "No, I have to go. I have to research this." He turns on his heel and stomps to the door.

"Tutor, wait." From somewhere inside me I must have summoned some authority because he pauses, but does not turn. I rise and walk to him, placing my hand on his shoulder. I can feel an angry heat emanating from his slight frame. When Tutor was stomping his way to my door I noticed a slight limp. My curious nature craves an explanation for this, but my humble nature tells me it would be wrong to push Tutor now.

I am not this close to Tutor often. From here it is evident we are basically the same height. In fact, if I angle my chin skyward, I can whisper directly into his ear. "You are favoring your left leg. There is a story there, I'm sure. When you are ready to tell it, I am ready to hear it."

He nods once. When my hand leaves his shoulder, he doesn't hesitate to escape the room. Whatever that information meant to Tutor, it has clearly disturbed him. Quickly, I race out the door to follow behind him. I stay a distance behind, wanting to see where he goes. His feet carrying him along the dirt path out of my home and into town. Where could he be headed?

Tutor seems startled when he reaches a doorstep. But then he slowly nods, like he knows this is where he needs to be. He disappears into a house. I hurry up to the area, turning the corner I was hiding around. Clearly, my friend and tutor knows more than he was letting on.

This is Charlotte's home.

Chapter

17

*E*SELDA. *E*SELDA. *E*SELDA.

The name itself has become like a pulse for the king. The princess of Enchenda has occupied his thoughts so much lately his staff is beginning to notice his distracted nature. *Well, either that or they are shying away from me because of the disappearance of the chambermaid. Likely it's the second, but it's more fun to blame Eselda for the distraction. Eselda. Eselda. Eselda.*

Shortly after he met her he realized what she could offer him. Beauty. An interesting blend of humility and pride. And the promise of the vote of the second realm. Best still her humble upbringing keeps her from the knowledge of her own attractiveness. If he can earn her favor, she will be sure to vote the way he wants her to vote on all issues.

There is a reason women usually don't do well in a position of power. They are too easy to bend. A few kind words, a little flirting, and they are eating out of the palm of some poor man's hand.

He chuckles to the empty room. *A beautiful girl like Eselda might even be able to sway the votes of a few other men on the council. This could be grand.*

Doubt creeps into his mind unchecked. *But I must be wary. It would not do to let my heart, or other parts below the waist, lead the march. Eselda* can be allowed to occupy only my brain if I am to remain in control of the situation.

Men are fickle as well, that much we know. Men who allow themselves to be led by the heart, or by the genitals, are often consumed. In those cases, the woman has the power, and that is simply unacceptable.

As he sits in front of the family tree in his home, he promises himself one thing. *Eselda may occupy my mind, even take time from my day as I think of her. If necessary, she may even have a time in my bed.*

But I promise all the ancestors before me, Eselda will never occupy my heart.

Chapter

18

Eselda,

> *I have been thinking about our conversation following the council meeting and I have more I would like to discuss with you. If you are available, I'd be willing to travel to Enchenda and see you. My messenger will stay until you have finished reading this notice, awaiting your word.*

> *Logically,*
> *Jordyn*

SMILE AT THE MESSENGER WHO has brought me the letter. "Can you wait while I write a response?"

"Yes, Majesty." The man bows low.

I grab a parchment and quill from the table nearby, grateful I was in the study room when this man arrived. Quickly, I compose a response.

Jordyn,

No, that will never do. Jordyn, although barely my senior, is a king of his realm. He may have used an informal greeting in his letter to me, but I cannot do the same. I hastily tear the top off the parchment and begin again.

King Jordyn,

I have thought about our conversation as well. It would please me a great deal if you would visit us in Enchenda. I am available anytime your Majesty wishes to come this coming few suns. I look forward to your visit.

Humbly,
Princess Eselda

I read the notice over one time. Satisfied that the response is appropriate, I roll it and seal it with wax. I cross the room and hand the note over to the waiting man. "Thank you for waiting sir. If you visit my kitchen on your way out I trust you will be well fed and watered for your journey home."

The man bows low again. "Thank you, Princess."

When he is gone I allow myself to think of the last conversation with Jordyn. So much has happened since the meeting that I plainly can't remember all the details.

Hopefully, this will not be a problem when he arrives in Enchenda. I'm sure I can count on Jordyn to explain the purpose of his visit in more detail. With any luck, he will also be able to shed a little light on the topics I have uncovered since.

I am oddly surprised to find how much I want to see Jordyn again. Rarely in my life do I have contact with young men. Although lately, it seems to be happening more and more frequently.

A girl could get used to this kind of attention.

Chapter

19

THERE IS SOMETHING SATISFYING ABOUT gardening. Without someone to tend the garden, the weeds would overgrow and consume the life force of the edible plants. Without proper soil and technique, one could not hope to grow such a vast variety of vegetables all in one location.

This is a skill I learned from my mother, who tended gardens in the home of my father before they were wed. According to father, this is how they fell in love. Mother was tending the garden and he caught sight of her from his window. When he tells the tale it is love at first sight.

I have never felt that way, but the beauty of the story is that it makes things like that possible. That instant warmth you might feel when just seeing your destined lover for the first time. Will it be like lightning striking? My parents are that love story; two people entwined together in an embrace that no human can tear apart.

Of course, in reality, death broke them.

I turn my attention back to the soil in my hands, breaking up clumps as I run my fingers through it. The last of the peas have been harvested. I am turning over the soil in preparation for the next crop. The kitchen staff has saved me some garlic bulbs; I am excited to plant this delectable seasoning. I know what a flavor it can bring to the cooking, and it is an easy one to cultivate.

I dig my trowel into the soil, churning the deeper underlayer to the surface. When this rich layer, dark in color and cold to the touch, flips to the surface a small piece of earthworm comes with it. I dart my hand below the surface, in search of the rest of the creature. My hand closes around it. I dig my heels into the ground and stand. Using all of my strength I pull on the night crawler. I can feel it holding tight. Hopefully, the thing will not break further. I pull a little harder, the earth shifts around it. Before I can brace myself better for our change in momentum, the worm comes free. The sudden change sends me reeling backward onto my behind.

Laughter comes from behind me, turning my face instantly red.

"Well done, Daughter." Father pushes a bucket toward me. "Slide him in here, the kitchen will be happy to butcher him for our next stew."

I do as my king has ordered. Then I wipe my hands on the brown smock I have donned for gardening and sit back, resting my palms on the ground behind me. "Were you searching for me, father? Or perhaps just out for a walk."

"I was searching for you. I have not had a moment to meet with you about your meeting with Tin since your return. The last time we talked you had other things on your mind. I did not want you to feel neglected, but I was a busy man. I'd like to know what you discussed with the king of strength."

Father is being coy. He has not been too busy for me; he has been in bed. The doctor has been to see him at least three times since we met about the family tree. What a mistake it was to confront a dying man with something that would upset him. I will remain calm with him today. I take a breath of the calming garden air before smiling at him. "Honestly, Majesty, it was not much of a political conversation."

Thinking about the dinner, the way Tin's hand brushed mine, has my blush rising again. Then all at once, the memory washes over me like the cold water of the River Fraun. Tin's promise. Has he spoken with father? Perhaps Tin has asked permission to court me. That could be what father wishes to discuss. My heart gallops at the thought.

"You met with a king, one who was expecting me, and did not discuss politics."

"Well he asked my opinion, but I didn't know what I should say."

"What is that supposed to mean? You are a daughter of Enchenda. Your opinion is whatever opinion befits Fraun." Father sounds tired and irritated. I fear I am failing at keeping him calm.

"We hadn't discussed which option was best for Fraun. I was unprepared."

Gregario sighs. "So the king asked your opinion. You offered none. Then you left the home?" he summarizes.

"Basically."

"Basically?" The echo is a command to explain, I can hear it in his voice.

I slam my eyes shut as though I was slapped. "We ate a delightful meal and talked of our realms." Perhaps Tin hasn't spoken to father. What is he waiting for? Could he be losing interest? Was he merely pretending to be interested?

"What of the realms?" Father asks.

"He merely asked what people in Enchenda are like. He told me about strength competitions in Sarcheda. It was a nice meal, father. He treated me well." Wouldn't a father want to know his daughter was treated well by a possible suitor? Surely he notices Tin is my age and could be a suitor. Surely he does not begrudge Tin simply for his age like Mick and Larecio do.

"You are telling me you discussed nothing of consequence?"

"Have you spoken to King Tin, Majesty?" The question flies out of my mouth, an escaped butterfly I cannot hope to catch.

"No. Should I be expecting communications from him?" he asks his guard clearly up.

"I know not, father. I merely wondered why you seemed to doubt my recitation of events." There is my answer. Tin has yet to speak with father. Perhaps he overstated his feelings? Good, I don't need the hassle anyway.

"Eselda have you given any thought to betrothal?"

Wait, what? Keep calm. Keep calm. Keep calm. Why do the people in Fraun continue to ask about my love life? Could this be normal questioning or was I wrong to assume father hadn't spoken with Tin? "No. Why do you ask?"

"Daughter you have grown into a beautiful woman of eligible age. You are awaiting a throne. You would be a fool to think no men will be interested in you. I merely want to know if there is one who has already expressed an interest or one who you perhaps fancy."

"I have no such thoughts, father. I will fall in love, as you did, and marry one who is fit to help me rule Enchenda. Fear not." Anger builds in me. Why does no one trust me to do what is right for Fraun? It's as though everyone is waiting for me to bring our entire history crashing down. As though by merely not taking a spouse I am capable of unweaving everything that has come before me.

"Tell me what happens if you take a commoner for your beau, daughter."

"The commoner becomes Enchenda royalty. He would attend council meetings with me, as he is the king. I would still attend, as I am royal blood. Is that what information you seek, Majesty?" The title drips with sarcasm. I am a princess, but I am also your daughter. Stop talking about my love life as policy.

"It is. What happens if you marry a prince?"

I know this answer, but what prince does he speak of? Marchenda has Carsen, although I cannot recall how many annuals he is. Farcheda has Hector. No, that's not right. Hector is married. Although he does have a son, Patt. Technically Patt would be a prince, although one too young for me. "If I marry Carsen..." I pause to allow my father to point out another prince. He does not such thing, forcing me to continue the answer, "...then he would become the king of Enchenda. He would lose all claims and rights to the realm of Marchenda and sit on the council in my stead. Although I have royal blood, his royal blood would be sufficient."

Gregario nods his agreement. "Tell me, daughter, what happens if you were to take a husband who is already a seated king?"

I small flame of hope ignites. A smile sneaks to my lips, which I cover by wiping my brow, glistening from the heat of the forgotten gardening. He could be speaking of Tin. "Our realms would unite and I would again lose my seat on the council in favor of my royal blood husband."

"I see you have considered all the options, daughter. But the repercussions are stated like one giving an answer to their tutor. You speak not like a queen who is considering her realm. Think, daughter, what happens to your people if you marry the king of strength." Father's voice is a knife pointed at me.

I pull back from him, frightened of his sudden anger. He knows something. Otherwise, why would that example be thrown out with such ease? "Father, you are far ahead of my heart on this matter," I speak with a calm I do not feel. My own heart has galloped away like a race roach. I hope to calm my father. Certainly, this anger is not good for his condition.

"Perhaps that, daughter, is the problem," he says. "Leave this garden. Return not to this haven you have created until you have thought about what your people need of you. My time draws to a close and you must prepare to be the queen Enchenda needs. It's time to stop being so selfish, daughter, and embrace the humble nature you're able to speak of with practice."

I could not have been more insulted if my father had pierced my heart with the trowel. Selfish? The future queen of humility, selfish? I clamor to my feet, tears stinging my throat. I will not cry in front of the king. "I fear you simply do not remember what it was like to be young, father." I deliver the line like a slap and run for the house before he can see me cry.

Doubt begins to creep in. What if he is right? That parting line was bold. It was probably stupid. Was it selfish? Am I selfish? I sink to the floor behind my closed bedroom door. How can a selfish princess even hope to become the queen of humility?

Chapter

20

I N THE GARDEN, GREGARIO WHISPERS a response to his angry
daughter. It is not for her ears, but for Gregario's heart. "I fear you
have no idea what is coming your way. Being young can't help you
in your pending heartache."

Gregario sighs as the memories of his own innocent youth flood
his brain. *Dancing women, beautiful women, I certainly had my pick. I
remember my tutor, Den, teaching me the ways of Enchenda. How angry
Den was when I dared to take out the woman he had his eye on.*

How angry I was when they had to wed.

*It was this very garden I ran to that night when my father told me why
the couple's wedding had been rushed. This is the garden where I literally
crashed into the woman who would later be my wife.*

*What would have been different in my life had I married the other
woman?*

*It's silly to think it now. Stefan would never have allowed the other
marriage to happen.* He chuckles. *The old man would've swallowed nails
if I had even asked for the other hand.*

*Ancient history. It does no good to dwell on it. Rubina was a beautiful
woman and a remarkable queen for Enchenda. The other woman, she*

simply was not to be. I learned to love Rubina. When it comes time, Eselda will learn to love whomever it is best for her to be with.

The old king rises, feeling every day of his life in the old bones. His daughter will need to wed, that much is certain.

Perhaps it is time for him to choose a spouse for her.

Chapter

21

I FLOP ONTO THE BED IN my room, stomach down, and bury my face in the puff of pillow. Without question, this has been the longest, most confusing three moon cycles of my life. The school visit was the last time I was anything resembling normal.

Wait, that's not right. Jordyn arrived in Enchenda unannounced for the school visit. That cannot be classified as perfectly normal, now can it?

I roll over letting my hair flare out around me on the pillow. A sigh escapes my lips. Despite my honest attempt at keeping my cool yesterday, my father lost patience with me yet again. I know my father is seeing the doctor at this moment, I saw the man arrive. I had hoped to take my mind off father's health by meeting with Tutor, but he failed to show up again.

That's another problem altogether; what to do about Tutor. The last time we spoke I made it clear that another missed meeting would not go unnoticed. But how much of the fault for this one lies with me? In keeping with my apparent knack for angering people, Tutor's last meeting was a total disaster.

I play the conversation again looking for the threat that worked him up. Tutor's first outburst had occurred at the mention of me wandering the town. Could this simply be a case of another man in my life feeling like I cannot handle myself? Could it be that Tutor is worried I will discover something about him in town? Could he be protecting some secret of my father's?

Tutor's anger had intensified at the mention of Charlotte's name. So that eliminates the possibility he was worried merely about my safety. Surely he knows an old woman would pose no threat? But could she have something to do with Tutor himself?

Obviously, Charlotte holds secrets of my father's in her weathered hands. Tutor obviously knew I had unraveled that secret. Is it possible this old woman is hiding something else? She knows of the age markers. Perhaps Tutor has been a tutor to more than just me. Perhaps father's "taking care" of Charlotte includes providing her with a solid education. Is that what Tutor is hiding? It certainly fits.

I try to recall the rest of our conversation, turning the information as I turn soil looking for rich bits to bring nutrients. Tutor's body language was stiff throughout the conversation. In retrospect that was probably an indication of whatever malady he was hiding. I can easily call up a picture of his limp in my mind and replay it. As he was storming toward the door, his back muscles had first drawn my attention. Where did a private tutor work up muscles of that caliber? My eyes had then been drawn down his backside and that was when I noticed the limp. Tutor had been keeping his weight unevenly on his right leg, accommodating the left.

Standing that close to him, pointing out his limp, I had noticed a pleasant smell. Something pleasing and light, like sunshine. Somehow knowing his true age has me seeing him differently. I guess since he has always been in a position of authority over me, I had assumed he was much older. It shocks me to learn he is so young. Yet as I picture him in my head now, I'm further surprised that I missed the signs.

The slight muscular build, the thick light hair, the youthful energy radiating from him. I close my eyes and try to bring the smell back to my senses. Sunshine and hard work. My entire body warms as I think of the way he trembled beneath my hand when my breath graced his ear.

Then he left here and went to see Charlotte. I'm standing before

I've fully formed the thought. Charlotte will give me the answers Tutor hides. The riding cloak is snuggly fit to my shoulders before doubt can settle there. Everyone in my life is hiding things, Charlotte is revealing. She will be able to tell me something. I will not leave until she does.

Chapter

22

OUTSIDE MY HOME, THE AIR is chillier than it has been. The days are shortening, meaning the cold weather is drawing closer. The sun is still shining and no clouds mar the sky, but the people of Enchenda are piling extra wood and preparing fabric for layers. Soon the cold will come, and it does not do well to be caught unprepared.

I walk with a new determination, my bare feet striking the dirt in a rapid rhythm. I march past the house where I taught the men of the lift and notice the contraption being utilized on a nearby cart. Further up the road, a young woman is struggling with something in a yard to the right. My training takes over and I feel my body slow, despite my desire to get to Charlotte quickly. The woman is yanking something in a small garden. Even as I try to talk myself out of helping, I feel my feet approaching the woman. "Is there something I can be of assistance with?"

The woman turns, surprise registering on her face as she recognizes me as her princess. Already hovering low to the ground, bent over something, the woman tries to bend lower in a bow. "Princess Eselda, I am not needing your help Majesty, but thank you."

"Would you take the help of a neighbor were it her offering?" I ask, squatting beside the woman.

"Perhaps," the woman answers hesitantly.

From this angle, I can now see the woman is pulling on the root of a weed which has taken residence in her garden. She must have pulled on the head of the plant at first, dislodging it. This makes the task of removing the root much more difficult. I crack my knuckles. "Well, you are in luck then, neighbor. I live just up the road and I came to help." I lean in and grasp the root below the woman's hands. "We shall pull on three, together. Straight up toward the heavens, lady. Ready?" I feel the woman's grip tighten.

"One…" I plant my feet securely "…two…" I lock my elbows "…three!" We both pull with every bit of strength we have. The weed does not release all in one movement. Instead, it shifts slowly. I give hearty tugs, grunting under the pressure.

Finally, the weed is separated from the ground. I take deep breaths to restore my lung capacity. Beside me, I hear the woman doing the same. She recovers first. "Thank you, Majesty."

"Happy to help. Good luck with your garden, maiden."

Having detoured, I now feel as though I must travel even faster. I am moving so swiftly, holding my rusty colored skirt in my hands, that I nearly run into a child as I round the corner into the town square. "Oh, excuse me," I call. The child, undeterred, continues to run full speed up the road. I force myself to slow down and take in the entire square with my eyes.

There are fewer people out this afternoon than last time I was here. A shopkeeper is brushing the dirt from his stoop. There are a few women walking, one holding the hand of a smaller child. Someone is picking strawberries from the bush near the edge of the square, across from my chosen path of entrance. Two small boys, maybe the same ones I saw on my last visit, toss a cherry pit back and forth. The boys are taking one step back after each toss, testing how far away you can be from another person before you drop that which they are asking you to save. As I resume walking, at a slightly slower pace, my eyes fall back to the strawberry picker. He is now standing and I recognize him immediately. My desire to see Charlotte fades as I change course and head right for him.

"Jordyn!"

"Good afternoon Eselda. I trust this is a good time for my visit." He smiles, the gesture reaching his blue eyes.

In the short time since I have seen the king, I had forgotten how tall he really is. The top of my head could fit snuggly inside the king's armpit. He is wearing brown traveling pants and a white shirt, which is open slightly at the neck. He is wearing some kind of chain there, but I cannot clearly see what it is. "How did you get here?" I see no sign of a traveling animal with him.

"Ladybug, actually. I was walking through Renchenda and a nice ladybug offered me a ride to Enchenda in exchange for food when I arrived." He holds up an aphid he must have found among the bushes. "I was on my way back to the edge of town to pay the insect. Care to join me?" Jordyn hoists the bug into his right arm and offers me his left elbow.

"Gladly." I slip my arm through the offered limb and allow myself to be lead around the strawberry patch outside of the Enchenda town square. A few steps past the opening the bright red of the ladybug comes into view. A few steps farther and it is clear the creature sees us as well.

"I thought you had turned your back on our deal, King of Renchenda." Unlike the roaches I have heard many times, the ladybug's voice is low pitched and deadly. It makes me shudder.

"I would never do that. I am, after all, the king of wisdom." Jordyn bends low, placing the restitution on the ground in front of the ladybug. "What would be the wisdom in causing problems with another species?"

"It would not have been wise, King. Thank you for the food." The ladybug grasps the smaller species, turns, and hustles off out of sight.

"What a beautiful breed," I say.

Jordyn stands, wiping his hands on his pants. He turns his attention to me, looking at me properly from my messy strands of hair piled on my head past my rather orange dress and down to my naked and dirty feet. I feel insecure under his gaze, fidgeting as he watches.

"Have you been working hard this morning, Princess?" he asks. "You have a shine about you."

I blush deeply and cast my eyes on the ground. "I was walking rather quickly, I suppose."

"For what purpose? Where were you headed?"

I look back up at the king, but the sun falls into my eyes and I have to squint. "Into town. I was in search of my tutor. He failed to show up for our lesson."

"So you were worried about him?" Jordyn's face scrunches up under the confusion.

"It's no matter. I had no other business this morning, I thought I would seek him out and perhaps get some answers." I look around the little clearing we are standing in. Around us grass grows tall, keeping people out. This area is flattened, and there is a piece of wood that must have been dragged here off to the side. I gesture toward it. "We should sit. You have at least one mark on me, I have to stare up at the sun when we speak."

Jordyn laughs. "I had noticed my neck tilts at an awkward angle to inspect you as well. Let us sit."

I stand beside the wood to let the king sit first. When he does so he slumps slightly, I wonder if this is to give off a relaxed air or a further attempt to get closer to my height. He turns his upper body toward the right, leaning back on the stalk of a plant growing behind the wood. I sit beside him and allow my posture to relax as well.

"Last time we spoke, Eselda, I mentioned betrothal to you. I wonder if you've learned anything new on that topic or had any further insights." Jordyn's position continues to appear relaxed, but his eyes flash with a curiosity that interests me. Are all in his realm this interested in conversation?

"Everyone has been speaking of my love life lately. It seems to be everyone's favorite topic of conversation."

"Oh?" Jordyn questions, "Who else is asking?"

"My father, my tutor, you, and King Tin." I had not made up her mind to mention the meeting with Tin, but it slips from between my lips.

"Interesting. My apologies for bringing it up again. We can talk about something else if you would like." Jordyn turns his head and looks at the ground, the gesture makes it clear he is uncomfortable.

His offer is moving. Many others in this position would try to convince me that this conversation is important and worth having. Jordyn has faith in my decision. For this reason alone, I will talk to him openly about it. "I have done nothing but think on this topic, honestly," I whisper.

Jordyn's blue eyes return to my face. "Go on." Somehow it does not come out as the command from a king, but the reassurance of a friend. This is a safe place to talk.

"I know what happens to Fraun and Enchenda depending on whom I choose to marry. But what of love? Our ancestors filled our heads with the idea that we will one day be slaves to an emotion so great we would literally die for it. I have never felt such a pull toward another. I often think I feel something, but how will I know when I feel that?" The words gush from me, pulled toward the tide of a logical listener who will not judge. "King Tin professes to feel something as well. He desires to ask permission to court me." Although he certainly has not rushed to make good on that. "At least that's what he claimed. He has yet to speak with Father."

"When did he claim this?" Jordyn asks.

"I had dinner in Sarcheda not long ago, maybe seven suns. Toward the end of dinner, he asked if I were being courted, said he would like to do just that." I drop my eyes from Jordyn's, embarrassed to be having such a conversation with him. I feel the blush, fast becoming a characteristic of my face, creep into my cheeks.

"What was your opinion of King Tin?"

"I'm not sure."

"Before he mentioned courting you, what had you felt about the evening?"

I think back. "I found him interesting. I felt warm when we were talking, I wanted him to continue talking. What does all that mean?" I dare myself to return my eyes to Jordyn's face. He is looking off to the right, eyes narrowed. Perhaps he is thinking.

"I do not know what that means. I know what hate feels like, it is the age marker I fight against each day."

I watch as Jordyn tenses under the chosen topic. I am afraid to move. Am I about to hear a firsthand account of what I will face when I am under the malicious age marker?

"Hate boils in your heart, quickens your breathing, and drives your adrenaline to spike. Hate fuels your body to act on every indiscretion. To think on every mistake. You feel hate in varying degrees for different people. One thing is constant, hate dominates your mind if you let it."

I could not hope to comment even if I wanted to. I am frozen in fear, my eyes locked on the king, new appreciation for what he is battling coursing through my veins. Then he turns his head, just a little, and those sharp blue eyes come into my vision again.

"Hate I understand, but of its counter, I know not."

He turns away again. I silently pray for his voice to continue, for his eyes to find mine again. *Please, Jordyn, you can trust me.* When I cannot wait any longer, I speak. My voice is quiet, soothing. "Perhaps love is as strong as its antagonist. Love then could warm your heart." I reach out and touch the king's chest, feeling the beat of his heart beneath his ribs. "Love could quicken your breathing and spike your adrenaline as well. Where hate may feel harsh when this happens, perhaps love will feel soft and free."

The king still keeps his gaze steady, but I feel his heartbeat quicken. He is listening. I slide my body closer to Jordyn and continue in an even softer tone. "Love will fill our hearts to act on every impulse to be with the one we love, perhaps to ignore their every mistake and flaw." My speech is rewarded. Jordyn lifts his chin and meets my gaze. Warmth spreads out over my entire body.

"Perhaps, like its reverse, love is also felt to varying degrees." I move my hand to the center of his ribcage, flattening my palm. "I feel it right here as I talk to you, compelling me to move closer to you and heal your pain. It stands to reason that love would devour you as well if you let it."

"The power of hate scares me, Eselda. What if love has the same power?"

"I am sure it does. But how can I fear something with such promise?"

Jordyn dips his head toward me until our noses are practically touching. He closes his eyes and sighs. "I feel it now. Thank you for helping me find it. This may be just what I need to fight the hate inside me."

Jordyn leans closer yet, his lips finding mine. The short kiss is enough to spark bursts of flame all over my body. I have never known such a feeling.

When Jordyn sits back to his relaxed position, I have to stop myself from pulling him back toward me. Instead, I take a deep breath and fight with my body to force it back into my original position as well. "You're welcome. Just remind me of this when I am twenty annuals and struggling with my inner monster." I try to force my voice to be light, but the kiss has left my head somewhere in the clouds. It sounds forced.

Jordyn laughs. "I will do just that. I must say, Eselda, the wisdom and logic you displayed there would make a citizen of Renchenda proud."

"Truly?" Praise from their king? Am I worthy of that?

"Of course. Applying the principles of hate to love is remarkably wise. I'm surprised I did not think of it myself."

"Don't feel too bad. Had you not been consumed by your age mark, I am confident you would have discovered it as well."

"There is that humility you are so fond of here. You cannot take the praise without returning it." Jordyn chuckles. "It is a beautiful trait. I shall try to adopt it as well if we are to be friends."

"Is that what we are to be?" I ask. Instead of blushing and looking away, I keep my eyes fixed on Jordyn. He is still smiling, but somehow it is uncomfortable. Perhaps even a little sad.

"I fear it is all we can be, Eselda. What would happen to our realms if we were to be anything more?"

He speaks the truth, I know. After that moment we just shared, I do not want to chase him away by asking for too much. Friends I can do. "I want to be your friend, Jordyn. We will be the best of friends."

Jordyn said you can feel hate in varying degrees for various people. That must be true for love as well. Therefore, I must not feel guilty for having feelings for other people. I can even help this whole betrothal thing along by acknowledging my feelings as they come. I feel some love for Jordyn, but didn't I also feel a little for Tin? Maybe even for Tutor?

"I am glad you feel that way. I want to be your friend as well," Jordyn says. Again when he smiles I see sadness. Then again perhaps I am only hoping there is a small grain of sadness for the love that cannot be allowed to bloom.

"Now, friend, shall we head to my father's home and dine at his table? We can talk more about Fraun after dinner?" I ask.

"Lead the way, Eselda."

Chapter

23

Y HEART FLUTTERS SO FAST I fear it will fly right out of my chest. Jordyn and I are walking back toward my home, hands clasped between us, talking about Enchenda. He is so eager to learn everything about my realm. "That is my father's home, ahead," I point out.

"It's only slightly larger than the homes of the people nearby. Your family did well in keeping themselves humble to the people they serve."

"It is really only larger because of the people who live in it. Aside from my father and myself, there is a lady in waiting, a cleaning employee, and a few who care for the roaches. They all can live in the home if they like. We also have a room alongside the kitchen where a warm bed, water, and meals can be provided for anyone in Enchenda in need of a place to stay. It's been used from time to time but is empty at the moment."

"People do not take advantage of that?" Jordyn asks.

"I'm not sure why they would. If you can find someplace else to sleep you would leave that room for someone who cannot. It's quite simple a concept, really."

"Interesting."

I pull the door to my home open. "I should really head to my room and freshen up."

"Could you point me toward the room we were speaking of? I'd really like to see it."

I point through the doorway across from us. "The dining room is through there. The kitchen door is on the right wall. The spare room is to the left once you are inside the kitchen." I think through the dress I would like to put on, what I wish I could do to my hair. "On second thought, I can go with you. I should tell the staff you are here anyway."

"No, I can handle it. Trust me, after the Castle Fraun this little house should be the perfect size to navigate." Jordyn enters through the dining room doorway, ducking slightly to enter, and disappears from view.

Who am I to argue with a king? I drop my hair from its tie and run my fingers through it to untangle the curls as I walk. I brush my hands over the skirt, dislodging stray dirt. When I reach my room I grab a black overskirt and tie it around my waist. A quick turn in the reflecting wall brings me satisfaction. Next, I use a small bowl of clean water nearby to wash my face and other exposed skin. There. Fresh enough for dinner with two seated kings, assuming the one I'm related to is well enough to join us for dinner.

Back in the dining room, I find father and Jordyn have already been seated. "Eselda, so glad you could join us," father greets. There are plates piled with salad before both kings and another at the empty place in front of the fire. I take my seat. "King Jordyn, it is an honor to have you at our table. To what do we owe the pleasure?" When father reaches for his fork, I do the same. I realize how hungry I am and have to force myself to chew slowly and be presentable.

"I have been thinking about the future of Fraun. Obviously, your daughter holds the key to our kingdom remaining at five realms, I was interested in speaking to her of this," Jordyn explains between bites.

The key to the kingdom? That seems a little overzealous.

"What opinion have you on these issues?" Gregario asks.

"The same opinion as you, I am sure. The princess must have an heir, in case of accident or death--"

"Are you lecturing me on marriage and babies as well? Where are your heirs, king of wisdom?" I snap. The two kings turn their attention to me, falling silent for a beat.

"Do you approach twenty annuals, Princess?" Jordyn asks, quietly.

"No, I approach the end of my patience with people trying to plan my life." I stand up quickly, almost toppling the little chair. "If you two wish to discuss what I should or should not do, you can do so without me. Good evening." I leave the room quickly but stop just outside the door. I hope one of them will call me back into the room. Perhaps follow me out.

"You were saying?" Gregario prompts.

"Oh, yes. I was saying Eselda needs an heir. I fear King Tin will win her heart, leaving us with only four realms. Four realms could vote in a tie. Four realms could change our way of life. It is not wise to have an even number of realms, sir. I merely came to see if my fears were becoming reality."

"King Tin is not the only one who could cause this, I feel as though I need to remind you of that."

"True. However, regardless of my feelings on the subject, I am wise enough to know this would be bad for Fraun. You have no need to fear my intentions, good king. I merely wish to help in any way that I can," Jordyn says.

"You strike me as a good and honest king, Jordyn."

"Thank you, Majesty."

"Have you ever met with King Mick on your own?" Gregario asks.

"I have not. Have you?"

"I have. He doubts the good of King Tin. How feels Renchenda on this topic? You are as much their neighbors as we are, perhaps you have seen or heard things. Perhaps you have even met with King Tin on your own."

"I believe Tin struggles with his age marker more than I, he allows himself to fall victim to it at times. However, I must say I have no reason or evidence to believe Tin is guilty of anything resembling rule breaking for Fraun. Like yourself, Tin is a king in Fraun. I put my trust in that title," Jordyn answers.

It is quiet for a bit. I assume both kings are enjoying the salad I abandoned. I am tempted to return to the table, finish my meal. I could also continue what I started out to do and head all the way to my room. Really I should do anything but stand here in the hallway eavesdropping on yet another conversation between two seated kings of Fraun.

"On the issue with my daughter, have you spent time talking with her? I find myself in a difficult position. She often will not speak with me, losing her temper as you just witnessed. I do not wish to choose a spouse for her, but I fear for Fraun I may have to if she cannot choose one herself."

What? My father could not would not choose a spouse for me. That cannot possibly be what is best for Fraun. What is he thinking?

"Eselda and I are friends. I wish not to break any confidences she may have trusted me with. However, I feel as though it would be acceptable to tell you King Tin expressed a desire to court your daughter. For reasons we have previously discussed, this should not be allowed. I hope you will think on that before he approaches you for permission."

"He will not be given my permission, Jordyn," father answers.

"Thank you."

"Again I must reiterate that you will not be given that permission either, good sir."

"And again I must remind you that I will not be asking for it, good sir."

I hear the change in the voices, they are deeper and more edged. Well good. Here they sit planning my entire life and discussing who I can and cannot marry. It's revolting. They should be ashamed.

"You demonstrate impressive control of your age marker. Are you approaching twenty-five annuals?" my father asks.

"I am barely twenty, actually. I believe my will to fight it is simply stronger than most."

"You do not wish to let your darker side take hold? I remember my own years fighting the beast within. I picked fights with everyone. In fact, the desire to give into the darkness was so strong some days that I would need to get in fights just to sleep."

"Never," Jordyn answers.

"I am impressed. You have earned my trust; I will give you this. Mick is thinking war."

In the hallway, the word makes my anger and likely my color leave. War? We cannot abide that.

"I had feared as much. What does he want from the council, assuming he wants something to avoid war?"

"A renumbering."

"In favor of his own realm?"

"Yes. Your brain has reached that quickly. You are truly wise."

"Obviously. Gregario, a renumbering cannot happen. Farcheda is known for being too quick, that would be highly unwise. I would not vote in favor of that," Jordyn says.

"He knows he will not have your vote. He needs another to vote with us."

"You favor a renumbering?" Jordyn asks.

"I am not so sure anymore."

I hear the chair scrape along the floor, indicating someone is rising. I turn to head down the hall. My feet move slowly like the new information I've gleaned is weighing me down physically.

"I enjoyed this meal and the chance to speak with you freely Gregario. I believe it would be wise for me to speak with Eselda again before I leave. Therefore, please excuse me," Jordyn says.

That is the last I hear before I'm down the hall. I do not stop until I'm lying on my bed behind a closed door. I am braced for a knock, for my name to be called, something. It takes a remarkably long time. My body relaxes, my breathing slows. I wait.

Finally, I hear the faint knock at my door and the voice of Eee call out my name. "What do you need, Eee?" I ask, my voice muffled by the pillow on the bed.

"King Jordyn is searching for you, Princess," the roach calls.

I sit up and run my fingers through my hair again. Then I cross the room and fling the door open. "Where is…" but there is no need to finish the question. The tall king is standing in the doorway, his blue eyes shining directly into my face. "Thank you, Eee."

"Eselda, can we talk?" Jordyn asks.

"Oh, you would actually like to talk to me now?" I step to the side and wave him into the room. I pull a chair out from under a table near the reflecting wall for Jordyn before dropping myself onto my bed.

"I am sorry if I offended you at dinner," Jordyn states. He sits in the offered chair.

"I am tired of everyone pushing me."

"I noticed that." He smiles. "But if your father dies and you have not wed, I fear many men will want to marry you for the title alone."

"You fear I will not be happy with these men?"

"I fear it will be bad for Fraun. Honestly, I hadn't really considered your happiness on the matter. I apologize for that as well."

"What do you propose I do then, Jordyn?" I throw my hands up. "All of you want to tell me what is wrong and what I cannot do. Would you please offer some advice on what I should or what I can?"

"Meet with Carsen, find a nice boy from Enchenda, or meet unwed men from the family trees still holding branches like that. You may find you have feelings for these men, but how can you learn that if you will not meet with them?"

"Why does this all fall to me?"

"You are a princess in a realm where there is no one else and your king is ill."

"There is no one besides you in your realm," I point out. "Don't people pressure you the same way?"

"Yes." He makes no further attempt to explain. Offers no advice on how to deal with it or what to do about it. He doesn't offer an explanation on why he can't take his own advice to meet someone nice.

"I want you to be wrong, but I feel I cannot say you are until I have tried meeting with these people. I suppose this is the price of being royal."

"It is. The people of Fraun deserve the best from us. They deserve a future. We must do our level best to prepare the Fraun for that."

"You make a good point."

"Of course I do, that is my way," Jordyn says.

I laugh at the true statement. It feels good to laugh with him.

"I am still your friend, Eselda. I want what is best for you, but it must also be wise for Fraun." Jordyn rises. "I have a long journey ahead of me. Can I trust we will remain in touch?"

I stand up in front of him. "We will keep in touch." I offer the king my hand. He shakes it, but I pull him into a hug instead. He smells of rainwater and air. "Travel well, Jordyn."

"Thank you. See you soon."

The door clicks softly behind Jordyn and I flop back onto my bed. Today I learned what power love and hate can have. I have learned you can catalog your feelings of love, felt to different degrees, and perhaps I can use this to find a prince suitable for my kingdom. I have also heard a word I never wanted to hear. Can war truly be on the mind of King Mick? Is that ever best for a kingdom?

Honestly, I cannot imagine a situation where war would be an option I would condone.

Chapter

24

I WOKE UP THIS MORNING WITH the desire to find Charlotte burning in my soul again. I need to ask her about Tutor. I cannot be stalled again. I dressed quickly and hurried to the town square. But when I arrived at the door, there was no answer. I drop myself onto the stoop in front of her home and watch the morning unfold.

The sun is just now beginning to rise, sparkling off the drops of dew on the grass square. A group of hunters traipses out of one house, long swords tied to their backs. Men with cutting implements take to the grass, laying on their bellies to be sure and cut it low enough. Mostly, it is quiet and peaceful. I could easily let myself slide back into sleep, but I fight the pull of my eyelids.

"Princess Eselda?" a small voice questions.

I turn my head to find a young girl, blonde and small. She is probably approaching ten annuals, if not already there. Her brown eyes are flecked with green and she wears the most enchanting little smirk, one not yet marred by the realities of life. She is also standing on the doorstep of Charlotte's home. "Good morning young maiden. I am actually waiting here to speak with Charlotte. Do you know the woman?"

"Charlotte is my mother," the girl answers.

My mouth drops open. "C-C-Can I speak with her?" I ask, my voice rising in pitch.

The girl spins on her heel and enters the now open front door, calling for Mother as she jogs through the little house. Beyond the girl I can see Charlotte standing in the kitchen, hunched over near the stove. She issues a small, tired laugh. It is followed by a cough that wracks her small frame. When her coughing ceases she stands tall. "I knew you'd be back, Princess. Please come in."

The young girl steps out of the way to allow me entrance. The fire has just been lit, it is sparking wildly but not yet giving off much warmth. Charlotte is holding a teapot, waiting for the flames to get themselves under control before lowering the metal into them. She is dressed in a nightgown, the bare material brushing her ankles. Her long gray hair is to her waist and slightly curled, as though the braids I last saw in her hair have caused the crimps to remain permanently. Her eyes looked clouded, but I cannot tell if it is worry, fear, or illness that causes this today.

"Have a seat, I'm just preparing tea. We can chat."

I hear the door click closed behind us, leaving us alone in the house. "I met your daughter," I challenge.

"Ah, I feared that may come up. Silly girl was told to say I was her Aunt if anyone asked. Still, I suppose that would've made you ask questions as well." Charlotte shakes her head, drops the tea kettle into the flames, and sits at the table across from me. "Let's have it then, say what you must." She reaches up and parts her own hair into two long skinny halves on either side of her face.

"I am a royal member of the House of Enchenda, madam. You were shunned and told to bear no children." I try to make my voice sound authoritative and stern. Truthfully, inside my nerves are shaking and frayed.

"That much I know child, what plans have you of dealing with us?" Charlotte begins to braid one segment of hair. Her fingers work efficiently.

"I do not know. I will have to speak with the king," I answer. What other choice do I have in the matter?

"Well, then I have no fears. Gregario knows of the child."

"I would love nothing more than to tell you that cannot be true. I fear with the last tale you told me checking out…" I taper off, sure my meaning is cutting through. My father has been keeping much from me, no wonder he is worried I cannot handle Enchenda. Look how easily he spilled the talk about his own battle with royal blood to Jordyn. "That young child has royal blood?"

"Shhh." Charlotte places a finger to her own lips. "She doesn't know that. Keep your voice down." Charlotte removes the finger and leans closer to me, her hands resting on the table between us. The braid she just finished begins to slowly unravel at the ends. "No one around here knows this family is anything other than ordinary, including my daughter. You'll keep that to yourself, or your father may change his mind about our situation."

I hesitantly nod. Charlotte relaxes back in her chair and finishes the braid, affixing it with a length of string from the table. The braid is sloppier than the last one I saw. Perhaps the girl braided the last. "Tell me the story of the girl," I say.

"Sawchett is her name. If I tell you the story, can we continue to have our anonymity once you are queen?"

My father has been guarding this secret for years, evidently. No further harm can come of this promise at this time. I nod. "I will make our tea this time, you tell the story."

"Very well."

I have remarkable recall. I find the silver mugs exactly where they were last time. I busy myself grinding some leaves I pull through the open window.

"I grew up not knowing I was any different than anyone else around here," Charlotte says. "I attended the school like everyone else, beginning at five. I don't know how it is for you, being royalty and all, but around here girls start looking for a mate around thirteen annuals. Just about the time a maiden turns fifteen and has hit all her age markers, she's usually found her spouse and they can wed. It keeps our population moving if you know what I mean."

I pour water over the leaves, not wishing to discuss the implications of that statement with an old woman. Yes, I know what you mean. Move on.

"One day I met someone in town, I was just shy of fifteen annuals myself. We spent the day together, talking about nothing. We were friends. I told myself we could be nothing more."

My sadness returns as I think of Jordyn. But Jordyn is a seated king, his reason for us to be nothing more is that it would be bad for Fraun and leave us with only four realms once my father passed. One can assume that there are other reasons in the world, but I can't think of any. "Why could you only be friends, Charlotte?"

"Plainly, his job would make things difficult. Let's leave it at that. He is not the girl's father. I bring him up only because he introduced me to the father. Shall I continue?" Charlotte asks.

I nod.

"Anyway my friend and I saw each other often, we would stroll the realm and talk about all things. He was a great companion. One day, on such a walk, we came across his father. His father was known to be a strict man and I had seen him on a few occasions. He recognized me, greeted me warmly. I fear he spoke to his son about me, however. After that, the boy was different." Charlotte's eyes look sadly to the right.

Possibly because I was already thinking of him, the movement of her eyes reminds me again of Jordyn. He always looks to the right when he is deep in thought. The sadness ebbs a little when I picture him doing that. I bring a mug of tea to Charlotte and take a sip of one myself.

"When I turned fifteen annuals the boy had me over to dinner. I foolishly thought he was going to announce that he'd figured something out, we could be wed. Instead, he and his father introduced me to another man. This man, Den, worked inside the royal home. Just as now, that was a noble profession. He was a good solid man with a good solid work ethic. It was clear Den had the blessings of my friend and his father to court me."

"Why would he need their permission and not that of your own mother and father?"

Charlotte throws me a dangerous glare for the interruption. "He didn't, of course. Not technically. But this was a family I was obviously close with, as I was having dinner in their home. I think it was the honor of the thing. For me it was a way to make it obvious; I could not have the son but I could have Den."

"Weren't you sad?" I know I was. I pretend not to care that Jordyn can so easily dismiss me as a friend and ignore those feelings. It hurt to hear him tell my father he would not ask to court me.

"I was. Sometimes I still am, when I think about it. But it was for the best, Princess. Trust me on that." Charlotte takes a sip of her tea and begins braiding the other half of her hair. "Anyway, I was telling you about Den. There is no question I loved Den. Shortly after meeting him, I felt all the signs within me whenever we were together. My mother noticed I was acting differently. That is when she chose to tell me about my past, my real past. She explained to me, as I will have to explain to Sawchett, the truth of our shunning. She told me about Gregario and Stefan, the story I have already related to you."

I nod. My head is swimming with the new world I have been learning and I find myself leaning toward Charlotte's voice, eating up the story like a starving man.

"When my mother told me I was shocked, I felt betrayed. It was Den who comforted me. I poured out my feelings to him, I told him everything."

"Everything," I echo the word reverently. This one little word has so many implications here. I turn them all over in my mind.

"Everything," Charlotte repeats the word with a veneration to match my own. "I probably should have been concerned. He could've revealed it to everyone. He did not. Instead, he pulled me into a hug and he promised to keep my secret.

"He even told me that I could use him as an excuse. We could tell everyone that he was unable to bear children. That way, he told me, the shame would be his." Charlotte finishes the final braid and ties it off.

"What a humble gesture," I say. I know that coming from me, the princess of humility, this will carry much weight.

"I told you he was a good man," Charlotte says.

"That's true you did. So you married Den?" I push the story onward, eager for the next tidbit. If they had promised one another no children, where did Sawchett fit in?

"We did. Your father attended the wedding, actually. It was a nice gesture, although one that proved rather tough to explain to a few local women." Charlotte chuckles at the memory. "Greg and I began staying in contact, he helped with food when we needed it. I think he needed the family connection as much as I did. It was a rather odd friendship. I can only describe it as strained. We were so obviously on different paths. Den and I were forced to be careful in our own bedroom, we could not make children. Greg and Rubina were having the opposite problem, with all of Fraun pressuring them for an offspring."

I can relate well to that pressure.

"Den and I made a mistake, though. One I tried to hide even from Greg. I became pregnant. The thought of giving the baby to Greg to raise, since it would have royal blood, crossed my mind. He needed an heir, I needed to not have one. Perhaps it would be best. It was only thoughts of my mother's struggles, being forced to live a life she didn't ask for, that made me keep the baby away from Greg. I pushed him away, refused to see him or let him visit, and hid all signs of the pending infant from him."

This story has taken a strange turn. The math does not work out. Why would Enchenda still need an heir? Clearly, Sawchett is younger than I am. "What happened to this baby?" I ask, finding I crave the answer.

"He died at birth." The answer is clipped, curt.

I pull back from the change in tone. Perhaps talking about this is too painful? "I'm sorry."

"It's no matter. When Greg found out that I had hidden a child, he was furious. He threatened to withdraw his family's support from my life. We didn't speak for ages and my family got by just fine without his help." Defiantly, Charlotte drinks her tea.

"What changed?" I use my gentlest voice to remind Charlotte I am not my father. I am not the enemy. Give me a chance and I will do what is right.

"You were born," Charlotte answers.

"Me?"

"Yes. Your father changed a lot after your birth. He reached out to me, he began helping again. I think seeing you helped him understand what I went through. For a while, things were well. Then two things happened to change all that. Your mother died and Den lost his job. Although unrelated events, they each took their toll on someone from my tale. I handled Den's termination poorly, as did Greg handle the death of his wife."

"I remember that, my mother's death I mean. I was close to ten annuals."

"You were. Anyway, Gregario and I had a huge row. Really we haven't spoken since. I was eager to make him miserable, as he had made me with the fight. I also wanted Den to be happy, I think. Either way, I must admit Sawchett was no accident. Once she came to be I knew there was no chance Greg would ever speak to me again. If help comes now, it is often delivered by a staff member. He knows of the child, but he has never met her. He refuses to. It's all well and fine, he keeps our secret buried deep. But the other kings, they cannot know. The council would order our deaths. It is the only way."

How revolting. That cannot be true. The kings are good people.

Wait, according to father, they don't have to be good people. They merely have to protect their trait. The council I have met is not like the council I imagined. They are not rational when speaking of royal blood. Perhaps what Charlotte says is true. Perhaps Sawchett is not safe if they know. "I will keep your secret, Charlotte. You have my word."

"Thank you, Eselda. I cannot tell you what that means to my little family."

"What became of Den?" I ask, glancing around the room for signs of another soul.

"He died a few annuals past. He was older than I, he grayed shortly before Sawchett was born. He never even heard her speak, she was not yet five annuals as he lay dying here on the floor." Charlotte glances to the curtain, the memory overtaking her.

I can see water building in the woman's eyes. "What will become of Sawchett when you pass?" I ask.

"I suppose I don't know."

"She will live in my home," I state. What did I just say? I don't know the first thing about children. Then again it was wrong of my family to disown this woman. I can make this right. "I can raise her. I know a good tutor who will see to her education. No one needs to know she is in my home until we are ready to tell them." As I say it, I feel the idea taking hold of me. Another girl in the house will be nice.

"But Greg…" Charlotte lets the protest fall into the room, unfinished.

"He is not long for this world. I can keep this promise, I assure you. Let me figure out the details."

"Thank you." Tears fall down Charlotte's cheeks. "I cannot tell you what this means to me. To think one of my family will be accepted by one of yours. It's too much to take." Charlotte stands. "I must think on this. Princess, be well." She plants a kiss on my forehead and disappears behind the curtain hanging in the home.

Not sure what else to do, I rinse the teacups and set them upside down to dry. I quietly leave the house. Outside, the sun has risen in the sky and people flood the town. As I head back toward my house, I feel excited about the future.

I will set my grandfather's mistake right.

Chapter

25

M Y BARE FEET PAD SILENTLY down the cold hallway. Early this morning Eee woke me with a message; my father is too ill to attend breakfast at the table but desires a meeting. My heart is beating rapidly against my chest. I am confident I know what the king wants to discuss. After all, I overheard him tell the king of wisdom that he plans to choose a spouse for me. The thought of having such a conversation, one that will surely be full of emotion, while he is sick in his bed scares me.

I reach the door to my father's bedroom and tap lightly on the wood. "Enter." His voice sounds so brave and strong. A man who sounds so powerful cannot possibly be sick. It gives me a burst of adrenaline to carry me through the doorway.

The room is dark, preventing me from seeing the king clearly at first. When my eyes adjust to the darkness and allow me to see him, I gasp. Lying in the bed, looking pale and weak, is a man I don't associate with my strong father. This man is a shadow of what I have grown to know. His hair is completely white, his skin sagging around his face. His head is propped on the pillow, not being held high as I am accustomed to seeing. When he coughs, the sound is rough and wet. I sit on a chair at the foot of the bed and reach an arm out to touch the king's leg. "Father, how are you feeling?"

"Old." He chuckles, forcing another bout of coughing.

I choke on the giggle bubbling up my throat as it catches with the tears I am trying to swallow down. "What can I do?"

"Become the queen Enchenda needs. Meet with Prince Carsen, Daughter. Allow him the chance to speak to you about the future he envisions for Fraun. Decide if this is a future you can be a part of." Again, coughs rack the old man's body.

This is no longer an argument I wish to continue. "I will meet with him, father."

"This is about Fraun, daughter."

"I will talk with him about the future we can build." What can it hurt to have similar conversations with Jordyn and Tin? A future warrants looking toward.

"Another thing, there is a council meeting in two suns. Mick and Tin have agreed to revisit the issue of a patrol. You will attend alone. You will need to stay strong."

"I will, Father." I consider the confusing issue, smiling at the ease of the new decision. "I am in favor of a patrol," I tell him. Somehow this feels like a meeting of equals this morning. I already know he will not argue with me on this decision.

"That is your choice." Father closes his eyes. They are closed for longer than a normal blink. When he opens them again they are misty with tears. "It is a wise choice, Eselda."

"Father, I spoke to Charlotte again." I hope he knows I wish to discuss this openly, not argue. "She told me of Sawchett."

Sadness crosses his eyes briefly, but he recovers. "That is something the queen should be privy to. What are your thoughts on the matter?"

Any fear I had anticipated at this revelation is mysteriously absent. "Sawchett, with her royal blood, will be raised by me and my staff upon Charlotte's death."

Gregario nods, the gesture painfully slow. "So be it."

It is this show of faith in my decision, no discussion or debate, that builds my royal nucleus. I feel my chin rise regally. "It is time Charlotte and her family were accepted by the royal family who serves her."

Gregario's eyes close slowly, and a tear slips down his cheek unchecked. "Very wise," he whispers.

That is the second time my king has complimented me on wisdom instead of humility. Perhaps he tires. "You look as though rest is vital, Father. Is there anything else I should know?" I feel the weight of the question fill the room. What else is there preventing me from leading Fraun alone? I am giving my own father permission to leave me, despite my heart's desire to force him to stay forever.

His eyes open slightly, as though he cannot quite see my face clearly without squinting. "You are ready, even if more secrets should fall into your path."

"I will leave you to rest then." I walk to the head of his bed and lean to kiss his forehead. "Sleep well, Father. I love you."

A second tear joins the already fallen one on Gregario's cheek. "Thank you, Majesty."

I slip out of the room quietly and close the door behind me. I rest my palm on the door at my back, smiling in acknowledgment of the regal term used by my father and king.

I am ready.

Chapter

26

"GOOD SIR," MY VOICE ECHOES throughout the walls of the stall house, a place no royal regularly visits.

The young man who had been crouched near a stall, fixing its door, jumps at the voice. When he stands upright and faces me, he is rubbing a sore spot on his head which he'd just knocked on the stall. "Princess, good morning." He stumbles for the appropriate greeting. "How may I serve you?"

"I am in need of transportation to Renchenda."

"I had heard of no such journey, Princess. None of our roaches are--"

"You will ready them, I will away today." I turn on my heel and walk back to the entrance of the stall house. Spying a nearby rock large enough to use as a chair, I set my rump on it and cross my ankles. Seeing that I intend to wait, the man hurries off to ready a roach.

I allow my shoulders to slump a little once he is out of sight. There really is no explanation for why I feel like traveling to Renchenda. I simply need a friendly face and Jordyn is just that.

Of course, I'll have to tell him I agreed to meet with Carsen. That could be uncomfortable.

Why uncomfortable? Surely Jordyn doesn't feel as I feel. I call up the memory of the strawberry field with a smile. The warmth of that kiss.

Somehow the memory makes it a more beautiful day. The sun is just beginning to rise. There is a dew covering the grass, so each blade is glistening with its own light. I am wearing a cloak with a hood this morning, as the weather is cold before the hour of high sun. Underneath the cloak, however, I wear a dress with minimal caps for sleeves. When the sun is at its highest point later, and bringing its heat to my body, I will be ready.

Perhaps Jordyn will have a solution other than Carsen. In the quiet of my home's backyard, alone, I can allow myself this fantasy. Perhaps Jordyn will find a way in which we can court each other. I think again of the kiss, and a smile flies to my face. Perhaps there will be more of those kisses this afternoon. A bubble of laughter floats from my mouth. The sound is quickly lost in the vast expanse of nature surrounding me.

The small man returns to my line of vision and I straighten my posture. "Princess, I have a roach who says he can make the journey if you allow him two short rests along the way. He is afraid, however, that he will not be able to make the return journey tonight."

"If I am to return tonight, I am sure that King Jordyn will see fit to provide me transportation." I recall the beautiful ladybug he brought along and smile anew. "In fact, I'm confident he will."

"Very well, Princess. I will fetch the roach." The servant turns. Once his back is to me he mutters, "I know that expression in her eyes, someone fancies that king."

Chapter

27

CASTLE FRAUN, COMMISSIONED DURING THE time of Oberian the Second and built by Fraunians, is the only three-story stone structure in the kingdom. Honestly, it is a beautiful building. The people of Fraun take great pride in knowing that such a masterpiece was erected by the hands and ingenuity of their people and their people alone.

Jordyn allows his gaze to trace the room, taking in the details. The inset wall torches are spaced evenly to fill the entire room with light. The brickwork has intricate details carved into the lowest layers purely for decoration. Although Jordyn understands the logic behind reusing instead of creating better than most Fraunians, even the king of wisdom in his tortured state cannot deny the beauty of the palace.

The room Jordyn occupies at this time of the afternoon was designed as a ballroom for special occasions. Other than five ornate thrones of gold on a raised platform along one wall, there is no furniture in this room.

There are many rooms in this vast expanse of a home, but this is Jordyn's favorite. Typically, on any given day, it is empty of people and quiet. On a day like today, when the beast has taken control of the king's being, he can hide out here and not be disturbed.

Today, he is perched on the fifth and final throne, stewing in his own inner turmoil and wrestling to get it under control. It is in this chair, he knows, he would be sat for all major events in the kingdom, were any to take place. He has never rested here for anything formal in his lifetime. The young king cannot help but associate the metal with his mother, the last person to sit in the chair in front of others.

He runs his long fingers on the cold gold arm of the chair. *What would mother think of Fraun now?*

Doubtless, the council will regal one with stories of Aine, the ruler. Aine, the great queen of Renchenda. Aine, the logical. Jordyn remembers a very different woman, one isolated and cold. The mother he remembers expected nothing short of perfection from her only son. *Would my mother be ashamed of how I battle with the demon within?*

Thoughts of the monster cause the hate building inside Jordyn to respond like an animal leaning into the hand of its master to be stroked. *Mother is not here. She wasn't even here when she was alive. She was content to lock herself up in rooms on the top floor and leave me to be raised by a common father and a staff of common servants. No matter how loving they were, no one could explain the curse of the royal blood that would be my future.*

The anger builds to a steady boil in the king's blood and he raises his hand level with his head, fingers curled inward like a claw. He rationalizes with himself. "You do not believe these things your brain is telling you, Jordyn." Even as his voice echoes off the stone and back to him, he feels his fist begin to curl. *The monster is winning today.* "You can do this," he tells himself. "One moment of outburst, then we will be in control of the beast." He closes his fist tightly and brings it crashing down on the arm of the chair.

The sound is magnified by the silence of the room, echoing for seconds after. The outburst does nothing to calm the king. In a rational state, Jordyn would understand what is causing this controlled rage is nothing more than his age marker, but he is not rational right now. The anger takes hold and rails unchecked inside him.

He stands and crosses to the opposite wall, the only one with a window, in ten long strides. He rests his palms on the thick glass and looks out over Renchenda. The sun is on its descent across the sky now and from this vantage point, two floors up, he can see much of the realm bathed in its light.

He breathes deeply. *It is the logical air of Renchenda I breathe in and the beast I breath out.* Usually, on a day like today when the battle has raged on for hours, this is the only way Jordyn can win the upper hand. Isolate himself and focus on breathing. *This is not working today.*

Instead, thinking of isolation feeds the flames of anger even more. *Isolation, that's what this tower was really about. Our ancestors knew. They knew the dark pull of our blood. They were not proclaiming us better than all of Fraun by erecting this castle. They were using this brick monstrosity, this fortress, to lock us inside. We are doomed to be isolated.* He punctuates his thoughts by slamming his palm repeatedly into the glass. The thick pane does not give under his anger.

A figure emerging from the woods connecting his realm to that of Marchenda catches the king's eye. He shakes his head to clear the fog of anger, shields his eyes from the sun with his right hand, and squints at the figure. *Whoever dares to cross into my land today is riding a roach and traveling light.*

As Jordyn watches the dainty face turns upward, taking in the full view of the impressive structure. "Eselda," the name escapes Jordyn on a sigh. He closes his eyes and rests his head on the glass. In this way he allows himself to remember the feeling of her slender hand on his chest, recalls her words.

"…love would devour you as well…"

When the king lets out his breath again, the beast is under control.

"Perhaps love is stronger than hate," he sighs.

Chapter

28

THE CASTLE FRAUN HAS ALWAYS been a beautiful sight. Today, after a full day's rather uncomfortable journey across the kingdom, bathed in the setting sun, it is enough to take my breath away. I feel a moment of pride and awe. Someone of my size, or perhaps even smaller, was able to build such a large monument.

I glance upward again, taking in the full height of the building. I wonder what the view from the top floor would be like. The times I have been in the castle, I have either been on the first floor or the second. There is a window on the second floor, which I have looked out before, but never have I been allowed higher. "Maybe someday I will ask Jordyn to let me up there." I practically giggle at the thought.

As if he heard his name spoken, Jordyn suddenly appears at the base of the castle. He waves his arm in greeting as the roach closes the gap between us. I dismount and pull Jordyn into a hug. "Oh we've had such a long journey," I tell the king. "I do hope you have food and water for my tired friend here." I indicate the roach I traveled on.

"Absolutely, I do. It's so nice to see you Eselda." Jordyn looks down at the traveling companion. "Good sir, thank you for bringing my friend to me. I was not expecting either of you today, although I am grateful for your timely arrival. Allow me to find someone to bring you a meal while you stay here in the shade of the castle and rest."

"Thank you, King Jordyn. That is most kind of you," the roach responds. Jordyn wordlessly offers his arm to me and leads me into the building. The roach scurries to the shade and gives in to the desire to lay down and sleep.

"Eselda, I don't know what brings you to Renchenda today but I frankly couldn't have been happier to see you just now." Jordyn positively beams down at me.

He is happy to see me. But happy as a friend or happy as one who feels something more? "Well, friend, I had a rather eventful day yesterday and I wished for someone to talk it over with," I explain. I watch carefully for reactions to the choice of label for our relationship. Did he look sad for just a beat?

"Then allow me to suggest we find a quiet place to talk," Jordyn says.

"Please, can we visit the ballroom?" I ask. "I long to look out that window again."

"We can." He leads the way to the room, pausing only once along the way to send someone to fetch the promised food for the roach. When we arrive, he opens the door to allow me to enter in front of him. I dash across the room, directly for the window.

It's thin and yet I have no doubt it is strong enough to support my wee frame. Despite the fact that it's a childish gesture in front of a man I am trying to impress, I press my entire frame flat against the window to peer out at Renchenda. "It's so beautiful, Jordyn. How do you not spend all of your life in front of this window?"

Jordyn moves across the room to stand behind me. He looks out over the scenery, taking in the view as I must be seeing it. Renchenda is a vast space, but no more people live here than my own realm. To me, the homes seem very scattered. Each person in Renchenda is asked to care for a large lot. Many of them have trees and bushes reaching as tall as their homes, they would have to stand on their houses to trim those trees.

"I do spend a lot of time here, but I also spend time out among the people." Jordyn places a hand on my back. "Now, Princess, tell me what you wish to discuss."

I turn and smile up at the king. "Shall we sit?" I ask. Jordyn nods before turning away from me. I flop down into a seated position on the floor.

Jordyn releases a hearty laugh. "I thought you meant to sit on the thrones," he says.

"I don't think I could sit there. My father is still king," I answer.

"Honestly I feel odd sitting there myself, I still feel it as my mother's seat." Something dark plays across the blue of his eyes. I turn my head, searching for a source of light that would cause that trick. I find nothing. "Surely you didn't travel here to talk of our thrones." Jordyn sits beside me on the floor, his long legs stretching toward the window.

"No, I didn't. I came to talk about promises."

"Promises?"

"My father requested to speak with me yesterday. He is not doing well, Jordyn. I fear he really may be leaving this world soon."

Jordyn reaches out and takes my hand before speaking. "We knew he was ill." This fact, simply stated, may have been taken rudely by others. Some may not be as familiar with Jordyn's way of relying on facts in difficult situations. I understand he intends to comfort.

"It's different, somehow. Seeing a person who is sick begin to fade away right in front of your eyes is so much harder than knowing it may happen soon," I explain, my voice ringing with sadness.

"I suppose that is true."

"I cannot be a child any longer, Jordyn. It is time I became the queen that Enchenda needs."

"I understand. My mother had never made plans for me to take over. When she died, it was a surprise. It is good that you have time to process this pending change before you take the throne," he answers.

The sadness in my eyes deepens, but this time it is directed at Jordyn. I squeeze the hand I have been holding. "Oh, that's right. I had forgotten how you took the throne of Renchenda. I am so sorry to burden you with this, Jordyn. The memories must be very painful."

"No," he answers. "I have made peace with my past. If you can learn from anything I have to offer, then it was worth the lessons I learned."

"That is so wise," I gush, awed by his capability to think logically in all situations.

"If you are going to insist on telling me every time I say something wise, I fear you'll have no time to talk of much else." We both laugh at the truth behind the statement. It is Jordyn who recovers first and moves the conversation forward. "You spoke of promises?"

"I did. I didn't know what to say to father when we spoke. He was so frail and sickly. I had not the strength to argue with him again about betrothal. I made him a promise." My voice trails down to nothing.

"What promise?"

"I promised to meet with Carsen, listen to him talk of the future, and give him a chance." I cannot bring myself to ask what I want to know: Do you have any feelings about that?

Jordyn chuckles, "You had me scared he wanted something more from you, the way you presented that information."

I look up from my lap, meeting Jordyn's eyes. "You have no opinion on this promise?" The hope I had been holding onto, the hope that he would have a different solution entirely, begins to fade.

"Of course I have an opinion."

"Let's hear it then." The hope begins to send off small sparks, enough to prove it is not dead. Will he resuscitate it?

"I told you. I believe that Carsen is an intelligent choice for you." Jordyn pours cold water over the flame of my hope.

I try not to show my disappointment. "That is true."

"You wanted a different answer?" Jordyn questions.

"I am not really sure what I want. I do want to do what is best for Fraun, but how am I to know what that is?"

"That is a good question. I cannot tell you that. I can tell you that Fraun will need someone to keep the balance in our kingdom. In order to do that, we cannot be left with an even number of realms."

"As would happen if I were to marry a seated king." I get it. Let's skip the lecture. I cannot look Jordyn in the eye. Instead, I turn my head to the window.

"Yes," he touches my arm lightly, drawing my gaze again. "There is no one in your realm who has royal blood. There is no one to take on your role if you do not."

"Someone else could take it?" This is new information.

"Of course. A few times in the course of our history someone from an alternate bloodline has taken the throne. If your father had a brother, for example, the brother could take the throne upon the death of your father. Or that brother's child. It has happened before."

"Anyone with royal blood would do?"

"I suppose. Why do you ask?"

I drop my voice, "I have heard talk that others exist. Others who have not been tracked on our family trees."

"You would need proof. The council would need to accept the lineage of this person, once that has been done they could serve as a ruler."

Perhaps this is the answer. What if Sawchett could be groomed to take over the throne. I could leave it all in her hands and then the pressure is simply gone. I could move to Renchenda, be with Jordyn. I could...

"Eselda," Jordyn is watching me carefully, "you will be a fantastic queen. I feel the need to point that out."

"But if I didn't need to be...if someone better suited were available..." my voice trails off.

"The council would need to accept the lineage of someone else before that would even be possible. It is not a timely solution."

I rise. "I feel as though you have given me hope in a situation that felt hopeless such a short time ago. Can I see your family tree?"

"My family tree?"

"Your lineage chart. It is painted here in the castle somewhere, yes?"

"Yes." Jordyn's single word answer still rings with hesitancy.

"I am very interested in lineage. I have studied my own at great length and found some interesting things. I'd like to have a look at yours to see if similar things exist. Perhaps while we look I can tell you about what I have found on mine."

Jordyn rises. "You have ignited my interest, Princess. Follow me."

Chapter

29

AS IT TURNS OUT, THE lineage tree for Renchenda is painted on the wall of a windowless room on the first floor. I can decipher no use for the room, other than to display the chart. As with my own, this chart is painted in the delicate gold scripting letters. The chart begins in the same way as ours; Oberian and his wife Alicia at the top, Oberian the Second below. From the second sprout his three wives, Suzeth, Ramona, and Rebekah.

It is from the branch of Rebekah that this tree, however, grows. Rebekah had two sons, Renchenda and Sarcheda. Standing on a contraption made of wooden dowels strung between two large pieces of wood, I run my finger along this line. "I never realized Renchenda and Sarcheda came from the same mother." I turn away from the wall to look at my handsome host.

"Sarcheda was his younger brother," Jordyn says.

My eyes resume their trace of the lineage. I take in the many names, starred and circled. Both women and men have served this realm. My fingers brush up against a name, Tawn. This name draws my eye for many reasons. Both Tawn and Kriep, husband and wife, are circled. Tawn has a black smudge, the kind I am quickly becoming familiar with, above her name. It is too small to hide an entire name. What have we here? "Tell me of this."

Jordyn leans down toward me so I can feel the heat of his breath on my cheek. "Oh, that is quite the tale. Tawn was a seated queen of Farcheda at the time she wed Kriep. Kriep, as you can tell, was from a line of Renchenda blood that was not serving the throne at the time." Jordyn follows the line up with his finger, leaning around me to do so. He is practically enveloping my smaller frame with his large one to reach around. His finger returns all the way back to Renchenda and his wife. Even he is not this tall, he must be standing on a lower rung of the wooden contraption.

"Renchenda and his wife had three children. The rule passed to his oldest girl, Alexa." Jordyn's hand points to the far right of the wall, away from the subject of my query. "As is the custom in most realms, this caused the other two children to live in the common areas and cease to be tracked for many years."

I review the children he speaks of. The middle child, Markin, is noted as having a wife but no children. I wonder if this is truly the case, or if there are others of royal blood in Renchenda who are not tracked by the council or this chart. Three moons ago, I would've thought such a thing to be impossible. Now I know better.

"Eventually," Jordyn continues, "the bloodline of Alexa ran out." I take notice of the end he speaks of. Two children were born to this line, Malkin and Liseth. Neither had children, although both are shown to be married. "This is what would happen to your line," he simply states.

"Or yours," I point out.

"True. In cases like these, where there are no longer direct descendants alive to be royalty the council is forced to track down the lineage of the siblings. In the case of Alexa, the council sent someone who discovered Kriep, alive and well and living in Farcheda."

I turn my cheek slightly to look back at the spot I asked about. My face comes into contact with Jordyn's. Instantly my heartbeat quickens at the touch and my breath catches in my throat.

"In the interim, while his bloodline was not being tracked, Kriep had moved to Farcheda and married a princess there. Shortly after their marriage, Tawn had become queen of Farcheda. The pair already had two children before the council approached them about their Renchenda blood." Jordyn has lowered his voice with the contact, it is merely a whisper in my ear.

I trace the small black smudge on Tawn's name, feeling the cement grind under the padding of my fingertip. "What is this then?"

"Under that black paint, you would find a gold star. Tawn was a ruler of Fraun, but never in Renchenda. She would still have her gold star in Farcheda." Jordyn points to a black oval underneath Tawn's name. "This child, the youngest of the pair, remained in Farcheda with her parents."

"Wait, I don't understand. I thought Kriep was tracked down because Renchenda needed a ruler."

"He was. He could not be married to a queen of Farcheda and serve as a king here at the same time, you know this. Their oldest child, Freth," Jordyn indicates that name, circled and starred, "became our king."

I allow my eyes to follow the rest of the chart down, noting that all further relatives come from this man. Including, a few generations removed, the man currently pressing against my back to explain the history of his realm.

"What became of their youngest?" I ask.

"I am told he became a ruler in Farcheda."

"This is a great story." I smile. Jordyn pulls slightly back from my body, leaving my cheek feeling cold. "Freth was okay with living here while his family served in Farcheda?"

"More than okay with it. In fact, during his reign, Renchenda became the first realm for the only time in history."

"That really is remarkable," I answer.

Jordyn takes a step back, putting his feet safely back on the floor. I remain on the makeshift ladder, analyzing the lineage further. "In my own realm we see this black paint over a few things as well," I reveal.

"As you see it for Tawn?"

"More like as I see it here." I point my finger at the youngest child of Tawn again. "On our wall, the entire name has been removed."

"As I explained, this was done because that child is now tracked in Farcheda. They are no longer tracked here, they are Farcheda royalty."

"That is not the case with the names I see in Enchenda," I say, continuing to search the wall for more black spots. Finding none, I turn on the ladder so I am facing the king. At this spot, with my feet on the second rung of the ladder, I am actually taller than he.

"Why were those marks removed?" Jordyn asks.

"They represent people who have been shunned."

"Shunned? For what purpose?"

"I am told it is for dishonoring their families by having infants before they were wed."

"I was not aware that could happen." Jordyn looks genuinely confused. "Are there many people like this on your family wall?"

"Not many, no. There was one in the past that I know nothing of. But there was one more recently that I've become aware of."

"What happens to these women who are shunned?" Jordyn asks. "Does the council know of this? Do they receive any training? Do we monitor them at all? How many are we discussing?" The questions are fired rapidly, too rapidly for me to interject an answer.

This must be how Jordyn processes. I hide my smile by lightly biting the inside of my cheek.

"Why would this have been approved? What becomes of their bloodlines?" he continues.

"I can answer many of those questions. Would you like me to?" I ask, teasing him a little for his rapid-fire style.

The king stops talking and nods.

I step off the ladder. "The women are sent to live, not unlike the relatives you spoke of earlier, among the common people in Fraun. The council is often informed, although I'm not sure if it is expected. As for the bloodlines, it is my understanding that these women are asked not to have children."

I am familiar with the confusion playing across the king's face. It is the same emotion I felt myself when confronted with this very issue. I wait patiently, watching him think, something I am finding I enjoy.

Finally, he speaks. "How is it that you know of this while I do not?"

"I met a woman who was removed from my family lineage tree."

The effect of this information on Jordyn is obvious. His face melts into shock and he sits down on the ladder. "You met one." He shakes his head left to right as if the information needs to move an inch before he can catalog it and use it. "Fascinating."

"That is not the word I would have used." I chuckle. Jordyn glances up at me, confused by my reaction. "I have reason to believe the council knows not of this woman."

Jordyn rises and begins pacing in front of the wall. "We cannot speak more of this then. The council must be informed of all matters discussed between two members of royal houses. We are not to discuss issues like this outside of council. There is a meeting in a few suns, we shall bring this before council then."

"Wait!" I exclaim, stopping Jordyn's tirade. This is not at all how this conversation was supposed to go.

He turns to me, pacing forgotten for a moment. "Why? This is a council issue."

"Jordyn, they cannot know. To know that a woman who was given direct orders from a seated king broke those orders? No, Jordyn. We cannot condemn this woman to death."

"What orders? She had a child, you said. You said this made her an outcast. You said they lived among the commoners. The council needs to know this woman exists."

"Jordyn, please. There is more to this story. Sit, I will tell you the tale." I try to calm the king with my hands, gesturing to the floor.

"I will not. I'm sorry, Eselda, but we cannot discuss this alone. If you want to tell the tale, you must tell it to the council."

"Jordyn there is more to this tale than you are hearing. It makes my family look…" I search for an adequate description, "…unclean."

I can see the anger rise up into his face. I watch as his eyes darken like the sky before a storm. "Eselda, I am a king in Fraun. I will not be found to have conversations about policy outside of council. If you have become aware of an issue in Enchenda that requires a decision, you will need to discuss that before a full council."

"Okay, okay. You are right." I concede, fear of the anger forcing my hand. "I will think about bringing it to the council."

"Thank you." Jordyn takes a few deep breaths. I silently watch him as his eyes return to their clear blue and his face relaxes. "I'm sorry." He continues to look at the ground, but his voice has lost all trace of anger now. "I lost my temper there; I fear it is partially the age marker." When he looks to me, I meet his gaze and give him a small smile which he returns.

"I feel strongly about issues of the council being brought before all representatives of Fraun equally. The process we have undertaken works only when we allow it to. When we find ourselves questioning the process or looking for shortcuts, we do not allow the system to work," he explains.

"I hadn't really thought of it that way."

"I find it is the only way to believe in the vision of the brother's. To follow it with nothing short of perfect intentions."

"Can I summarize what I have learned from your lineage tree today?" I ask. I wait for his nod before pressing forward. "Sarcheda and Renchenda were brothers, meaning their family lines are very similar. However, because of our divisions of realms, none of Sarcheda's bloodline is traced here."

"Yes," Jordyn states, crossing his arms.

"You also have branches here that appear to end. But, as is with the tale of Kriep, we know that to not always be true."

"That is accurate." Jordyn's eyebrows rise with the unanswered question. He is wondering where I am going with this.

"Furthermore, the bloodline currently reigning here in Renchenda is a direct lineage to Farcheda as well."

"That I am."

"So how are we to know for certain that the issue I am facing, a woman who is royal blood but not tracked on my lineage tree, is not also true for other realms? Including this one. How are we to assume our lineage trees are accurate when there is so much confusion in the process?" I am tempted to squeeze my eyes shut in case his face turns angry again.

"It is not our task today to question the accuracy of these bloodlines. It is not our task to follow them to their ends. It is our task to recognize our place among them and step up to lead our realms." Jordyn keeps his voice even, controlled.

"You said yourself that other people with royal blood if they were recognized by the council, could lead."

Jordyn steps closer to me and takes my hand. "I did say that. You said this was a story you didn't want to share with the council. How could they accept the lineage of this woman if you will not tell the story?"

I sigh and my shoulders slump. Of course, he is correct. There is no obvious solution here. Charlotte's story cannot be brought to council because of the negative light it casts on the house of Enchenda. But Sawchett cannot be prepared as a princess without such a recognition. The depression is a pool so deep I could drown in it. There is no way out of this.

Jordyn steps to my side and wraps his arm around my shoulder. I feel myself melting into the touch, resting my head on him. "Eselda, I am a smart man," he begins, "Your objection to ruling Enchenda, I fear, has more to do with me than with blood or self-confidence." He pulls back from the embrace enough to hook his finger under my chin and turn my face up to him. "Is that accurate?"

Leaving the ruling of Enchenda to someone like Sawchett while I move to this beautiful castle with you just feels perfect. You could attend council meetings and make decisions for us both. I'm sure Sawchett could handle the pressure. My solution would be easier. I cannot find my voice to say any of this. Instead, I nod.

"I feared as much." Jordyn sighs. "Eselda, I am not the right match for you." He drops my chin, but my gaze does not falter. "No matter how you feel--" he shakes his head. "No matter how we feel." He emphasizes the changed word, correcting himself. "We are better for Fraun as equal rulers of two realms."

Despite my sadness, I cannot help but nod. Jordyn continues. "The people of Enchenda will need you when your father passes. You are a face they trust to get them through the sadness of losing a king. The council will only benefit from two minds such as ours sharing a table. We are both smart, you are humble. You are going to make a fine queen of Enchenda." Jordyn places a kiss on my forehead and steps back, putting space between us.

"You have made your point," I state. "I fear I may have traveled here today to find an escape. My path is not going to be easy."

"It never is."

"But as usual, friend, you have helped me. I believe I am ready for that journey now."

"I see it in your face that you are ready. I will fetch you a ride home and see you at council next. Think about your issue more, decide if our fellow kings need hear it." He turns to leave the room.

"Jordyn?" The sound of his name softly leaving my mouth turns him again in my direction before I even realize I spoke his name aloud. "I know I should not ask this. I find I cannot help myself. Humor me. If I were a commoner in Renchenda, would you have wanted to court me?" My voice is merely a whisper carrying what is left of my dreams of what might have been. A pain begins in my stomach, thick and hot. What if he laughs at the thought?

Jordyn closes the space between us and pulls me close. I close my eyes as he leans in, so by the time our lips connect I only feel it. The warmth spreads through my entire body and I lean into him, deepening the kiss.

It is Jordyn who pulls away. When he leaves the room, I know he gave me the only answer he is capable of giving.

Chapter

30

THE MORNING OF THE NEXT council meeting arrives. The sun is rising over the beautiful kingdom, but the cold has begun. The people of Fraun have kept wood burning stoves running as they slept, and will be waking soon to feed the flames. Outside, people pull on warm cloaks to complete their daily chores and shoes adorn the feet of children, an unusual sight to be sure.

It has been a few suns since my visit with the king of wisdom and the kiss which signaled goodbye and yet my father has not risen from his bed and is resting quietly. Having been taking on much of the duties for leading the realm, I was exhausted when I reached my bed last night. I gave orders to a manservant that I not be woken today. It is this manservant you would find standing on the front lawn of the home in Enchenda, toe to toe with Tutor, anger crackling dangerously from one man to the other.

"You cannot keep me from her. Until she is crowned, I am her personal tutor," the younger man's voice rings out. This argument has been building for a few minutes, the men are close to solving it with their fists if another solution does not present itself soon.

"I have my orders. If you will not leave, I will have no choice but to make you leave," the other voice is lower, more controlled, but equally as dangerous.

"You are a traitor if you would make me leave. I am not a threat to this house," Tutor yells.

"If you try to shove your way in, that makes you a threat."

"Get out of my way!"

"Make me!"

Behind the older man, sprawling out in both directions lies my family home. An opening in the wall to the man's left is covered with curtains which part in one swift movement as I thrust my head out the open window. "HEY!" I bellow.

Both men freeze and turn their full attention in my direction. "What in the name of Fraun are you two arguing about?" I ask.

"Majesty you asked not to be disturbed and this man wanted to wake you. I could not let that happen," the manservant explains.

"Yeah, well done on that," Tutor says. He claps the man enthusiastically on the shoulder. "Princess, I need a word. Will you meet me in the garden?"

I nod once and disappear back into my room. "Never a moment of rest for me and I'm not even Queen yet," I complain to my reflecting wall. Speaking with Tutor was actually on my list of things to do today. Admittedly I had planned to wait until a decent hour of the day. It is for this reason that I allow myself to be summoned to a meeting with him.

I mentally rehearse what must be said to Tutor as I walk the halls. It is my belief that, since I will be assuming the day-to-day operations of a queen, I no longer require tutoring services. I do feel sadness at having to cut ties with my old friend. But in truth, I cannot fault myself for this. Tutor has been putting enough distance between us lately. This is for the best.

Dressed in an orange colored long sleeve dress that sweeps the ground and wearing black shoes on my feet, I enter the garden to find Tutor sitting on the bench by my vegetables. I sit beside him. "Good morning, Tutor." He blinks at the edge of authority in my voice.

"Good Morning, Majesty. Sorry to have woken you."

145

The wry smile on his face suggests otherwise. "You certainly don't sound sorry," I tease.

"Fair point. It could not be helped."

"Then I shall listen to what you came to say, out of respect for our past. Then we have business to discuss."

Tutor turns his brown eyes away from me, as though something interesting was transpiring in the garden. "Eselda I have come to tell you that I can no longer be your tutor. In light of new information I have recently received, I feel I cannot be of service to you any longer." His eyes catch the sunlight as he looks up from the garden. "I am not at liberty to say much else. It is my hope that you will let me out of my service immediately."

I recover from my shock in time to return the stony expression to my face. "What service have you been completing lately that I should let you out of? In my pressing time of urgency, you have been absent." I coat my voice with anger and authority.

"That is true. Perhaps that will make it easier to let me go."

"Perhaps. Tell me what information you have received and I will decide." No more secrets.

"I cannot do that, Majesty."

"I am your princess. You will tell me." I catch myself just shy of stomping my foot in an immature show of frustration.

"With all due respect, Princess, I cannot."

"When I am Queen, I can force you to tell me or have your head."

Tutor sighs, "If that is what you wish, we can discuss this again then."

Oh, this is not working. I must try another tactic. I soften my voice. "We were friends once Tutor, before you stopped coming around. Can you not tell your friend the truth of this decision?"

Something softens in his expression. "I have learned things which I wish I could share with a friend. Things I cannot bear alone. I wish I could do that, Eselda, but believe me when I say you don't want to hear this truth. I must refuse." He stands to his feet, sighing with the effort. "Ask me again when you are Queen if you feel like demanding it. But know that you still will not want this truth then, as I do not really want it now. Good day, Majesty."

I brush the arm of the man as he leaves, but he slips his arm from my fingers before I can gain purchase there. He never once turns around to look back. I find the sadness is overwhelming, another friend lost. I allow myself a moment to reflect.

You could always make me laugh, I will miss that most. You pushed me but always knew when to let something rest. It's the end of our time together. Shouldn't someone feel that sadness?

Of course, it's also the end of the skipped lessons with no explanation. The limp you cannot explain and the secrets you refuse to talk about will end now as well.

When I rise from the bench, I am no longer sad. "I am in no further need of a tutor anyway," I state for my own benefit.

Chapter

31

T IN SITS ALONE AT THE head of the council table, tapping his fingers rhythmically. He has never in his reign as king been this early to a council meeting. He arrived before the shadow has even begun to reach the building, indicating it is time for the meeting of the council. The king of strength is aware such an act will not be lost on his comrade of speed. In fact, the act was carried out for this purpose.

Speed is such an undesirable trait to have alone. What good would it do one to be quick? You could run from a fight, sure, but why run when the strength of Sarcheda can guarantee you the win?

Tin is eyeing the doorway when Jordyn's lanky frame fills it. *Wisdom, now that is a quality I can use. Wise enough to know the strategies of the enemy in war. This is why I must always try to keep Jordyn on my side.*

"King Tin, you are early today," Jordyn greets. He offers his hand to the slightly older king. Tin accepts the hand and they shake.

"I thought it would do me some good to sit here and think in the room where great men before me have sat to think," Tin explains as Jordyn takes his seat.

"Great women have sat there as well," Jordyn points out.

Tin acknowledges this comment with a simple wave of his hand. "Have you been thinking any more on the patrol?" Tin asks, hoping the fact that they are in the council room will be reason enough for the rule-abiding king to discuss policy.

"I have. Let us wait for our partners in leadership and I will share my thoughts."

Having no other course of action to suggest, the pair settle in to wait. Jordyn absently stares at the table while he ponders. Tin continues to focus on the doorway. Both men are lost in thoughts of what they want for the future of Fraun. Neither king seems aware their colleague's opinion differs so much from his own.

After the passing of some time, King Mick enters the room. As is his style, he is moving fast. "Gentlemen, this is two meetings in a row when I am not the first to arrive," he points out in lieu of a greeting.

"Perhaps you are losing your touch in your old age," Tin challenges.

"I am not late, that much is certain," Mick answers, taking his seat. "Have either of you heard from--" the man is interrupted by the arrival of King Larecio and Princess Eselda, who enter the room laughing. All eyes in the room turn to the pair.

"Good afternoon everyone," Larecio heartily calls as his eyes sweep the company. He turns back to Eselda. "Apparently they were waiting for us."

Tin sits up straighter in his chair. "Well, let's begin. I have an issue from our last council meeting that I feel we should revisit. The idea of a patrol to provide safety to Fraun. Are there any further points on this topic?"

Chapter

32

I LOOK AROUND THE ROOM, TAKING in the faces of the kings of Fraun. They are a proud bunch; their faces tell me that. King Tin, to my right, is seated regally in his chair today. He is holding his gaze steady as he also stares down the men from the table. He is wearing his stubborn desire to argue like a cloak.

To my left King Mick is equally ready for a challenge. He is stiff-backed and wearing a smile one would expect after a large meal; altogether satisfied and happy. To his left, King Larecio holding up to his realm's trait looking full of mirth. To my own eyes, the man looks like he doesn't belong in this group, being the only one to not wear a serious expression in the crowd. Lastly, my eyes fall to Jordyn. I know that look he wears all too well. The king of wisdom is formulating an idea.

As if he heard my thoughts, Jordyn clears his throat. "I believe I have some insight on this topic." All eyes in the room turn to Jordyn. "When last we met King Mick proposed we begin a patrol to keep Fraun safe." Everyone nods their agreement with this statement, although no eyes move from Jordyn's face. He continues, "The disagreement came when we began to talk about what we would train this patrol for, and therefore where we would train them." Nods again.

"I believe I have an idea. By themselves, none of our traits may be suitable for a patrol. However, can you imagine how powerful a patrol would be that was strong, humble, quick, mirthful, and wise? Why they would be unstoppable." Jordyn's eyes travel the faces of his colleagues.

I take the opportunity to do the same. I see some smiles and nods, but Tin has turned his face to stone, revealing nothing. Jordyn and I lock eyes as he finishes his point. "Perhaps our solution is simple. Perhaps a troupe of the best Fraunians from all of our realms should train up together. The patrol group could spend a few suns in each realm, learning skills of that realm in turn. By the time they had visited all five realms, we would have a strong patrol who knew the Fraunian land better than any seated here. They would truly be the best protectors we could offer."

Here the young king stops talking and sits back, taking in the room again. There are many more nods this time. Larecio speaks first, "What a delightful idea, Jordyn. I could see my son enjoying his time training a guard."

"My son as well would enjoy his time with such a training," Mick states. "But what of Enchenda?" The older man turns to me. "Would you feel comfortable training a group of men in the ways of Enchenda and how to be humble?"

The question drips with something bitter I cannot name; he speaks as though trying to harm me with his words. "Why is it only Enchenda you worry about, Majesty?" I ask. I feel something grab my hand and give it a comforting squeeze. Without looking down, I squeeze back and hold on tight. At least someone supports me.

"You are the only one seated at this table with no male presence in your realm to train."

My defiance is obvious, I square my jaw and raise my chin. "You assume two incorrect things, King Mick." If it is confrontation the old man desires, I will gladly deliver it.

The man smirks at me. "Is that so? Well straighten me out then, maiden, go ahead."

I make a calculated decision to let my voice ring out with all the authority I can muster. Still, my nerves set my body to tremble. I hold tight to the hand, the show of support helping me stay grounded. "One, you assume a lady as myself cannot possibly have anything to teach this patrol. In this, I assure you, you are sadly mistaken and outdated. I can bring a patrol up to speed on many things around and in Enchenda. Things I could teach that patrol you yourself may even benefit from, good sir.

"Secondly, you assume there are no young men anywhere in my village. Again, you are mistaken. Good King Jordyn did not suggest at all that the people training these patrols would need to be of royal blood. True, Enchenda has no young men with that in their veins running around. But I assure you, sir, we do have men in our realm."

Mick smiles. "I suppose I underestimated you, milady." He glances around the room. I take the opportunity to look down and see who the hand belongs to. It is that of King Tin. I smile at him shyly. He returns one of full force before taking his hand back. My next glance is toward Jordyn, as though my eyes were pulled there of their own accord. He is watching the exchange. My face reddens.

"It sounds as though our wise friend here has come up with a solution that we can all agree upon," Tin says. "What say the council?"

"I agree." Mick startles the room by agreeing with the king of strength. "Call the vote, Tin."

"All in favor of beginning a patrol that would spend time training in each of our five realms and serve all of Fraun say 'aye'."

"Aye." The room echoes with the word.

"The vote is unanimous," Tin notes. "Now the matter of details. How many men will each realm send and where should they report?"

I clear my throat. "As far as I am concerned there is no reason why the patrol should not begin training in the first realm and move onward from there." There are nods of assent around the room.

"As for the matter of numbers, I believe no more than two from every realm would be sufficient to begin," Mick adds.

"I can stand behind that number," says Larecio. "Call a vote, leader."

"All in favor of sending two men each to begin training for patrol in the first realm within five suns say 'aye'." A wide smile occupies Tin's face as he calls the vote.

"Aye."

"Again, the vote is unanimous. Send me your men," Tin glances at me, "or women within the next five suns. I will begin training them at that time. After a time, I will send them on to Enchenda for phase two of their training."

I cannot help but feel pleased with the way this meeting has transpired. In contrast to our last meeting, we have actually accomplished something today. Maybe I misjudged what it means to be a member of this council. Perhaps, although it has been a rocky lunar cycle, I am actually prepared to be the queen my kingdom needs. Perhaps--

"Questions of our policy regarding royal blood have been recently brought to my attention," Jordyn states.

My good feeling deflates instantly. We weren't supposed to bring this to them until I said I was ready. It was my choice to make. I cannot control the increased breathing, the redness that creeps into my face, or the glare I shoot across the table at the king.

Jordyn continues, "I think it befitting of the council to discuss the issue of unneeded relatives becoming common citizens."

"Where is this coming from?" Larecio questions, not unkindly.

"No specific place. As I mentioned, it has merely been brought to my attention. For example, I know it is not lost on this council that three of our members here have no offspring to assume the throne upon our deaths."

"Damn right you haven't. We need to speak of that," Mick says.

What are you doing, Jordyn? Why bring that up? Mick needed no inspiration to get fired up again.

"I thought we were discussing that. It has been brought to my attention that if the realms were to track their royal blood properly there may be other citizens fit to serve," Jordyn states.

"How would that be possible?" Larecio questions, propping his elbow on the table and leaning forward.

"I can give you an example," I blurt, eager to steer the conversation to safe grounds. "If my father had a younger brother, what would have become of him at birth?"

Mick plays along. "He would live among the common folk unless he is needed to serve the throne."

"Exactly." I offer him a smile for helping with the example before hurrying along. "Now let's say my Uncle continued to have children. I don't know about your realms, but Enchenda wouldn't know."

"Of course not, we don't track the legacy of every commoner in our realm," Tin agrees.

"Exactly," I continue. "Therefore, although I have birthed no children it is possible that upon the untimely death of my father and myself that my Uncle could have royal blooded children ready and able to serve Enchenda."

The news silences the room. Likely there are many men trying to find the flaws in my thinking, but they will find none.

"Fascinating," Mick breathes. "Jordyn, you among us are the smartest. Do you agree with this logic?"

"How could I not? There are no flaws there. Do you see why this issue was one I thought best to bring to the council?"

"I don't see what you want us to do about it," Tin says. Again the men around the room bob their heads up and down.

"I propose that our council select a representative of each realm to look into and update the lineage charts in our realms," Jordyn suggests.

"Jordyn, what a lovely idea!" I cannot help myself. Jordyn has discovered a safe way for me to have Charlotte added to the wall without having to tell her tale.

"It was a good idea, no need to get that excited," Mick chides. I offer him a shrug.

"All in favor of a representative from each realm updating the lineage charts say 'aye'," Tin bellows.

"Aye."

This time the vote is not unanimous. Tin continues, "All those opposed, say 'nay'."

"Nay." Mick glares around the table at those who did not vote with him.

"The motion carries five votes to one. Let it be known that Farcheda is not in favor of this new law, but will comply accordingly."

"So noted," Mick mumbles.

"Excellent." Tin smiles around the room. "Any further business?" He allows the silence to monopolize the room before he stands. "If there is nothing further, I call this meeting of the council of leaders adjourned for another lunar cycle."

Immediately the room begins to empty. Tin places a hand on my arm. "Can we talk?" he asks.

I notice Jordyn's steps falter as though waiting for my answer.

"Of course, Majesty," I answer. I think I notice a slight shaking of Jordyn's head, but then he is gone from the room.

Tin turns his chair in my direction. "How have you been?"

"Fine, thank you. How have you been?"

"Busy. I am sorry I haven't yet had the chance to speak with your father."

"Regarding what?" I ask. Immediately, I regret the question as the memory of Tin's promise at dinner comes back to me. "Oh, right. About...that. It's fine, really," I stammer.

Tin's face crumples. "You no longer wish to be courted?"

"No, it's not that. It's...well, this is hard. My father feels..." I stop, breathe, and start again. "My father and I feel that I should probably give Carsen a chance. Both kings have accepted this. We are actually meeting for dinner tonight. I'm sorry." The words rush out of my mouth quickly, before I can choose to stop myself.

Tin, for his part, looks devastated. His head and shoulders slump. "I understand. I should've acted with more urgency in the matter." He touches my hand. "Please let me know if anything changes."

"I certainly will. I'm sorry about this change of our plans, Tin."

"You owed me nothing, Princess. Think not on it."

It was easier to dismiss Tin's offer when I believed he was speaking in haste. I should explain to him that I had convinced myself his mind was changed on the matter. I never meant to hurt anyone. There must be a way to explain this. "Tin, let's be honest, we could never be." I shamelessly steal lines from Jordyn. "Sarcheda and Enchenda, they need us both to rule and be strong."

Tin gives me a puzzled expression. "What makes you think they would not have us both?"

I lay a hand on his shoulder, leaning toward his ear. "If we were to be together, our realms would lose one of us. A king and queen must rule together from their realm."

"Our realms could unite."

"Leaving four realms would be unwise." It is what I have heard but my confidence wavers under the king's austere expression. "Wouldn't it?" I question.

"I suppose so, but things could change." Tin grasps my hand. His hazel eyes flash greener today than I remember, hypnotizing me. "We would be the most influential Reign in years. I can't remember the last time a king and queen seated together both had royal blood. We could still both sit at the table for council meetings."

"We could?" Is that a rule? When was the last time that happened?

"Why not?" He leans toward me, our noses practically touching. Is that hope I see in his eyes?

"We could make the rules," he whispers.

"The council would vote for that?"

At this, the king bristles. He drops my hand and rises, the mood broken by his sudden anger. "The council is full of fools making decisions from their own past." He grabs my hand again this time to pull me to my feet. "I want to make decisions for the future of Fraun."

"I do as well." Perhaps people misjudge Tin. Perhaps I did.

"Good." He moves closer until our noses are touching again. "You have this meeting with Carsen. You see which way he looks when speaking of Fraun. But if he is looking to the past as well, you remember that in Sarcheda there is one who does not."

I can find no words under the weight of this simple request. I nod.

Tin leaves the room and I am left with a puzzle of options spread before me. Jordyn, who says two seated royals cannot court. Tin, who argues that is an outdated rule that would not stop him. Carsen, the prince I have not met as an adult.

What is truly best for Fraun?

Chapter

33

NSIDE THE CARRIAGE, I AM wearing my finest clothes. My soft green gown, the color of Enchenda, reaches to the floor. The long sleeves are tight to my skin but have caps on the shoulders. The bodice of the dress is black and tight, nicely showing off my curves. On my ankles, in my hair, and around my neck I wear matching silver chains. They are thick ropes, looped in a decorative way and catching the moonlight beautifully.

I have never been to Marchenda before. For this reason, when the roach-drawn carriage pulls into its borders, I am on full alert to take in new information. The homes are small, but well lit from inside. I can hear the sounds of laughter and smell food cooking. My stomach growls in response.

The front gardens of the homes are well tended. In Enchenda one often sees small, low landscape. In Sarcheda the homes were very dark and had much space between them. In Renchenda there were tall trees marring the vision from one house to the next. Marchenda appears to be the realm most closely resembling my own.

The carriage pulls to a stop in front of a small home puffing smoke into the air. The home is surrounded by a wooden fence and the front yard is immaculately maintained. This home looks like an inviting place.

Like my own, this one is clearly repurposed from giant materials. I can see it in the unequal roof slats, the scratched doors, and the oddly sized lanterns. It doesn't detract from the home's charm in the least.

The front door opens and a man emerges. He looks to be about my height. He has brown hair and carries himself well. He is dressed in a pale yellow shirt and brown vest. He wears slacks of brown as well. By far the most handsome feature on the man, however, is his expression. He wears the most relaxed, comfortable smile that I have ever seen. It truly reaches all the way to his brown eyes.

The door of the carriage opens, and the man holds out his hand. "Princess Eselda, I assume," his voice is smooth like the Sarcheda chocolate.

"Prince Carsen?" I question, hopeful.

"That is what they call me. Please, call me Carsen." He reaches out his hand and I place mine delicately inside. I allow myself to be pulled from the carriage.

"You have a beautiful realm."

"Well, thank you. We are happy with it," he answers.

"You have reason to be."

"Are you hungry, Princess?"

"I am. But please, Carsen, call me Eselda."

"Alright, Eselda. Let us head into my home where we can eat." He turns and heads toward the home, leading me. The interior of the home also resembles my own, although there are more windows here. The hallway we travel is almost entirely covered in glass, a view which I would love to stop and take it were it not darkening outside. We do not stop at the dining room that we pass. Instead, Carsen leads us to the backyard where a table has been set for two people.

The backyard is unlike anything I have seen. Instead of grass or garden, there is only a gray surface marred by symbols. "What is this ground?" I ask, stomping my feet on it. The surface has no pliability, holding fast under my heel. It is warm, hard, and echoes back the sound of my stomp.

"Isn't it remarkable? The scouts brought it back from an excursion. The Giants used this material for everything. The scouts tell me there are spots beyond Fraun where this material is all you can see in every direction. Even the bravest scouts fear to cross it."

"What is it?"

"I know not its name. This chunk was found toppled and broken, they knew I would find it fascinating," says Carsen.

"What are the symbols?" I ask, gesturing to one colorful streak near the prince's feet.

"I am told they are old letters the giants used." Carsen points to the table, set flat on the surface. "Shall we sit here? I know there is a chill in the air tonight, but I find this to be my favorite spot."

Imagine being so large that this entire slab, which spans the prince's vast yard, would seem small to you. These large markings would be merely letters you used in communication. The rare glimpse into the world of the giants is alluring. "It is beautiful out here. Thank you for choosing this location."

The precise second my bottom touches the seat food is delivered to the table. The orchestrated delivery is flattering. Smells waft up from the bowl in front of me, garlic and onion filling my nostrils.

"I hope you like earthworm, Eselda. I am told this soup is delightful, the staff we have here are great chefs." Carsen's ever-present smile is infectious and find myself turning on my own.

"Earthworm stew is something I'm very familiar with, it smells delightful." We each take up a spoon and begin eating. Soon, the silence grows uncomfortable. What should we discuss? How do I broach the subject of futures?

Timidly, I choose a conversational thread from my dinner with Tin. "Tell me what you do here in Marchenda for fun, Carsen."

Carsen puts his spoon down and gives his full attention to the conversation at hand. "Many things. We tell stories often, it's something we excel at actually. I enjoy going down to the school area and telling tales to our younger citizens. Each of us has a different style of story we like to tell. I personally am more partial to those with a good life lesson."

"I've never met someone who told made-up tales for the amusement of others. Would you tell me one?" Most of the tales used in the schools around Enchenda are those that really happened, like the story of the brothers. It is our practice to regal those old tales that have been shared time and time again. It is rare to find someone who makes them up, particularly with no notice or warning. I find the idea tantalizing. I lean on my elbows toward the prince.

"I suppose I could tell a short one. Let me think a minute."

I watch as Carsen stares up at the sky, eyebrows drawn together as he concentrates. His face is lean, his eyes are a startling dark brown, the color of the dirt in my garden. He has a strong jaw; he is certainly handsome in his own right.

"I have one," he states, returning his eyes to me. "Once upon a time there lived an old frog family."

"How many were in this family?"

Carsen laughs lightly, "Three children and two parents. But let me tell the story to the end before you ask more questions. The young boys grew up together, as close as brothers can be. The family often played in the pond outside their front door and their Mother doted on a beautiful lily that grew there. No one else could sit upon this lily pad, except for their Mother."

The prince's voice is soothing, a warm sense of calm washes over me as he talks. Although I have no brothers to speak of and no Mother at home to dote on anything, I find myself smiling at the idea. I lean closer still to the prince.

"As it came time for the boys to leave their parent's home and strike out on their own, their Mother was suddenly taken from them." The sentence is a brisk clip. I gasp at the abrupt sadness that pierces my heart.

"The boys were devastated," Carsen acknowledges. "In their grief, the oldest suggested they each take a part of the lily pad that their Mother had so loved to their new home. He reasoned that the memory would bring them joy whenever they saw it.

"Eager to preserve a part of her, the boys tore up the lily pad. Great care went into ensuring the pieces were of equal size. The boys each took their section of lily to their new home, around the further edges of the pond."

160

"That's rather sweet."

"It was, at first. The day came to pass that the lily, being a living plant, died."

"Oh no." I am surprised at how dejected I feel. I place my hand over my heart, I can feel it beating underneath the material. "The boys must have been so sad."

"They were unquestionably dismal. Here was the last piece of their mother, and each one thought that he had done something wrong to cause his part of the lily to die. No boy was willing to admit he had killed the plant. So each one continued to pretend that his part of the plant was alive and well, further upsetting the others who believed this strengthened their fault in killing it. The boys grew apart as a result. The father, when his death finally came, had none of his three boys by his side."

"How terrible." Please make it at least to see me return home tonight, father.

"It was. From this sad tale, however, sparks a lesson we can all learn from. Sometimes our desire to share something beloved, no matter how equally we share it, can kill what we love and be our ruin."

The message hangs in the silence of the backyard for a moment. "Wow. You made that up?" I ask.

"I did. You couldn't tell?" Carsen chuckles. "I'm not even sure how a lily grows or if you could tear one up."

"It rang like a true tale." I flop back in my chair. "The Mother dying, it was so sad. Then the children lying to each other…" I trail off.

"Of course I base it on things real people have done. That is the mark of a good tale. But the point, for me, is always the lesson." He smiles. "I fear the last of your stew has likely gone cold as you listened to the tale."

"You even added the part about the father dying alone. I only have a father. That thought pulled on my heart."

"You forget; I only have a father as well. That part was as personal to me as it was to you." The quiet quality of the prince's voice on this note snaps me back to reality. I take in Carsen's face again, there is a new dreamy quality to his eyes.

"Telling tales makes you happy."

"It does."

I reach out and take his hand, resting on the table. "Thank you for sharing it with me." I squeeze the hand.

Carsen squeezes back. "My pleasure."

"How old is your father, if you don't mind my asking."

"He just recently grayed, actually. So he's barely forty annuals. Is it the same for King Gregario?"

"I suppose not." I shrug. "Honestly I do not even know my own age." The truth slips out in a whisper. "I know I have passed the fifteenth annual, but I cannot recall when that happened."

"I am nineteen," Carsen admits.

"You have one annual left." The statement trails up at the end, turning it into a sort of question.

"Less, actually." Fear looms behind Carsen's expression.

It is a fear I recognize. I wonder how long I have until I am waking up and facing the dark age head-on. "I fear the age markers." The honest statement slips out of me easily, offered to the prince like glass to be cared for.

His eyes meet mine and he nods. "As do I. My dreams carry such dark thoughts about what may be awaiting me." Carsen is speaking in a low voice. I am forced to lean closer to hear him. "At times I think it cannot possibly be as bad as I imagine. Other times, I fear I may be in for a nightmare."

"Have you known anyone who passes through this marker? Someone you can talk to?"

"Only King Jordyn."

The name, so often running through my mind, sounds strange from the mouth of the prince. "You know Jordyn?"

"He has had many a conversation with me about preparing to lead my realm."

"I suppose he has had the same with me," I offer.

"King Jordyn is a good man." Carsen smiles, squeezes my hand, and rises. "I am going to take our empty plates inside. Excuse me for a moment."

As Carsen traipses inside with an armload of dishes I stare at the giant's scrawl on the flooring. Imagine someone who was large enough that this writing came from a pen. The pen would have to be my size. I trace my toe along the writing nearest me. My foot could have made these marks.

"Fascinating isn't it?" I startle at the voice. When I turn to look at him, I see his cheery demeanor has returned. "I often wonder what the symbols were for," Carsen says. "Were they labeling something? Claiming ownership? Telling a tale?"

"I'm surprised and a little impressed with how long it has lasted. The Giants have been gone from this land for many generations and yet here it remains, preserved." I turn my chair to better face my companion who has moved his chair away from the table and slouched slightly. He is the picture of relaxation. "It makes you wonder," I muse, "what will remain of Fraun after we are long gone? What will whoever begins after us find of ours?" I return my gaze to the symbols in silence.

"Nothing."

I turn back to Carsen. He is still staring at the ground. Perhaps I imagined the single word answer. "Excuse me?"

"Nothing will remain. A generation of people who live after us will find nothing of ours." He turns his eyes to me. "Isn't that our intention? We use only what we need and make nothing. Therefore, the next people to come will find exactly that."

"We have the Castle Fraun." I smile, trying to lighten what suddenly feels like a dark mood.

"That we do." He clears his throat and returns his voice to a lighter quality, the smile back on his face. "That will be our legacy then."

You are perplexing, Prince of Marchenda. You put on the mask of someone relaxed and happy, but there is much lying behind that facade. I would welcome the chance to see that hidden layer. Who is the man when he feels not the need to be mirthful for his realm?

"Carsen, I have had a lovely time. However, the night grows long. I hope you will call upon me again." Although it sounds like a formality, the sentiment is true.

The prince pulls me into a hug. "Count on it, Princess. It was refreshing to share my thoughts with someone so like myself. I will be calling on you soon."

I allow myself to be escorted out of the home and into the carriage. Once I am seated, Carsen places a warm kiss on my cheek. I smile at him before the door is closed and then I wave as the carriage pulls away.

Carsen is a good man but I must admit that kiss lacked the spark I felt in Renchenda.

Chapter

34

HAVING MET WITH CARSEN I feel I am no closer to knowing what needs to be done for Fraun. What if I decided not to choose a husband? Could I lead my realm alone? Surely they will continue their friendships with me even then. I would not truly be alone, per say. My thoughts are racing each other through my head as I pull open the door to father's room. They are the very same thoughts that occupied the hours in which I should've been sleeping.

"I'm glad to see you well this morning, father." I take a seat on the edge of the bed, patting him on the leg. In truth, he doesn't look well at all. Under his eyes there are dark circles, giving the impression his eyes are sinking into his skull. He is frail, blanched, and weak. I will my face to betray none of this.

"Tell me how went the council meeting and the dinner." His voice is a breathy whisper and is punctuated by a cough.

"The council voted to train up a patrol in all five realms, Jordyn's idea."

"Naturally." The king tries to chuckle, and another coughing fit ensues.

I wait him out, unsure how to help. "Yes. The vote was unanimous.

I need to send two men to Sarcheda to begin training. I am going to head to the village today and find some willing volunteers."

"Check at the edge of town by the fields. There are many men there who are a young age, they often look for work."

"I will do just that, father, thank you. The council also voted to update the lineage charts in all the realms," I say.

"For what purpose?"

"To help find all available citizens who may have royal blood within their veins. You know how concerned they are with the lack of heirs in some of our realms." I try to keep my voice worry free. The last thing father needs right now is more to worry about.

"Did you tell them of Charlotte?" he attempts to prop himself up on one arm, but wavers dangerously and drops back to the pillow.

"Of course not, father." I pat his leg. "Fear not, that will be taken care of."

"What of the meeting with Carsen?" he asks, a glimmer of hope in his eye.

"It went well." A sparse blush begins on my cheeks. "Carsen is a good man."

"Is he courting you?"

The blush deepens. "I believe so. I asked him to call again."

"You make me a happy man, Daughter."

Am I an awful person for letting him root this small happiness in exaggeration?

"Father, I have business to attend to and you look like you could use some rest. I will visit again tonight." I kiss his cheek before leaving.

The trek to the village is uneventful this time around. The people of Enchenda seem to be holed up in their homes against the cooler air. I am wrapped in a warm cloak, my hands shoved deep into the pockets.

Not only do I need to find a few volunteers for the patrol, a task which may be harder than I anticipated because of the lack of people braving the cool air, but I need to find someone willing and able to update the lineage tree as well. How does one just stumble upon someone capable of good communication skills and an ability to write, a task not taught to all in school?

I reach the edge of the village square. Despite the cold, there are four young men, bundled up and fidgeting to stay warm. "Good morning, Princess," the tallest of the group greets. "Are you searching for something this morning? My friends and I can handle any household task and all we ask is for one warm meal each." Clearly the leader, he has stepped away from the huddle of the group.

My eyes search the faces of the men. The leader stands two clicks over my own head. His eyes are kind but his face is stoic. He looks to be older than me, but father had mentioned the men here to be young and looking for work. Behind him, the other three men are shorter than I. To the far right the man has a sad expression, like a wilting flower. The middle man, the shortest of the bunch, wiggles continuously like a flag in the wind. The man to the left seems almost shy, turning his face away from me. I address their leader, "The task which I seek to fill today would require more work than a simple household chore. I need only the bravest souls; ones who are able and willing to travel all of Fraun. I search for someone who finds it in himself to be strong, humble, quick, happy, and wise."

"Something like that would require more compensation than a single warm meal," he answers.

"Three warm meals a day and a place to rest your head," I promise.

"You mention all five qualities of the realms, Princess. Would I be correct in assuming this job would require someone who is willing to work for other realms in our kingdom?"

"You would. Would such a man exist in this area of the realm? I am in need of two."

The man turns, facing those gathered behind him. "Kristopher, Michael you should head home." The man in the middle opens his mouth, taking a step forward. The leader speaks before he has a chance to object. "Michael you have family here. If the princess is asking for someone who can travel, that is not your lot. Who will care for your sister if you are gone?" The man, Michael, seems to agree. He hangs his head and leaves the clearing.

The man on the left, the one who had been looking downward

instead of at me, speaks. "Thank you, Lance. I...uh...I am not ready for that."

"Kristopher you will be, someday." The leader, Lance, uses an amiable tone.

I can hear emotion for the men he leads in his voice. Yet, when he turns to face me there is no trace of that emotion in his expression. "Tell us more about this job."

I look to the man remaining, he continues to look dejected. "What is your name, sir?"

His cold eyes light upon my face, briefly, before returning to the ground. He does not smile. "Danyel."

"Danyel does this seem like a task you would be willing to hear about?"

"There is nothing left for me here in Enchenda, Majesty."

"Enough about him. I can handle him. He will not go if he is not willing, trust in that," Lance interjects, stepping between Danyel and I. "Now tell us more of this position."

I watch his expression as I explain. "Fraun is beginning a Patrol. The men and women who make up this patrol will be from all five realms. They will travel throughout Fraun training with the various leaders, learning the skills and characteristics all realms have to offer. Once their demanding training is finished they will then be a Patrol for Fraun."

Lance's eyes betray nothing. "These men, this Patrol you speak of, they will be expected to travel forever. Once they are a Patrol they will be all over Fraun. Trained in all realms, living in all realms, these men would have no realm to call home."

"That is true. They would be citizens of Fraun itself."

"More prepared than any other, that is for certain."

"Lance, who cares where we call home? Enchenda offers nothing for us." Danyel steps forward. "I'm in." He offers me his hand.

I hesitate. Should I accept a man who clearly takes this task to alleviate some personal sadness? Do I have a choice? I shoot out my dainty fingers and wrap them around his offered hand. "Excellent, Danyel. They will be lucky to have you. Do you have transportation that can take you to Sarcheda?"

"I'm sure I can procure some."

"Good. King Tin will expect you by tomorrow. Please make arrangements to be there on time." My smile is not returned to me.

"Will do, Majesty." The boy bows low before leaving the small clearing. I return my focus to Lance. "What are your thoughts on our Patrol, Lance?"

"What is the council afraid of?" he challenges.

"What makes you think we are afraid of anything?" The personal pronoun was a nice touch. Perhaps I consider myself a member of the council after all.

Lance chuckles, the sound is hollow, dying at our feet instead of echoing around us. "You begin a patrol and train them more than any other in Fraun. You share them equally among all the realms. This speaks of a culture preparing for war."

I shiver at the word. "You have the wrong impression, sir. The council merely wishes to prepare for anything that may happen. There is nothing pending on our horizon, I assure you."

"Regardless of your reasons, I think it's about time Fraun organize something. I'm in." He offers his hand and I shake it. "I have transportation. I'll be at Sarcheda before sunset today," Lance says.

Look at me. I completed my first assigned task from the council in less than two suns time. As I turn to head home, I notice Sawchett drawing water from the town supply. "Good morning, child," I call.

"Hi, Princess."

"Can I carry that for you?" I offer my arm for the bucket, noticing how heavy it looks with water reaching its rim.

"Thank you." Sawchett transfers the bucket to me carefully, spilling only a few drops of the water. "We live right there." She points.

"I remember."

"You can leave it out here if you want. My Aunt will bring it in."

"Actually I'd like to come in if it's alright. I really should say hello to Charlotte." I wait for the small child to step out of the way and nod before I enter the home. Inside a fire is warming everything, bringing a bright light to the crevices of the house. Is that dust covering the table? I run my finger along the surface. The motion leaves a line in the gray layer and my finger covered. That is concerning. "Is your Mother ill?" I inquire.

"She'll be alright, won't she?" Sawchett asks, her lower lip beginning to quiver.

I bend down until my eyes are even with that of the smaller maiden. "Where is she?" Sawchett merely points toward the closed curtain. "I'm going to go see her. Sawchett, whatever happens, you must trust that you will be cared for."

I leave the girl in the little kitchen and push the curtain aside. "Charlotte?" Beyond the curtain, the scene is much like that at my own home. The woman is up to her chin in blankets and looking worse for the wear; gray hair, sunken eyes, and sagging skin. "Milady, how are you feeling? Is there anything I can get you?"

"Princess, is that you?" Charlotte croaks out.

"Is it, Aunt. What can I get you?" I ask. Charlotte tries to sit up. Instead, I sit on the edge of the bed. "No, don't get up for me. I'll come to you. Tell me, how are you feeling?"

"Old," Charlotte chuckles.

She is the second person to make that joke in a fortnight. I fail to see the humor. Can one truly feel old? "Can I get you anything?" I repeat.

The old woman shakes her head, no. "I'm all right child. What are you doing here? I fear I can't handle more questions about my past right now."

"I'm here for you and for the girl. She was fetching water in the square. She seemed to need help. Once I got here it was clear we share concerns about your health."

"I am afraid of dying and leaving her to bear witness to that," Charlotte says.

"What can I do?"

"Take her with you."

There are so many reasons to deny that request: the king will not allow it, I am not ready to raise a child, no one at home has prepared for it. The ferocity of Charlotte's gaze burns at me. I cannot turn the woman down. "I will."

Charlotte's eyes close. "Good. Tell Tutor that I have taken care of it."

"Tutor?" Curiosity piqued, I tap the woman to wake her. "Do you speak of Tutor the man or the profession?" When the answer is not immediate, I shake her slightly. "Answer me, woman."

Charlotte's eyes flutter open. "The man, silly girl."

"How it is you know Tutor?"

Charlotte's face registers shock for a moment. "Did I say that? What did I say?" Confusion flits across her tired face.

"You said you know Tutor. How is that?"

"He came here. When Sawchett was born he came to tutor her. Your father arranged it." The answer is clipped.

Is Charlotte lying? Why would someone lie about that? "You say Sawchett has some training from him then? She was not a child of the school?"

"No, no. She went to school as well. He only came sometimes. He helped both of us. I think your father did it from guilt."

"I will ask him of this," I promise.

"Your father or Tutor?"

"Whichever I find first. Know you where I can find Tutor?" I push to my feet.

"I do not."

"Is that honest?" I ask.

Charlotte's eyes lock on my face again. "It is the most honest I can be."

"Fair enough. I will send in the girl. You will take your time saying your farewells."

Back in the main room of the house, I lay a hand on Sawchett's little shoulder. "Your mother would like a word with you." When she departs, I find an empty wooden crate and begin tossing in articles of clothing that look like they must belong to the young one. The mention of Tutor's name has my mind working like a water wheel, constant and spinning. Why would he be worried about the girl? What does he have to do with Charlotte and Sawchett? I know the only person who can answer this to my satisfaction is the man himself. But where do I find him?

"Princess," the small voice breaks into my trance. I turn to find

Sawchett is standing in the room, her eyes filled with water. "I am ready now," Sawchett whimpers.

The small frame is shaking slightly, but Sawchett's shoulders are pulled back tightly. Her chin is raised. Taken as a whole her body language communicates a girl much older than her years ready to face the world. What impressive strength; where did she find that?

Without giving myself a chance to overthink it, I drop to my knees and open my arms to the girl. Sawchett runs to me, gladly accepting the hug. "It's going to be alright, little one," I coo, brushing the blond locks with my fingers. I feel the girl's trembling crescendo under my encircled arms. "It's alright to cry." The girl gives in to the urge and covers my shoulder with tears.

There is something about having to stand strong for another that makes you feel substantial. The sudden surge of power makes me feel more like royalty than I ever have.

Chapter

35

THE DOOR TO MY HOUSE flings back on its repurposed hinges faster than I meant for it to, slamming against the wall. My eyes take a moment to adjust to the darker front room. When they do, I see the small form of a servant bowing at me from the corner of the room. I recognize the woman I dined with and rush to her side. "Linchanta..." her eyes register shock at the use of her familiar name, "...this is Sawchett." I step aside to reveal the young child.

"Who is she, milady?" the servant asks.

"She is a friend of mine and she is to be treated as you would treat me. She will have a room of her own, we will need someone to fetch her more clothing, and I will see to her having a personal tutor." My heart flutters with doubt. How will I answer the questions she will ask?

But there are no questions. Linchanta merely nods, although her eyes do not leave the small one. "One more thing," I add, "my father need not be troubled with the news of another mouth to feed."

This pulls her eyes from the face of the child. They snap to mine. There is a question forming there, I can see it. Whatever it is, she swallows it down. "Of course, Majesty."

The new formal title slips into my ears easily and coaxes a small smile. I hide it by leaning down to the girl. "Sawchett I have other business to attend to, but Linchanta will take good care of you. If you need anything, please ask. This is your home and you should be comfortable here."

"Can I play outside?" The girl's voice is weak and trembles slightly.

"Of course." I ruffle the hair of the little blonde. "Linchanta will take you out to my favorite garden once she has shown you the room you'll rest in. Sound good?"

"Thanks, Princess."

"Honey, call me Eselda."

"Thanks, Eselda."

"You're very welcome, Sawchett."

Linchanta offers her hand to the little one, "Sawchett, would you like to follow me to your room?" Sawchett places her little hand, and by extension her trust, in the offered palm. Together, they leave, heading for the little room beyond the dining room.

Another order of business taken care of. As I turn towards my father's bedroom, I see Eee scurrying across the floor. "Eee," I call out, halting the roach in her steps. "Do you know the man who used to tutor me in my youth?"

"Yes."

"I need to speak with him. It's urgent."

"I could have him tracked down." Eee begins to move again, in the same direction she was previously headed.

"Eee," I again pause the roach merely with this word, "don't take 'no' for his answer."

"Yes, milady."

Chapter

36

"HOW IS HE FEELING THIS afternoon?" I ask.

"About the same, Majesty. I am not sure how much longer he can hang on," the caregiver answers.

I bustle in like a hurricane wind, practically knocking the door off its second-hand hinges. "Father..." my voice trails off as I take in the sight of him sitting upright. "You look surprisingly well." I bend to kiss his forehead.

"You were expecting me to be gone from this world?" he asks lightly.

"I didn't truly know what to expect," I answer, sitting in the chair beside the bed.

"Tell me how your expedition went." He breaks into a fit of coughing that he cannot control. I hold tight to my stony expression, not wishing to show the fear he puts on me with this illness. I command myself to stay strong for my king.

When his coughing has subsided I continue as though uninterrupted. "It went well. I found the two men who will represent Enchenda in the patrol. Both promised to be in Sarcheda by tomorrow nightfall at the latest. I have yet to find a scribe, but an idea has come to mind."

"What, pray tell, was that idea?"

"I am thinking it may be wise to request that Tutor fill the position."

The idea had fleetingly crossed my mind, this much is true. But until I spoke the words aloud I had not decided what to do with the thought. Tutor is well versed in both reading and writing. In addition, having lived among the common people but worked among the royals he would be a wise choice for the conversations that must be had with people for this job. In truth, having now heard the thought aloud, I quite like it.

"That is one idea. Is he no longer providing tutoring services?"

"He is not. I felt as though he was no longer needed. He agreed with my assessment of the situation." I feel the pull and tug of my younger self wanting to ask if father agrees with this decision as well. I bite back the bitter urge to ask him.

"It sounds like you have things handled."

"Thank you, Majesty." My eyes water at the unexpected praise. I blink too quickly, a fruitless effort to control the tides. "I'll let you sleep." I rush out of the room before he can respond.

Back in my own chambers, I lean on the closed door and sigh. How regal is it to melt at every praise offered? I must learn to fortify myself against such praise if I am to be taken seriously as a queen.

I saunter to the window and place my palms flat on either side of the opening. In this manner, I am peering out over the walkway to town when I hear a loud crashing noise from the side of the house. Turning my head to the left, I see the head of a large creature come into my view.

A gasp escapes my lips and my hand sails to my mouth. The creature is brown, large, and leads with long hooked grippers. There are multiple legs, I count three on each side as the creature barrels toward town. I am numb with panic. Something in my mind screeches at me to move, get help, or aide in some way but my feet remain firmly planted to the flooring. I watch in horror as the creature approaches a group of boys kicking an acorn around in the street. From my room, I shriek, "Get out of the way." The voice is lost in the thin air.

I am left to watch in revulsion as the creature rapidly closes the gap between itself and the children.

Chapter

37

*T*HE TOWN IS BUSY. THERE are children playing nearby, he continues to see one or the other of the boys step into his line of sight from around a corner. According to the directions he received when he arrived in town, that is the direction to the princess' home as well.

Tin takes the corner at a reasonable clip. His eyes waste no time locking onto the ant progressing down the walkway. He takes in the whole of the creature, noticing its length is more impressive than its stature.

Instinctively, Tin steps into the path of the ant.

In his haste, he knocks one of the small boys back away from the road. When the ant collides with his body, Tin has already squared his feet to accept the weight. In this way when he stands under the creature he is able to lift the body and send the ant sprawling to its backside.

It takes effort for the being to right itself. In this time the king of strength never removes his eyes from the offending beast. He knows from his practice in the ring with different creatures that he must remain dominant to keep the pest moving. He holds his arms out at sharp angles in a show of size. He breathes heavily, being sure to make it sound like a war cry.

The showing is effective. The ant, once righted, scrambles away into the brush behind the houses. Thanks to his knowledge of the Fraun map, Tin knows it is heading for territory beyond their limits.

I regain my ability to move at the sight. I dash for the door and out of the house, all the while shrieking the name of the king of Sarcheda. From the end of the walkway on my front lawn, I see the king reach for the small boy. His eyes scan the child quickly, looking for injuries. Finally, the boy rises. I arrive on the scene just in time to hear the boy thank the king, "Mister that thing would've killed me. Thank you."

Tin notices my arrival, his shoulders tighten and he stands a little taller. "If you were a bit stronger you wouldn't have needed me." His voice, hard and edgy, does not match the scene I just watched unfold.

Curious.

"Tin," the king turns his head to fully look at me. "That was…" my mouth is unable to form adequate words. "It was…impressive." I settle for the first word I pull from the jumble in my brain. Once the word leaves my mouth I am disappointed in the choice. That wasn't the word for what I saw. Heroic would be better.

Tin waves off my compliment. "Ants are something we see our share of on the outskirts of Sarcheda," he says. "They can be dangerous when they are lost from their group, I think it's panic at being alone. Most of the time they mindlessly follow one another."

"I have never even seen such a creature. It could've hurt those boys if you hadn't been here."

"That's why we teach them strength in my realm. Boys that age could have handled such a creature in Sarcheda."

I think I just got a rare glimpse of what true character brews under the surface of this man, yet he tries to hide it from me now. Curious. "What are you doing in Enchenda anyway, King Tin?" I ask.

Tin visibly changes. His eyes and shoulders soften. He smiles at me and allows his eyes to trail my figure. "Actually, I came to see you."

I blush under the survey of the handsome king. "Oh? What can I help you with?"

"I know you had your meeting with the prince yesterday. I wanted to be sure you knew I was serious when I said I had a desire to court you. Clearly, I should've made it my priority in the beginning," Tin says. "What says the good prince? Does he look to the future of Fraun?" Tin asks.

I think of the giant remnants making up the back garden. *Past.* I think of the impressive story, not one based in past but one made up on the spot. *One with even a lesson someone could learn from in the future.* "I think he does," I answer. "But he hasn't yet forgotten the past. He seems to understand how to learn from it."

"What can we learn from a past full of old men who believed in outdated ideals?" Tin challenges.

"What ideals do you speak of?" I soften my tone in response to the sharp one taken by the king. I take a small step back. It would do me well to remember he is of a malicious age.

"This marriage fiasco. Do you know how many times I've been questioned by our council of leaders about my personal life and relationships?"

I shake my head. Although I'm sure I could guess.

"Who says a man is only really a man when he has a wife and children? Am I not fit to lead the council table because I do not possess those things? They talk of renumbering to remove me of my right, I know they do. What crime have I committed?" Tin asks.

That is exactly what I've been saying. I take a step toward the king and reach for his arm. "You are right. There is no crime in being alone. Certainly, if there is you are not the only one committing such a crime."

"They hold these archaic beliefs about meeting outside their council room, they undermine me when I speak out of turn, and if you need help with an issue in your realm they are not available." Tin shakes off my arm and turns away from me. "There was no one to guide me when I reached twenty annuals. No king, although they are all my elders, was willing to help me with that. I had to learn this on my own."

That's odd. Jordyn has initiated conversations with me on the same topic. Even Carsen mentioned meeting with Jordyn. "Not even Jordyn was able to offer guidance?" I quietly ask.

Tin wheels around to face me again. His eyes are troubled by anger. When he speaks his voice is low like thunder before a storm. It is a warning. "He is not the man you think he is."

I take a step back, feeling my heartbeat quicken. "You do not get along?"

"We are different people both battling the same monster." The king shakes his head, rolls his neck, and looks back at me again. He takes a deep breath. "I am sorry. The state of the council gets me irate. Sometimes I wonder how we'll ever set it right again."

"Do you truly feel there are that many problems?"

Tin steps closer and takes my hand in his. He leans close until his breath falls upon my lips when he answers. "You've been there. Don't you see it?" I feel his need to have someone on his side pulsing through his body.

It must be so hard to sit there in charge of that group and remain strong. I squeeze his hand. "I think I see some of it."

At the show of reinforcement, the king leans in further until our lips touch. The sudden display of affection shocks me and the kiss is broken before I have a chance to recover. Tin straightens but does not step away. "I'm sorry, was that inappropriate?" Something in his tone of voice tells me he doesn't care in the least whether it was appropriate or not.

"Perhaps a little."

The king smiles and takes a step back. "Well, dear Eselda, I should probably head back. I have a patrol reporting to me soon. I merely needed to see you for myself to see where your prince's loyalties lie."

His loyalties?

Tin reaches for my hand, kissing the back of it lightly. "Until we meet again."

As quickly as he came, the king is around the corner and out of sight. I stand firm on the spot after he leaves my head fluttering with betrothal, kisses, councils, and rules.

Is it time for some of the rules to be reviewed?

Chapter

38

OUR MORNING HAS BEEN TYPICALLY quiet. The clanging of the utensils on the plates and the snapping of the logs as they burn down in the fireplace are filling the awkward silences. Sawchett keeps yawning, likely because I continue to insist she rise at a decent hour of the morning even though I have not yet found her a tutor. I am interviewing another today, but if I don't stop comparing these men to the tutor I grew up with I will never find one.

"Your Majesty," a voice blusters into the room from the hallway. Two men enter one standing and dragging the other. The one in charge at the moment is clearly struggling, being the smaller of the two. He is pulling the writhing body of the other.

The body of the struggling man flips just right and his face comes into focus. "Tutor?"

"Tutor!" Sawchett exclaims, excitement lighting her little face.

Tutor must recognize the little voice. The fight drains out of him and he stops pulling against the stubborn foot soldier who insisted he come to see the royal family at the request of the princess. Not ready for the sudden stop to his protesting, the smaller man drops Tutor's weight to the ground. Tutor takes his time rising, never taking his eyes from Sawchett.

"Should I remain close lest he run again, Majesty?" the footman asks.

"No, you may go." I eye Tutor wearily. This is the most unkempt I have ever seen the man. He is wearing gray pants that appear to be dirty, he is barefoot, and his brown shirt hangs loosely on him. I can see a small bruise on his left arm, half hidden by the shirt sleeve.

"Sawchett, what are you doing here?" Tutor asks, approaching the young girl.

"Missus Princess Eselda says I can stay here," Sawchett answers.

"I welcome the company," I explain. "Sawchett, why don't you go see to the garden and let me talk with Tutor." Sawchett rises, hugs Tutor briefly, and dashes out toward the garden.

In the girl's absence, Tutor braces for a fight. He does not turn around, so I have front row seats to watch as the muscles in his back clinch. A bitter chuckle escapes. "Well isn't this a familiar scene?" He drops into the chair nearest him.

"How so?" I ask, reclaiming my own seat.

"Many a time I entered this room to find two people dining. One who was tired and unprepared for the day," he gestures in the direction of the chair Sawchett has just vacated, "and one seated regally ready to lead this realm to great things." He sweeps his hand across the table, pointing to me. He allows his eyes to flit to the empty chair at the head of the table. "Why don't you occupy his chair?"

What is wrong with his attitude today? "My father lives, Tutor."

"I'm glad to hear it." He reaches for a strawberry, plucking it from my plate.

It is openly rude; he is asking me to get angry. I force myself to stay calm. I will not play your little game. Today we play with my rules. "Tutor, I have questions for you."

"I figured that out when I was summoned. Well, summoned is not the right word. I figured that out when I was dragged out of bed in the middle of the night and forcibly brought here before you. What are you waiting for? Ask your questions."

There is so much anger in him. I try to match his hard tone. "This time will be different. This time you will answer."

"Fine."

"How do you know Sawchett?" I begin with what I perceive as a safe question. Clearly, he was pleased to see the child, perhaps this is a good foot on which to begin.

"I've tutored her for the last three annuals since she could speak."

"How did you come to be employed in this manner?"

"Her mother asked me to do it." At this comment, his eyes flash dangerously.

I know how this will make him feel, but the time for treading carefully has passed. "Charlotte?"

"That's the one," he answers.

This attitude is so unlike what I recall of Tutor. He is slumped back in the chair and leaning on the arm of the furniture. He is sporting disheveled hair and wild eyes. It could be that the struggle with the man who fetched him for this meeting roughed him up a little. Or it could be something or someone else has changed the man I remember into this creature before me. "How do you know Charlotte?"

"She lives in the village. You've been there, it's hard to miss her house. She's right on the edge of the town square." He indicates the direction with one hand, but his tone of voice tells me he's being sarcastic.

"Tutor you are disrespecting a member of the royal family of Enchenda," I say without raising my voice in the least. "What relationship have you with Charlotte?"

For a beat, I am not sure he will answer. I watch the storm play out in his eyes. His jaw continues to work like he is chewing on a piece of tough meat, his right leg bounces like there is a spring below it.

Finally, he sighs. "Did you know I wasn't raised here?" The question is delivered in a whisper.

The familiar voice is back. I let out a breath I didn't realize I was holding and lean toward him. I'm thankful he is his old self, even for just a second. I'm afraid more movement, like a hug, would break the spell.

"My earliest memories are of Farcheda. I was in Farcheda until I was full height," Tutor says.

Ten annuals, I note.

"I lived with a nice couple, both old. As I understood it, my parents had died and I was being raised by the family that had lived alongside them." Tutor sits a little straighter in his chair, leaning his weight now on the right leg. In response, the bouncing is immediately resumed by his left. "When I had just reached full height, we were forced to flee Farcheda in the middle of the night. The old man had stolen something from a neighbor. We feared being caught so we fled. We ended up in Renchenda.

"I was given to another family, a younger one, to be raised. Honestly, I think the old couple was afraid they would gray and die in my presence and leave me with nothing. I attended school in Renchenda. I have to tell you, Eselda, their schooling is amazing. The things they have those children doing is..." he pauses while he thinks of a word, "... inconceivable for someone from another realm.

"During that time, I made friends with many a man who went on to become a Scout. At fifteen annuals I decided it was time for me to take my leave. I wanted to see Fraun. I wanted to travel. I wanted to join the Scouts."

The scouts are a daring and dangerous group. Their task of exploring what lies beyond Fraun and bringing back items that can be reused has always brought me equal parts fascination and fear. I pull my legs up on the chair in a childish show of my engagement in his story, settling in for the tale as I probably did many times growing up.

"The scouts wouldn't have me. They told me I first had to find a place to call home, then I could walk away if I liked. They reasoned that I was walking away from nothing in hopes of finding a home among wanderers. It was an argument with many flaws, but my youthful energy did not translate well to arguing my case. They took me on a tour of Fraun. We visited the realms in descending order, but I never made it out of Enchenda.

"When I arrived here, I fell in love with the realm. The houses are quaint, the people are so nice, and I really felt at home here. I stayed for a while in the group housing off the town square near the strawberry patch. I was staying there when I met Charlotte. She made a habit, apparently, of visiting there. She explained once that a child she had lost would've been the age of the boys in this group home and she liked to give back by visiting. She took me for new clothes, new shoes, and food. She came back to visit me four or five times. She was impressed with how smart I was, likely due to my time in Renchenda. When I had been here for an annual and was tiring of day labor, she told me of an opening at the royal house. Her husband, a wonderful man named Den, knew of an opening for a tutor here."

During his tale to this point, Tutor's eyes had flit between the fire roaring in the fireplace and the table in front of him. He nervously tells his tale, but he tells it as one would tell an empty room. At this time, he turns his gaze fully on me as though remembering I am in the room. "I doubt you remember, you weren't much older than Sawchett, but I was given the job when I was about sixteen annuals and I've been your personal tutor ever since."

"I don't remember having anyone other than you tutor me."

"You would've had someone else for a few years when you first learned to speak."

"Did Charlotte continue to help you?"

"She allowed me to move into her home after her husband died, I helped care for Sawchett and tutored her once she began speaking."

"You never knew Charlotte was royal blood?"

He knee speeds up in its jostling and his expression hardens again. "Not until you told me." He adopts his angry tone as easily as one would put on a shoe.

"Do you have any opinions on that subject?"

"I do not." His gaze is piercing. It is his turn to ask the questions that need be asked. "Is it why you have brought the girl here?" He grinds his teeth as he awaits the answer. "Is she to be some kind of pawn for whatever you are planning?"

"I brought the girl here so she wouldn't need to see what is becoming of Charlotte," I snap.

"Are you grooming her as a princess?"

"It was not my intention, no."

"Then why summon me? Surely it was to tutor the young princess, prepare her to inherit the realm." His voice is thick with contempt.

185

Never in my life have I been spoken to with such hatred. "Tutor, I do not want you to be responsible for the education of the girl any longer. I had questions for you, that much is true. I had also hoped you had it in you to undertake another job, but now I fear it is too difficult a task for one so emotionally against royalty."

"I have spent much of my life serving your family. What makes you say I am against royalty?"

"I never had that thought before. But I realize you think less of Charlotte now that you know. This woman, she cared for you when no one else knew you. It sounds like you owe a lot to this stranger in your tale, and yet you seem enraged now that you know her truth."

"She lied." The words are spat from his mouth like seeds.

"She did. At the request of her king, for the betterment of her people, she lied." I look deep at Tutor, willing the man I know to be inside somewhere beneath the anger. "Can you honestly say you wouldn't do the same if I asked it of you?"

I find the scariest moment to be the one following this sentence. Can I, the future queen, ask things of my people? Will they follow me as they follow my father? Tutor rises and walks to the lineage chart painted on the wall. He stands ramrod straight, hands buried deep in the pockets of his gray slacks. I allow the silence to wrap itself around the room, a dark blanket on our scene. The silence stretches, folding over on itself until it has cocooned us both.

Deliberately, Tutor reaches his fingers out and caresses the black oval covering Charlotte's name. "She should be here," he whispers.

I want to jump for joy at the return of his familiar tone.

I walk across the room to stand behind my oldest friend. "How many others are missing, Tutor?" I ask. "How many, like Sawchett, never graced this wall?" I reach out my hand and lay it on his shoulder. "The council believes it would be wise to find out the answer to these questions. They have asked me to find someone capable of updating the lineage chart for Enchenda." I don't ask if he will undertake the job, I let the idea grow roots.

"She will likely die never knowing her name was once here," he whispers. "That is wrong. She should know."

"You're right, she should."

Tutor turns without warning, shocking me. My arm falls back to my side. Tutor is close enough that his foot lies between mine. "I would like to be in charge of updating this lineage tree, but I have one condition."

"I'll hear your condition."

"All names I find get recorded. No one can choose to leave one off the wall for any reason. I don't care if they were shunned, embarrassing, or dishonest. If I unearth proof of their royal blood, they get their names on that wall in gold ink." He gestures to the wall. "No exceptions."

I hold my serious expression for a beat as I pretend to consider his offer. Finally, a smile breaks out across my face. "I knew you were the right man for the job."

Chapter

39

SEVEN DAYS AND SEVEN NIGHTS pass. I notice Sawchett is already blossoming under the attention of the newly promoted lady-in-waiting, Linchanta. I watch the pair pull weeds from the garden, the sun bouncing off their blonde heads bent low. Sawchett sits cross-legged on the ground, holding a stubborn green plant by the base and pulling with all her strength. The servant smiles at her, making light of the lack of upper body strength, before helping her to yank the offender from the ground.

I sip my lemon water and return my gaze to the papers in my lap. Although the people of my realm are not noted on the wall in my home, or in any place where the council will recognize them, they do feel honor in their lineage. It is tracked by the medicine men in the village. I requested copies of any death notices or birth notices that come their way. This sheet, prepared and sent to me this morning, includes the fourteen deaths of recent days and the twenty-three births. This is good information for a princess, such as me, to have as I plan for the future. This means there are nine more bodies to clothe, nine more mouths to feed, nine future students to train, nine more people to protect.

How many more people can the small realm house before it can do no more? Will we run out of food or shelter first? I shake my head.

Certainly, the council will see fit to allow us to assemble more homes before people are without living quarters. I will see to it.

Sawchett's youthful giggle pulls my attention back to the garden where the two young ladies have managed to free the weed. Sawchett proudly holds it over her head, a sign of the struggle overcome. "Well done." I clap for the show.

"Would you like to help, Eselda?" Sawchett asks.

"Actually…" the voice floats from the far reaches of the yard like seeds on the wind. Gentle, calm, and beautiful. I turn toward it in time to hear the end of the sentence. "…I'd like to steal her away if it's not too much trouble."

My eyes light upon the brown hair glowing in the sun and I smile. "Prince Carsen, to what do I owe this pleasure?" I rise and stretch out my palm, which he wraps warmly in his own.

"I was hoping to speak with you a moment."

I notice the uptick in pitch at the end. Not an order, but a question. I nod once. "Let's speak over there." I point in the direction of the side yard, away from the prying ears of the girls.

We walk in silence. Once we are around the corner of the house, Carsen sits down on the ground. He gestures to the space beside him and I sit as well. "How are you feeling today, Eselda?" he asks.

"I am well, thank you." What is he doing here?

"I have a proposition for you," Carsen blurts, reaching for my hand.

"I'm listening."

"I was speaking with King Jordyn."

My Jordyn? I mean my friend, Jordyn? I cover any emotions with a smile.

"He has offered his blessing and his castle should you choose to accept."

"Accept what?" I squint my eyes, trying to decipher the puzzle Carsen has begun laying out.

"I have been privy to the fact that your time to rule fast approaches and that the council is concerned. Were it not for this fact," he blushes, "I would never rush this."

"Carsen…" I spin my hand so it is now holding his as well as being held by him. I squeeze once. "...stop being apologetic. Let's have the thought on the table and we shall work around it."

Carsen leans in close. He veritably whispers, "Princess Eselda, will you be my wife?"

I wait to feel emotion. Warmth and love at the question, anger and frustration at the askant, anything. Instead, I feel nothing. It is the shock of this lethargy that holds my voice in its prison. My eyes drop to a spot on the ground and I freeze.

Carsen begins to panic, he presses forward. "I don't mean to be presumptuous. Like I tried to explain, I would never have rushed this were it not for the politics. But Eselda, I really do have feelings for you. Our date showed me what an amazing woman you are."

He squeezes my hand briefly, but I cannot react. His pulse quickens and his breathing picks up. "I played the scenario out in my head, you know, like a good story. I imagined taking you out on many occasions. We would grow to fall desperately in love and then we would wed. But when I talked with Jordyn," at this name my cheek twitches slightly, "he pointed out that this plan could take more than an annual. What if then we were unable to have children right away or that took annuals atop that. This is a long time to wait, he reasoned, if I already know now how I feel."

Finally, I feel able to move. I turn my eyes to his face.

"You are beautiful," he blurts. "Your hair has this lovely red tint and your eyes are the color of a shamrock."

I shake off the flattering comment. "After one dinner, you already feel as though you could spend your entire life with me?"

"I do. You are an amazing person whom I am just barely getting to know."

I can appreciate that. But what of the future of Fraun? There is more to this than two people, one of whom may be falling in love. "Was this a business proposition or a proposition of the heart, Prince?"

"A little of both, I'm afraid."

"Then we better talk details of our business." I slide into the body language I have learned from Tutor; back straight, shoulders hunched slightly forward. Carsen will feel as though I am closing in. I will get honest answers. "Which of us is to rule Enchenda?"

"You."

"What is to become of you?"

"I will be your king, but this is your realm."

"What becomes of Marchenda?"

"They will need a ruler, but my father is not dying yet," Carsen answers.

As opposed to my father, you mean to say. "He will soon. What then?"

"We will just need to have children."

Oh. Despite my desire to keep the pressure on him that one makes me sit back. I let my shoulders slump. "I am starting to think no one will be happy until I do just that."

Perhaps this is the only way to end this incessant focus on my love life. Perhaps this will allow me to actually run my realm without pressure. Jordyn...wait, that reminds me.

"What did any of this," I ask, "have to do with the king of wisdom?"

"What is he if not a good sounding board for all things logical and wise? Who better to help with a decision that needs to be analyzed?"

I can't argue with that.

"I knew how I was feeling, but when he explained the situation as the council sees it I knew it was unwise to wait. Both of our realms need more rulers quickly. I'm only trying to speed up what I know would've happened eventually, Princess," says Carsen.

It is this comment, delivered with such confidence, that finally brings the warmth. It begins in my stomach and slowly spreads. "We would've married eventually?" This time the question is playful.

"That's how the story goes." He sounds relieved. He reaches for me, placing one hand on either hip and scooting closer until there is no gap between us. There he freezes. I wait him out for as long as I can stand it before I close the gap and plant a kiss on the lips of the prince.

Carsen rests his forehead on mine. "I can love you, Eselda. If you will let me."

I think about my life as of late. A queen must make decisions for her realm. There must be a child, a child within wedlock, and it must come from someone who can serve Enchenda with me and not be tied to his own realm. It cannot be a king whose loyalties lie elsewhere in the Fraun. I begin to nod my head. "I will marry you, Prince Carsen."

A smile of pure happiness fills his face as he pulls our foreheads apart. This time, it is Carsen who kisses me and the kiss is deep. I cannot help but feel small tendrils of smoky sadness wind their way through the warmth of the moment.

When the kiss breaks, Carsen's smile is somehow wider. "Jordyn has offered us the castle Fraun for the announcement party."

"Announcement party?" What else did you two plan without me? Was there no doubt that I would say yes?

"Yes. It is customary to announce the engagement of any member of a Ruling family. In this case, a special case, all of Fraun will delight in the news. What better reason for a party?" Carsen says.

"What else, pray tell, did you boys plan?"

"Nothing else, Eselda. Only that there is to be a party, and you are to be the star."

I smile a little as old dreams of dancing all night by moonlight fill my head. "We are to be the stars, you mean."

"How could I hope to compete with you?" he teases. "Would you like me to work out the details of the announcement party with Jordyn?"

I shake my head. "No, I will handle that. You speak with your father. I will be in touch." I rise from the ground, and Carsen scrambles to get up in my wake. "I shall write to our friend now and begin planning."

"When will I see you again?" Carsen asks.

"Soon." I plant a small kiss on the cheek of my promised and head quickly to the house.

There is much to do.

Chapter

40

King Gregario of Enchenda
and
King Larecio of Marchenda
are pleased to announce the betrothal of their only children
Princess Eselda
and
Prince Carsen.

A Ball is to be held announcing this to all of Fraun on
the next full moon in the Castle Fraun. We hope you and
guests of your realm will join us for the celebration.

HE CRUMBLES THE PARCHMENT IN his fist and lobs it into the roaring fire.

Second place.

He doesn't even try to fight the dark malevolence as it takes hold, instead he lets it engulf him. As he rises from his chair, he swipes at it and sends the heavy wood smashing into the far wall. He stands, breathing deeply, and letting the anger grow roots.

This will not do.
I knew this was possible, but I thought I had more time.
No, this will not do at all.
I will fix this.

Chapter

41

OUR HOUSE IS BUSTLING WITH activity. On the lawn, shivering from the cold, nine bakers sit with samples of their treats. In the front room of the home, thankful to be out of the elements, six musicians await their audience. They bear instruments and play soft notes to prepare. In the dining room, in front of a warm fire, seven dressmakers display their craft to an overwhelmed version of me.

I have already made decisions about material to cover the tables, what time of day to hold this ball, and what beverages to serve. I am now trying to decide on which dress would be just right. This decision, which would've been my favorite task as a younger girl, is getting lost among all the things to be done.

I finger the soft fabric of the simple pink gown again, smiling as it slips through my fingers. Pink is the color of a girl, immature and unprepared. I can no longer be that girl. I am announcing my engagement to a prince.

I look to the deep purple gown again, heavy and adorned with small white pearls. The sleeves are full length and would extend past my wrists to cover the backs of my hands with the small triangles of fabric. The skirt is shaped to flow out around me, brushing the floor and giving me the appearance of a large purple bell from the waist down. The top is cut very high, almost to my neck. I frown, I could never wear something that hot and restricting.

Next along the line, the blue gown. This one comes lower, dangerously so. What a fiasco I would be if too much skin were showing in front of the council and important members of Fraun. I sweep my eyes onward.

This next dress is yellow and has no straps or sleeves. The bodice is tight and wrapped with jewels. The skirt layers have been cinched to give the appearance of many layers although it may be only one. I reach out a finger and brush the fabric. It is cold but soft. "I would like to try on this one." I hear the other six dressmakers sigh as one.

The dressmaker, behind closed doors, helps me into the small gown. It is zipped up my backside as I face the reflecting wall. The bodice hugs my frame, giving focus to the curves I am learning to embrace. I run my fingers over the billowing skirt, smiling. The color plays well with my dark curls, cascading over the bodice. "Do I look like a princess?" I whisper to the mirror.

"No, Majesty, you look like a queen." The woman smiles and bows.

"I'll take it." I nod. "Now help me out of it and I will show you the girl you are to dress as well." As we begin working on zippers, I continue issuing direction. "She is to be in the same color, but something more simple. I want her to match with my house, but she is to look like a girl. Light fabric, plain, soft. Then you will go to Renchenda and prepare my fiance's suit as well. Use touches of this yellow among the black."

At this, the woman's hands freeze. "Renchenda, Majesty?"

My eyes widen. "Did I say Renchenda?" At her nod I rush to rationalize the error, "My mistake, the party is in Renchenda. My betrothed is in Marchenda."

The woman widens her eyes, just once, and bends to gather the dress. I quickly slip back into my house dress, a more understated black garb. "Thank you, madam." I quickly leave the room, glad to escape the embarrassing error. In the hallway, I wave to Linchanta to bring Sawchett in for her fitting.

I dismiss the other dressmakers with my fondest apologies, then signal for the next group to be brought in. I close my eyes and run my hands across my face, trying to wipe away the exhaustion. When my hands come away it is a local medicine man standing before me. "May I help you, good sir?"

"I have news for you, your Majesty."

"On with it then, it's a busy day here."

"You may want to sit, Majesty."

"I am fine where I stand, thank you. What news do you bring?"

"The woman you asked about last time we spoke, Charlotte?"

I nod. I fear I already know why he is here.

"She has passed, Majesty."

Tears spring to my eyes. With much effort, I hold them in. It is silent in the room as I wrestle with my composure. My mind springs to the story Carsen weaved about the frog father. "Was she alone?" I ask, my voice shaking.

"A man named Tutor was at her side," he answers.

Well that, at least, is a comfort. "Thank you for the news." The man receives the hint, bowing gracefully from the room. I make a triangle out my fingers and blow into it as I fight with my emotions.

I wish there had been more time to get to know Charlotte. After all, she is my Aunt. My blood relative. But I cannot allow myself to be selfish. There is someone else here who will feel this loss. Perhaps even more than I have felt it.

I trace my steps back to the dressing room, pausing outside the door to take a stabilizing breath. I can do this.

When the door opens I take in the sight of Sawchett as she is now. In front of the reflecting wall, a dressmaker beside her with a string wrapping around the girl's arm. Her excitement is palpable. It's a terrible feeling, knowing I'm about to ruin that.

"I need a moment with the girl." Without question, the dressmaker scurries from the room. I gesture to a bench along the back wall. "Let's sit."

The girl doesn't even question me. She drops to the bench. I sit beside her and take a deep breath. "I have some news for you, and it's not going to be pleasant."

Sawchett's smile falls. "Do I have to leave?"

I reach for her, slipping an arm around her shoulders and pulling her close into a sideways hug. "Never, my dear. I love having you here. No, the news comes from the village." I pull away enough to allow me to look the girl in the eye. "Remember we talked about how sick your mother was?"

Sawchett nods slowly. She sits straighter and tears fill her eyes. She already knows the truth, but I must put it in words. There is no easy way to do this. "She has passed, Sawchett."

The tears are immediate. Sawchett flops down, burying her head in the folds of my black dress. Her sobs tremble her small frame and fill the little room. I stroke the soft sun-kissed hair and let her cry.

It is a struggle to contain my own emotions, but this is Sawchett's loss. I cannot lessen this pain by feeling some of it for her, although I wish I could. So instead, I maintain my calm while Sawchett falls apart.

Chapter

42

I N THE ROOM THAT IS becoming his prison, Gregario taps his finger impatiently on the bed sheet. "Try and stay calm, Majesty," the medicine woman coos.

"Where is she? Isn't this when she comes to see me?"

Growing old, he has come to realize, *actually means shrinking. I no longer have the strength to rise from this bed. For all intents and purposes, I am gone already. Is it too much to ask for an exit from this life worthy of the king I tried to be? Something honorable and graceful? Dignified even?*

A small knock on the door precedes the entrance of his daughter, bringing with her the smell of cinnamon. *Eselda looks weary and tired. I recognize the mask of strength she hides it behind, it is one I often wore myself.*

"Good evening, father." She bends, kisses his forehead, and takes her chair beside the bed.

"How goes our party planning?" he asks.

"It went well; many decisions were made. I have other news to bring you tonight, father. News that will not be so pleasant." She winces at the thought of repeating the news again but leans close to her father's ear so as not to be heard by the resident caregiver. "Charlotte has passed from this life," she whispers.

Internally the old man struggles to process the onslaught of memories rising within. *In recent years Charlotte and I had little to no contact. This is not what I want to remember.* He is smacked by the sudden memory of Charlotte, young and waif like with hair like wheat, dancing in her flowing skirts in the field beyond the strawberries. *She danced as though nothing in the world could break her happiness. She was the most beautiful woman I had ever laid eyes upon.*

The memory changes, he recalls lying in a field alongside Charlotte. The tinkling of her laugh reverberates through his ears as though it is happening now.

Even after I learned who she was, I have always loved this woman. The one who never truly existed. The mere memory of the girl who was perfect for me. The one I never felt related to. The one I had no connections of blood to, but just wanted to be with. She will forever remain frozen at this age, in this way in my mind. Separate from the child of my father's dark secret.

Eselda can see Gregario is processing information, so she slips quietly from the room. The years rush at him faster now as he allows himself to remember things long buried.

My father's face the day he ran into us in the village is equally as clear as the memories of my young Charlotte. But that memory has sharp teeth which bite at my happy thoughts.

His face showed eagerness and excitement to meet the girl his son had spent so much time with. But that mask had cracked and hardened instantly when she came into view. Even the memory feels confusing as it did then.

Then came the unveiling. Charlotte was revealed to be a daughter of Stefan himself. The king had taken over the planning of the rest of the situation, including Charlotte's future. Numbed by the turn of events and my father's bitter secret, I blindly followed.

In the wake of those events, Gregario had never spoken of them to a soul. The ache for the girl that no longer existed to him and never would again exist in the same way left him a changed man. He later married out of necessity and convenience for his realm. He forced himself to face forward and march onward.

Until today.

Today the old king finally glances backward and lets the sadness consume him.

Chapter

43

ANDLES BURN AND CAST SHADOWS upon my face in front of the largest reflecting wall I've ever seen. I am deep within the walls of the Castle Fraun, wearing my yellow gown and readying myself for the evening.

'...*there is to be a party, and you are to be the star.*'

The gown picks up the light from the candles and reflects it back, shimmering with its own beauty. The hair, wrapped around the diadem worn only when I am attending formal events, is flowing and light. I am the picture of royal beauty until the lights fall upon my face.

Don't get me wrong, I see the beauty there. My delicate features have been scrubbed until they are rosy. But the eyes...the eyes give away my true heart.

Tonight I announce a marriage of business, a marriage of convenience. The girl who once dreamed of a love story to end all love stories has accepted a fate absent of that. It is a fate I can resign myself to, but you cannot hide sadness like that from your eyes.

Enough. This is best for Enchenda and for Fraun. Carsen is a good man. He is a good match. He will care for me, love me, and make me happy. "You will feel happy about this announcement," I command my reflection.

Behind me, the door opens. In the reflection, I see Sawchett enter. "Eselda, can you help me with my hair?" Sawchett asks, holding up a clip.

The dress for the girl was made in a white with the yellow I chose an accent color. The dress has long sleeves and a high neck, it complements the girls' blonde locks well. She wears it like a little princess. I beckon to the girl, holding my hand out. Sawchett passes me the small jeweled clip and watches in the mirror as I expertly flip the hair up into a twist that leaves only small ringlets framing the delicate face.

"You look beautiful, Sawchett." In the mirror, I watch her eyes sparkle like diamonds, an expression only a little girl playing dress-up can muster. I remember the days when ball gowns and dances held as much joy for me as Sawchett displays tonight. This is growing up. Not an end to my childhood but watching it through the eyes of another.

Sawchett twirls in a circle, her dress flowing out around her. "I'm going to go dance," she proclaims. I cannot even hope to answer before she runs from the room to do exactly that.

I turn back to my reflection. I take a deep breath and throw my shoulders back. I will go out and face the people. There will be many people here tonight. Each king was invited, and each will likely bring members of their realm with them. Those of Renchenda, who don't have to travel far, will likely be greatest in number. But even my own realm, farthest away, sent rows of people traveling on roaches to the Castle Fraun this morning. My stomach flutters at the thought.

Again the door opens. This time in the reflection I see the king of strength himself. I talk to the reflection. "King Tin, can I help you find something?"

The king pushes the door closed quietly and closes the gap between us with remarkable agility. He stops just short of my body, his heat searing my back and shoulders. In the reflection I watch as he leans down toward me, closing his eyes and breathing in my scent. I close my own eyes as he whispers in my ear, his breath lightly brushing my skin and making the hair on my neck stand at attention. "I found what I was seeking."

My breathing quickens, my palms sweat, and my stomach flutters. "Why did you search for me, Tin?"

"I had to see you one more time before the announcement is made and I can no longer stand this close."

I feel the heat of his hand on my hip, his palm lying flat where the skirt begins. "I had to touch you before you belong to another and I no longer can," he purrs.

I keep my eyes shut tight and swallow the rush of emotion at the flattery. "King Tin this is hardly appropriate." I try to sound confident. My voice quavers slightly. I hope he doesn't notice. "I am announcing my betrothal to another tonight."

The pressure on my hip increases and I feel his free hand light upon my other hip. I open my eyes and catch his in the reflection for just a second before he spins my body around. The motion is quick, almost painful, a shocking reminder of his strength.

"Do you choose him freely?" he asks. His voice is suddenly harsh and demanding.

Fear begins to creep up my spine. "I...I do. Carsen is a good man."

Something flashes in Tin's eyes but he drops his hands and steps back. It is a small step, but the space it leaves between us is enough to allow me to breathe again. "Then best wishes to you both." He traces his eyes down the length of my body, almost sadly. Then he turns to leave.

He is halfway to the door before he turns back. "Eselda, the rules could be changed." His voice is pleading. "It doesn't have to be this way. Just say the word and we can escape all this."

My breaths are shallow as the comment echoes in the stone room. Reflexively I take a step toward Tin and the offered promise. Can the rules be changed? Is it this simple?

I stop myself. Think of what is best for Fraun. "Thank you for the offer, King Tin. I'm sorry. I'm betrothed to another," I answer.

Tin hangs his head, defeated. "So be it." His voice is quiet but somehow strong. He turns and leaves the room and all the air escapes me. This is going to be a long night.

Chapter

44

H E STANDS IN THE SHADOWS at the back of the ballroom. People from all over Fraun, dressed in their best clothes fill the room. Four men with various instruments play music together along the side. Some of the younger Fraunians dance gaily in the center. At the front of the room, two of the five heavy thrones are filled as Mick and Larecio sit, smiling and whispering amongst themselves. Everything about this scene conveys happiness.

The king of wisdom quietly takes it all in.

This is logical, this match. They are the appropriate age for each other. They are of similar backgrounds. They need each other to bring a future to their realms. The match allows for five realms to continue to have representation. It makes sense.

When I listened to Carsen talk about Eselda I knew, deep down, I could not take this from him. There is no reason why I should object to this betrothal, and yet I feel the anger raging within.

For the first time in his life, Jordyn is at war with himself about a logical decision. This puts him in a foul mood. He remains hidden in the shadows, hoping with everything he has that this does not turn out badly.

The music changes to clipped noises used to get the attention of the crowd. A young man stands tall at the back of the room and speaks loudly into it. "Presenting, from Enchenda, Princess Eselda."

The doors to the ballroom open and Eselda glides into the room. At first, Jordyn can't look. He breathes deeply and keeps his eyes focused on the ground. A young Fraunian bumps into him and his eyes land on her in the shuffle. *That yellow dress...the woman wearing it...they both glow.*

Just that quickly, the monster is caged.

Chapter

45

I TREMBLE WITH AN OLD FEAR. The fear of making a mistake, making a fool of myself in front of everyone. Walk slowly. Don't trip. I make my way to the front of the room where I shake hands with King Larecio and King Mick before standing beside the chair reserved for my father. The eyes in the crowd, which have followed me to this point, now turn back toward the door in anticipation of the prince.

The same man who announced me clears his throat and loudly speaks again. "Presenting, from Marchenda, Prince Carsen."

The doors open again. This time there is no one in the doorway. A gasp escapes the crowd. A few stray men run toward the door, looking left and right before shrugging.

Chaos ensues.

"What is going on?" I watch, confused, as people spread out to search the castle grounds for the prince. A lot of panic for one man who likely just changed his mind. I flop onto the floor near the thrones. As evidence of their focus on the prince, no one notices the decidedly unroyal act.

I turn my head as a pair of shoes stops beside me. "What is going on?" I ask again.

"People are worried. A prince is missing."

My spine stiffens at his voice. I turn my eyes up to the man I have been avoiding since the proposal. Questions I will not ask him fill my mind. *Why? Can't we...? Will there ever...?*

To add frustration to my sadness...tears begin building behind my eyes. I feel them burning back there. I want to tell him about Charlotte's death. I want to tell him I doubt this marriage. I want to tell him that Tin seems to think the rules can be changed. If they can be changed for that king, maybe...

The desire to share this burden is so great, I have to physically restrain myself. I wrap my arms tightly around my drawn up knees.

"Do you know where Carsen may be?" Jordyn asks.

I shake my head and feel my curls bob and dance. "I'm sure he's here somewhere." I shrug. "Perhaps he's changed his mind."

"He did not do that."

"How can you be so sure?" I don't add that I would have changed mine if another option had presented itself.

"The man I spoke to was clearly in love, just the way you described it to me once upon a time," Jordyn answers.

I blush at his words and cast my eyes to the ground. The guilt is overwhelming. Carsen really felt that?

"You don't run from that," Jordyn adds.

I whip my head back around to the king. "You don't?" Anger raises my voice. "That's funny, I thought someone wise once told me you must do what is right for Fraun and allow the system to work despite your personal feelings."

Jordyn does not shy from my gaze but meets it. He doesn't even blink. "In that particular case, the feelings did not befit Fraun. In this case, they do. The situation is not the same."

I rise. From here I'm close enough to touch Jordyn but I won't let myself give into that desire. "I remember what you said and I haven't forgotten what I must do for my people." I can feel the tension crackling between us like lightning.

Without warning, there is a scream and a commotion at the entrance to the hall. Jordyn pushes me behind his tall frame and faces the doors. I peer around the king, annoyed at him for treating me like a child. A man has run into the front of the hall, terror writ plainly on his face.

"The prince is dead," the man bellows.

Chapter

46

EVER THE RESPONSIBLE ONE IN a crowd, the king of wisdom has managed to get all party guests into the ballroom to keep them occupied and in one place while we collect details. Now, in the center of a smaller room off the ballroom, he stands surrounded by the kings of Fraun and the man who made the discovery of the body. I remain with this group, a representative of the House of Enchenda.

"Tell us what you discovered," Jordyn commands the man.

The man's eyes dance nervously around the outside of the room, taking in the varying faces that look on. King Larecio is sitting on the floor, wallowing in a misery none have ever seen him in. Jordyn, Tin, and I are in a small line directly in front of the man. King Mick stands beside Larecio, but his eyes are fixed on our conversation. The man swallows. "We were searching for the prince all over the castle grounds--"

"Who is we?" Jordyn asks.

"Everyone on your staff, Majesty," he answers. "I opened the door to the small room on the first level, where the prince had been getting himself ready for the announcement. I found him lying dead on the floor."

Jordyn jabs a finger at the servant. "Be more specific. What did you do? How did you know he was dead?" Jordyn's gaze is boring into the man, who shakes underneath it.

"I entered from the only entrance, and immediately saw him. He was laying on the floor and blood had pooled around him. I could tell it was coming from a long wound on his neck, which was sliced open."

At this, King Larecio lets out a long wail of pain. Jordyn remains focused on the man, but the attention of the other royals turns to the older king.

"We will look at this wound later, but what is your opinion? Could it have been something he did himself?" Jordyn quizzes.

Behind him, Larecio wails again.

"Jordyn..." I reach out and touch the arm of the king. He jumps as if slapped and looks down at the hand. "...take this conversation to the side of the room out of the earshot of the man's father," I request.

Confusion crosses his face.

"Please."

Jordyn and the man who made the discovery head for the side of the room. I follow and use my body to shield King Larecio from the view of this discussion.

"It was not one he could inflict himself, in my opinion. There was no weapon around. If he had cut it himself, what became of the weapon?" the man says.

"Was anything out of place in the room? Did you move anything?" Jordyn asks, his voice a little quieter now.

"No, Majesty. Nothing was moved and I moved nothing. I came straight to the ballroom to tell you and the others of the discovery."

"Did you shut the door behind you? Could anyone else have been down there since then?"

"No Majesty. I put a roach on guard at the door after I shut it with instructions to let no one pass without your permission."

Jordyn pats the man heavily on the shoulder. "Good man. Take us to the room."

I stand frozen just outside the open door. Jordyn and the servant have stepped into the room. I heard the king take a sharp and jagged breath when he entered. Fear for what must cause this noise from such a man has me grounded to my position. From this point, I can hear their conversation as it continues.

"I agree with your earlier assessment, good sir." The voice of Jordyn, shaky but ever professional, floats to my ears. "There is no way prince Carsen inflicted this injury upon himself."

"The wound is deeper than I remembered it being, Majesty."

"It is deep, someone used a sharp weapon to cause this. I cannot even look down at the body for clues. That deep gash and the awkward angle with which his body lies turns my stomach."

"I feel the same, Majesty."

"How long was Carsen absent before you discovered this?" Jordyn asks.

"Not long, Majesty. Perhaps three songs from the band. I had only enough time to search two other rooms before arriving here."

"Interesting." Jordyn's voice ticks up at the end and the word trails on. He is thinking.

"You are thinking that timeline will help us determine who may have killed the prince, Majesty?"

"I am thinking just that."

"So whoever did this must have been away from the crowd during that time," the man offers.

"That seems to be the case, yes."

"Who would do such a thing?"

I lean closer to the door, for this is the question I have as well.

"If I were to venture a guess, it is someone who has a reason to want the prince to not marry our fair princess there," Jordyn says.

My eyes slam shut. This is my fault.

"Who would not want them to wed?" the servant asks.

"I would hazard we are looking for a male, young, someone who perhaps thought they were a candidate for the princess if Carsen here were not in the picture."

A whimper escapes my lips. That cannot be, can it? What a terrible thing. My mind spawns a suggested culprit, but I will not acknowledge it.

"Do you know of such a man?" the servant asks.

"I can think of one or two such men," Jordyn admits. "More importantly, can you think of any?"

"Majesty, in the interest of being thorough, I must ask you something," the servant says. "Where were you when the prince here was killed?"

I cannot abide this. I burst through the doorway. "That is highly inappropriate, sir. The king was with me while you were searching the castle for the prince." The man steps back from me, fear written on his face. "How dare you accuse him of such an act?" I yell. "This man is a king, your king. Do you know what you are suggesting?"

Jordyn catches my raised hand, calming me.

"I only wanted to be thorough, ma'am," he answers, his voice quaking.

"He is not wrong to ask, Eselda."

"But you were with me. Perhaps it is good he is thorough, but tell him you couldn't have done this." I continue to trap the servant with my angry expression.

"I cannot do that," Jordyn says.

What? I turn my gaze to the king but not before I note the servant's mouth falling open in shock. Jordyn's blue eyes meet mine with pain.

No. No, stop talking before you say something that will forever change my opinion of you, Jordyn. Please.

"Carsen may likely have been killed before we knew he was missing. Until we know when he was last seen, I have no alibi. It could've well been me," Jordyn admits.

"Surely you would know if it was you, Jordyn." My voice is soft, a prayer spoken only to him. I close the small gap between us and rest my palm over his heart.

"I wish I could tell you I didn't do this. But things often happen in my dark states that I remember not." He reaches out a hand and caresses my cheek. "I was so angry with Carsen this morning when I saw him, the monster inside was hard to tame. I don't know what I may have done in a disassociated state if such a state were to have occurred. I'd like nothing more than to claim this wasn't me. I fear I just don't know that for sure."

"What do we do?" I ask, the first tear for this event finally falling.

"We let my man here investigate. He is wise, he will find the answer. Even if the answer is not the one we want him to find."

"Jordyn--"

"Eselda, it is what Carsen deserves," says the king. Jordyn turns his attention to the young servant. When he speaks again the earlier sadness is absent and he is all business, "Are you up for this task?"

"I have spent my life idolizing you, sir. I am seeing you in a new light today. If you had asked me yesterday if I thought you were capable of love, a feeling devoid of logic, I would have told you no. Today, after what I have witnessed here, I know that may not be the truth anymore."

I blush. Apparently, I did not imagine our spark.

"If you want objectivity, I can give that to you now. I fear I no longer know what you are capable of. Could it be murder? I am not sure. I consider it an honor that you trust me, Majesty. I will undertake this. I have a few questions for you though. Perhaps ones I should ask without the princess present."

"Ask me whatever you'd like. But I will make one suggestion. Do not let King Tin leave this castle without asking him questions as well."

Chapter

47

THE KING WATCHES THE SUNRISE through the window. He, as well as most of those in attendance at the party, has not been to sleep yet. Based on the questioning of the small servant man who has been put in charge of the investigation, he is a person of interest in this murder. *As well it should be. After all, I am the person who used the kitchen knife to slice through the throat of the prince.* He has to stop himself from smiling at the thought.

The lie I told earlier slipped so easily off my tongue, more so than I thought it would. I had dreaded having to lie about my involvement. I knew the questions they would fire: When was the last time I saw Carsen? Did I have any reason to want the prince dead? I wondered what I would say to such questions.

As it turned out, it was easier than I thought. Mostly truth, with some small adjustment. I even had the foresight to talk about the darkness that is my age marker, just in case.

Ironically, were someone to outright ask me if I had murdered the prince I would probably take credit. However, no one has done that yet. For now, my lies seem to be holding water.

He glances around the room, eyes lighting upon the princess.

This isn't over yet; it's only just getting started.

Chapter

48

OUTSIDE THE LARGE HOUSE, SNOW is softly falling. The rising sun tinges the sky a soft pink. People are inside their own homes, plumes of white smoke reaching for the stars. Sawchett knows the people are hiding from the cold as much as they are observing the day of grievance ordered by the council.

She overheard the conversation last night, this is "highly unprecedented" according to one lady. A day of grievance is often observed following the death of a royal. It is a day when the people will not work. For one full sun cycle, they will not attend school or shop. They will remain in their homes and think on the life they have lost.

Today, however, differs from the previous days of grievance. At the Castle Fraun yesterday, as the sun was rising, the council made an announcement to the room. Sawchett had been seated on the floor, nearest the window, her eyes drifting closed on their own accord from the long night. The prince had been dead for the entire night and the sun was finally making an appearance. King Mick had loudly declared that all of Fraun would be observing the day of grievance by order of the council of kings. The council would allow you to travel back to your homes and the day would be observed the next day, today.

Sawchett cannot help but be awed by such an act of power. King

Mick's voice had boomed through the room and not a soul had questioned him. *Had Prince Carsen possessed such a power? If so, what could bring down such a man?* She finds she cannot come to an answer to this question. Instead, she fiddles with the hem of her dress and thinks of other things.

The girl, having nothing else to do today, is seated on the ground in the hallway outside the princess' closed door. Already this morning she has knocked and tried to coax the princess from the chamber to no avail. Her mind replays the comfort offered by Eselda just a short time ago when mother passed. That thought leaves her grounded in this hallway. *The princess will emerge eventually and I will be on hand to comfort her when she does.*

Chapter

ON THE OTHER SIDE OF the repurposed wooden door, I sit facing out my only window. I am watching the white dusting collect and slowly bury the front lawn. I sigh and a white circle from my hot breath mars the glass. Tomorrow morning, I must sit around the council table at the emergency meeting, as is tradition following a day of grievance.

Nothing like this has ever been experienced before, at least not since Oberian II. Never have all five realms observed a day of grievance together. In this case, it was needed. All realms were in attendance on this occasion, all realms will feel the shock and fear. The council will need to discuss this, proceed with caution from this point. Accidents can be explained; they are not something to fear. But outright violence...

I sigh again. This line of thinking is not productive. The council meeting has my stress level rising like the snow. What will they expect of me? Will they expect to see me fall apart like Sawchett did upon hearing of Charlotte or like Larecio when the facts of Carsen's demise were revealed? I am not sure I have that level of sadness in me, although I feel pain at the loss of my friend.

My thoughts turn to King Jordyn, almost of their own accord. What of this problem? I chew on my fingernail, taking out the tension on the inanimate and unfeeling object. Two seated kings are the main suspects in a murder investigation. Surely they will both be cleared, I cannot possibly believe either man is capable of such an act. But my assurance of their innocence may not be enough for the council. It may not be enough for King Larecio, who could demand justice.

A soft knock forces me back to reality.

"Eselda, there's a lady here who says your father asks for you," Sawchett calls.

I cross the floor in few steps and yank the door open. The child topples inward. She must have been leaning on the door. Even as I right her my eyes fall to the medicine woman. "What is it? Is he…" my voice trips over my fears.

"He is alive, Majesty. He simply demanded I bring you to him, I couldn't delay him. I fear it is good for neither of you, but he insisted."

After a quick scan of Sawchett for possible injuries from her fall I follow the medicine woman to father's chambers. At the present moment, the bed looks as though it is swallowing my father. In fact, for the first time in my adult life, there is room enough on the surface for me to sit comfortably beside him. I do just that, sitting beside his legs and directing my head toward him.

"Daughter, I heard of Carsen's death." Father's voice is so low it is mostly air. I have to angle myself over his body to hear properly. I prop my arm up on the far side of his chest, so I can comfortably lean and appear to have an air of relaxation I do not feel. "When is the council meeting?" the king asks.

"Tomorrow morning."

"What happened to him?"

"He was killed." I hear the slight quake in my voice and cover it with a little cough.

"This is certain?"

I am afraid of the words not being adequate for the grave situation. Of the words bringing tears. Making it real. I merely nod.

"The council knows this?" he asks.

Again, a nod.

"Listen to me, Daughter. Mick will not stand for this. I know not the details of this death but I do know Mick. He will use this to scare you."

What does Mick know of my fears? "Scare me?"

"Yes. Find a friendly face to focus on and stay calm," he orders. It sounds strange, an order from the feathery voice. It is hard to believe I was ever scared of this man.

"Father, why would he try to scare me?"

"Because, daughter, the time approaches when the king of speed will call to renumber. This is something he needs support for. He will scare you then offer you safety. In this way, he could earn your support." The longer speech leaves father gasping for air.

I allow him a moment to regain his breath. "There's more you should know, but I fear it's not good for your health to inquire further." Father cannot find the strength to form words but he can muster the energy to trap me with a gaze that means business. Despite his frail form, I squirm under such a gaze. "A small bit more, and only because I hope you can offer advice," I say. "There is an investigation that has been launched into who may have killed the prince."

"Good." There is no force behind the word, I barely hear it.

"They even have a few likely suspects, or so I hear." This time I see the mouth move but hear nothing. "I'm concerned about how this will play out Father, because they suspect a seated king." No need to tell him they really suspect two of them. The advice will be the same either way.

Shock marks the face of the old man. He shakes his head in disbelief, opens his mouth and tries to speak. Words will not form. Instead, he holds up his hand and shakes it to draw my attention. I turn my eyes to the fingers. The first finger is stretched up tall, standing above the rest. He is asking me if the investigation focuses on the first realm. He is asking if King Tin is a suspect.

"How did you know?" I ask.

He merely shrugs.

"Yes, father. They suspect Tin. Will this cause more problems?"

A nod.

"They will call for the vote tomorrow, won't they?" I ask the question as quickly as it occurs to me that I already know the answer. This may be the proof Mick has been waiting on.

Another nod shows me father agrees.

"Which way do I vote, father?"

He shrugs then he reaches out with his hand and taps me on the forehead. It's as if he is telling me to use my own brain. What if that is not enough?

Tears begin to fall, striking the blanket covering my father. "I'm scared," I speak quietly, so quietly he probably doesn't hear. Then I feel his arms, frail and thin, wrapping around my shoulders. He has pulled himself up into a sitting position, despite how much of his energy that must have taken. He is giving me the support I need.

I allow myself to fall apart, for maybe the last time. Tomorrow, I have to lead.

Chapter

50

T HE COUNCIL IS GATHERED, ALL except Tin. Larecio is barely holding it together. He is flopped over on the table, head on his arms, sobbing. The pain is filling the room, affecting everyone gathered. Jordyn is pulled back from the table, his jaw steeled shut. He will not meet my gaze. Beside me, Mick is annoyed. His jaw works dangerously as though he is chewing something or perhaps grinding his teeth. He is the only one present who doesn't appear changed by the recent death.

The door slams open and Tin saunters into the room as though nothing bothers him. He heads directly for his seat at the table and casually drops into it. He takes my hand, squeezing it. "None of us can take the pain away, Princess, but do let us know if you need anything." He drops my hand and turns his attention to the table.

"I call this emergency council meeting to order. Have we an update on the investigation?" Tin turns to Jordyn, but the answer comes from Mick.

"I asked the investigator to report to me," Mick announces.

Tin's head, along with all the others in the room, turns to Mick. "Why? Did you find the king of wisdom incapable?" Tin challenges.

"The man explained to me that he had reason to believe that Jordyn may have been involved somehow."

The statement does exactly what Mick intended it to do, incites a reaction from all present. Jordyn's eyes close as though he is experiencing great pain. I slam my hand down on the table. Tin's eyes widen in shock. Larecio rises from his chair and squares his body at Jordyn. "You killed my son?" he bellows, his face reddening.

Mick rises from his chair, holding his own hands near Larecio in case restraining him becomes necessary.

"Jordyn, speak up. Defend yourself," I plead with the king from my seat. I can feel my body trembling. Jordyn remains frozen, his eyes shut and his fists clenched.

"Alright, enough," Tin barks. "I'm not one to stop a show of strength, but we need to hear the facts and draw our own conclusions first."

King Mick sits, practically pulling Larecio down with him. Larecio keeps his eyes locked on Jordyn. "What says the investigator, Mick?" Tin asks.

"Well, he says the culprit is likely a male who would have reason to want Eselda and Carsen unmarried," Mick answers.

"I feel as though that is an unconfirmed suspicion," I argue.

"True, Princess," Mick concedes with a dismissive wave of his hand. "However we all know that the malicious age could cause one to do things they wouldn't otherwise do. Add to that the question of who had access to Carsen. How many of the people in attendance know the rooms of that castle well enough to get in and out unseen?"

"Actually that depends on just how long they had to do that," Tin interjects.

"Well, my investigator tells me that Carsen was last seen when his father checked on him whilst he was getting dressed. That would be a significant amount of time before Carsen went missing. The first guests were just arriving then," Mick says.

"It will be hard to find alibis for anyone for that entire period of time," Tin states.

"Actually it isn't that hard for me or for Larecio. I met him outside the same room, we walked to the ballroom together, we were there until the announcement was made. We are each other's alibis," King Mick proudly explains.

"Did you actually see Carsen when you met up with Larecio?" Although he has not moved, the voice comes from Jordyn. All eyes in the room turn to take in the sight of him. As if he senses us watching his hands move up to hide his face.

"I did not. The door was closed."

"Are you implying I killed my own son?" Larecio asks, his voice taking on an edge at odds with his title.

Jordyn sighs, moves his hands, and opens his eyes, meeting the challenge. "No. I'm merely pointing out that your alibi isn't as solid as Mick would like people to believe. If Carsen was dead when you left that room it doesn't really matter where you spent the next stretch of your time."

"Now see here, I stand to gain nothing from this death except for chaos and anger."

"I fear I stand to gain the same, good sir. Yet I seem to be enduring your wrath and doubt," Jordyn says.

Tin interrupts, "Alright gentlemen, settle down. What of the rest in attendance, did they not have alibis?"

"With a timeline as large as you're talking, King Tin, I fear no one will have a solid one," I say. "Are there facts beyond this? Is there anything about the crime itself that will lead us to an answer?"

"Like I said, he tells me it is likely motivated by jealousy from someone who wanted to be in the place of the prince that night." Mick's eyes fall back to Jordyn.

"Well, that's hardly reliable, especially considering it was the king you stare down there who put that very thought in the man's head," I yell. "There are likely many who could come up with other reasons, but speculation does not indicate guilt."

"Who would want my son dead?" Larecio challenges, finally tearing his gaze from Jordyn long enough to turn it on me. "This is your fault, you know. Had you not agreed to marry him this never would've happened." He rises from his chair and points his finger menacingly across the table. "Someone killed my son to assume your throne."

Before anyone can get a word in or reason with the man he storms from the room. Mick, shrugging in apology, follows.

I drop my elbows to the table and cradle my head in my palms. "He's right. This is all my fault." I hope someone will correct me, point out a flaw in the argument.

I pick my head up enough to look at the two remaining kings. Neither has moved. No one will correct me, I'm not wrong.

This is my fault.

Chapter

51

WHEN THEY ARE ALONE, JORDYN turns his gaze on Tin. The anger he is feeling becomes dangerously obvious, zapping back and forth between them. Tin matches the stern line of the mouth and the harsh body language.

"I cannot prove anything with certainty, Tin, but I fear as though one of the people in this room is responsible for the murder of the prince," Jordyn says.

"Is that so, Jordyn? Do you think I don't know what affects you today? Do you think I can't read the signs of the age marker all over your posture? You lose the battle against your demon today, friend. Is there something you'd like to confess?"

"I have a moment I cannot seem to remember before Eselda's entrance into the hall. It is this missing moment, and this moment alone, that leaves me doubt. Can you say the same?"

"I cannot. I know my whereabouts for the evening. Do you challenge me?" Something in Tin's eyes almost looks as though they'd welcome that challenge.

"I will solve this puzzle, Tin, and I will bring the killer to justice."

"Even if it turns out to be you?" Tin asks.

"Even then."

"So be it." Tin rises, shakes his head at the other man, and leaves the room.

Chapter

52

OUTSIDE THE BUILDING, I FLOP down on a dry patch of ground underneath a large tree. I wrap my arms tightly around my knees and drop my chin on them. I am thankful the council did not have the presence of mind to call a vote on renumbering. I haven't decided how I will vote on such an issue. I try to take a deep breath and think logically, as Jordyn would. What is the purpose of having a first realm? Why does it matter what number your realm is or who is in charge of the council?

I think back through my old lessons with Tutor, reaching through the expanse of knowledge I've cataloged over the years. The king of the first realm leads all council meetings, maintaining calm and assuring all rules are followed. In the event of a tie, the first realm king can table his or her own vote in order to call for more discussion on the topic.

It's more than that, I am sure. There has to be a reason why the first realm is such a coveted position. I have a few more days to figure it out, the next council meeting is not planned for another half of the lunar calendar, about a fortnight.

"Eselda..."

The voice belongs to King Jordyn. I turn to find him walking toward me, a cautious smile on his face. He looks shaken up and frustrated, an expression that is foreign on his face. "How are you holding up with all this?" he asks, drawing up to stand beside me.

"I'm doing alright, thank you."

"Can I sit?" he asks, gesturing to the ground beneath his feet.

I nod and scoot my bottom sideways to allow for space between us. "What do you think of this investigation so far? What do you think happened?" he asks.

Strange choice of topic, considering his obvious discomfort when it was brought up at the meeting. "I do not pretend to know the answer to that. I know you couldn't have done this, it is not in your character," I answer. I watch his face. Something is different in him. He seems somehow more like himself than he was during the council meeting. I turn my body more in his direction and lay my legs down between us. "What do you think happened?" I ask.

"Well, obviously I believe the idea that this could be someone after the throne of Enchenda is sound. It was my idea, after all."

"Are you completely opposed to any other ideas?"

"Such as?"

"I'm not sure. Thinking up ideas is something you are more suited to than I, Jordyn."

He adopts the expression he often has when he is deep in thought, unfocused but concentrating. "What if someone has a plan to remove a realm from Fraun all together?"

"What do you mean?" I ask.

"Think about it. If your Father dies and there is no heir, we would have to absorb Enchenda into the other realms. Perhaps redraw the lines of our boundaries. This would leave us with four realms, changing things for our council."

"Why would my Father dying cause this to happen? With or without Carsen I will be there to take on the throne."

"Unless the plan was to take you out as well," he says.

"You think someone may be after me?" My voice betrays the fear I'm feeling.

"In fact, now that I'm thinking this through if Larecio dies soon

Marchenda would then be absorbed as well. This would leave our council with only three realms."

"But Jordyn, you forget, our council is in the process of updating lineage charts as we speak. I have already hired someone to work on Enchenda's." I rush to get the words out, eager to fall into a safety zone where I no longer feel like my life is threatened.

"Mine is in the process as well. I know this, you know this, and the council knows this. For that reason, we may be looking for someone who is not of royal blood. Someone who doesn't know the council is actively searching for members in the realms who have the blood in their veins who could rule in the event of the death of an entire line."

"That is a scary thought indeed. Do we have any way of knowing which commoners were in attendance at the event?" I know the answer even as I ask the question. I cannot even tell you who from Enchenda was in attendance. This would be an impossible list to compile.

"I wouldn't even begin to know who attended." Jordyn echoes the very thoughts from my head. "Besides, think on what we discussed in council, we are likely looking for someone who has knowledge of the Castle Fraun," he adds

"But as King Tin pointed out this isn't so much of an issue if the person had adequate time to make their escape."

"No. That logic doesn't track. If the person were new to the Castle and having to fumble their way about for directions someone would have been likely to see them. I had my entire staff on the premises that evening." He pauses, again thinking. "What if the offender is someone I employ?"

I am grateful for his brain coming up with a possibility that doesn't include a seated king. "Could you supply a list of your employees?"

"Do you know the names of all who work in your home?" he asks, not unkindly.

"I know most, but admittedly not all."

"I do not know all either." He is quiet for a moment before yawning and stretching his long legs out in front of him. Suddenly he appears relaxed. "You have given me some new ideas to ponder, Eselda. I feel better just having something to occupy my brain."

"I'm glad I could help." My voice gives away a sadness under the surface.

"Tell me what bothers you then," he prompts.

I think about arguing. I think about denying my sadness. In the end, staring into the deep blue of his eyes, I am grateful for the friend. "Things feel so much harder than even I thought they would be. It's all wrong, Jordyn."

"You mean with Carsen?"

"Yes, among other things." Now that I have begun sharing I can almost feel him taking up some of the weight I have been carrying. The words tumble out. "I agreed to marry Carsen only for convenience. But he was truly a good person and I am sad for the loss of his life. I wish there was something I could do to comfort his father and his realm and I'm absolutely terrified that everyone will think, as Larecio does, that it's my fault he is dead."

"You cannot let that bother you." Jordyn reaches out and pats me lightly on the arm. "Larecio spoke out of pain and anger. He will come around to see the truth soon enough, he is a good and fair man."

"The most infuriating part of this whole thing is that it's all about royal blood. I am getting so tired of hearing how precious that is. Carsen had it and look where it ended him. It's like the people of Fraun are completely obsessed with those of us who have it. Yet I fear there are many out there who have it and know not. I just can't wrap my head around what it is that makes this such a precious commodity worth killing another person over."

"It's not."

"Clearly it is to someone, Jordyn. Doesn't that thought scare you?"

"It does. I have as much of it as you do. What if this makes us vulnerable? Is that what you're thinking?" he asks.

"Yes. If someone gets it in their head to wipe out all with royal blood in Fraun, haven't we made their job easier by documenting it on our walls?"

"I suppose so, but they are in our homes. It's not as though everyone has seen them."

"It can't be that hard to see them. I have seen two."

"I've seen four." Jordyn drops this fact lightly, but it is not received that way.

My jaw drops. "You've seen that many?"

"Yes, at one time or another." Seeing my expression, he laughs. The sound is so light and airy compared with the darkness of our lives lately that it offers refreshment which I gladly take in with a smile. "It's not as big of a deal as all that, you'd have to take very good notes to remember them all. Seeing them once is not enough," Jordyn explains.

"I suppose. I guess I'm being irrational. There are so many secrets coming out lately and I'm scared of what will be left of my life when they are all in the open. It's starting to seem as though nothing is what I thought."

"Like?"

The prompt is permission. Jordyn is giving me permission to share my secrets with a seated king without the presence of the others from the council. "My tutor, who has always been someone I consider a friend, is hiding something. He walks with a limp, he won't answer questions, he doesn't want to speak with me, and he has new bruises when I see him."

"This worries you?"

"Yes. It's more what we were discussing the first time he refused to answer questions that have me worried. Remember the royal blood I told you about, the one that wasn't charted?" I watch for signs that he will stop me here. The first time I tried to bring this up, he made his feelings very clear.

"I remember." He smiles.

"I mentioned her to my tutor, asked him about her. He got very angry and stormed out of my home. He hasn't been the same since."

"That is curious."

"He admitted he knew her, she took him in when he was first in Enchenda."

"He's not from Enchenda?" Jordyn asks, his curiosity piqued.

"Apparently he was raised in Farcheda and even spent some time in your realm before coming to Enchenda."

Jordyn stops me, reaching out a hand and laying it on my leg. "What is his name? How old is he?"

"He would be a few annuals older than I, his name is Tutor."

"I will look into his background a little, see if there are secrets buried there. Would you like that?" Jordyn asks.

"I would. Thank you."

"How fares your father?" Jordyn asks with his typical abrupt jump in topic.

"Not well at all, actually. Our last conversation, yesterday, was too much for him and his voice left him. I am worried about him, Jordyn." Unexpectedly, I feel ambushed by my feelings. The tears rush from my eyes unchecked. I wipe them, but it only makes them fall harder.

Jordyn recovers quickly from his shock and acts on instinct, pulling me into a hug and rubbing a small circle on my back.

I take comfort in the arms of my friend, my stomach fluttering at his touch. Over his shoulder, I watch as King Tin leaves the council building. I see him glance in our direction but I do not have the desire to move away. Not even when he pauses in his walk to look a second time. Not even when it looks, from here, like he is suddenly angry.

Chapter

53

THE OLD STUDY ROOM IS dark, lit only by the single candle I have brought into the room with me. I have spread out old parchment rolls on the floor around me. I carefully unroll one, trace my finger down the writing as I scan for important details, roll it back up and toss it into a new pile.

I have been sitting here on the floor long enough for my legs to cramp up three times. Each of those times I have taken a short break while the blood rushes back to them, causing me pain I don't think I will recover from. Each of those times the pain finally subsides and I resume the search.

The pile of already searched documents that do not talk about why it would be important to be the first realm is growing rapidly. The pile of documents left to search, in contrast, is dwindling. With each new parchment roll, I become more frustrated. My hair is collected in a messy knot atop my head and sweat mixes with grime on my body. I am aware what a mess I am becoming, but I care not. This information somehow feels like it will help me make my decision in a fourth of a lunar cycle and yet it continues to elude me.

Frustrated, I throw the scroll, another that told me nothing new, across the room. Glancing down at my pile I see there are only ten left. I sigh and reach for another.

Nothing.

Another.

Nothing.

"This is hopeless," I yell into the empty room as I lob the newest useless scroll into the black. I flop back to rest on my hands, staring up at the ceiling. The information must be locked in this brain of mine somewhere. It has something to do with war, that much I remember. Something about the king of the first realm's role during the war. Something that makes him different, somehow, from the other seated kings.

My shoulders begin to ache painfully from the stress. I reach up and rub one. Perhaps I could write to Jordyn, he would know. I stand up, intending to head to my room to grab some parchment with which to write him. Just outside the room I nearly crash into the medicine woman. The woman's frantic expression requires no more information. I turn on my heel and run directly to my father.

When the door opens I fear I am too late. My father, pale and small, lies buried in the pillows of the large bed as still as death. "Father..." I sob, suddenly finding I have no more words for the grief sitting on my chest. I rush to his bedside, taking his hand in my own and kissing him on the forehead.

As my lips brush his skin I feel it, the faintest of pulses in his wrist. "Father?"

I hold his hand as the life leaves him. I sit close enough to hear the ragged last breath pass his lips. When it does, the sobs leave me and I cry long into the night, holding the hand of the man who was once my king.

Chapter

54

*E*NCHENDA IS SAD TO ANNOUNCE *the death of their king, Gregario. However, in his stead, we welcome the Queen Eselda. Eselda, the only daughter of Gregario and Rubina, rest her soul, is a staple in our community. She is humble and will lead Enchenda to greatness, without a doubt.*

The announcement arrived this morning by messenger. The king steeples his fingers over the paper, smiling to himself. *The queen will have people in an uproar. She is now one small accident away from wiping all royal blood from Enchenda. Yes, the business of finding the queen a suitable king will be in high demand now, that is certain.*

She must be in a tizzy. Surely she has noticed death seems to be tracking her everywhere she goes.

It's almost as if it stalks her.

Long live the queen, if she can.

Chapter

55

"**A** SECOND EMERGENCY COUNCIL MEETING IN one lunar cycle? This is getting ridiculous." King Mick's voice booms throughout the council chambers.

The day after the death of my father has passed. Yesterday, his day of grieving was observed only in Enchenda and Renchenda. If I were feeling normal I would probably appreciate the show of support from Jordyn. Instead, I barely acknowledged it. Now we sit around the table once again for the emergency meeting required after a day of grievance. This time, it is I who am barely present. I am focused on the table in front of me and have yet to respond to anything said.

"You know as well as the rest of us do that this meeting is required, Mick," Tin states. "Eselda is now a queen and will be welcomed by this council."

"True. Can we discuss other business during this meeting once that's settled?"

"What did you have in mind, old man?" Tin goads.

"What is going on with the patrol I have sent you? I want to know if they are being trained and what they are training on."

"The training progresses swiftly, actually. They are quite a strong bunch. My boys have trained them in combat and on the various animals we encounter. They should be ready to progress to Enchenda for phase two of their training any day now. I fear this is not a good time for Eselda to be taking them on, however. Should we wait a few more days?"

"The hell we will," Mick bellows, rising from his chair. "I'm not giving you any longer than you should have with them. They are not to be your personal army." Mick turns his attention to Larecio. "Didn't I warn you he'd try and pull something like this?" His eyes are back to Tin before the king of the fourth realm can even nod. "I'll take my turn with them, we'll bring her back in later after they've been to all realms."

"She can handle it," Jordyn interrupts. "In fact, I'm sure it will give her something to focus on. It could be good for her."

"Kindly stop talking about me as though I'm not in the room," I say, quietly but forcefully.

"What say you, Majesty?" Tin prompts, his voice softer and kinder.

"Send them my way in two days' time," I order.

Mick sits heavily in his chair, defeated.

"Then it's decided, we proceed as planned. What else have we to discuss?" Tin asks.

"I have another topic," Mick states. "What says the council to a renumbering?"

This time it is Tin who vacates his chair. "What reason have you to take this position from me?" His voice drips with hatred.

Suddenly I cannot stand another meeting like this. Another time when the people who are supposed to be leading Fraun sit around a table and fight. I push myself up, slowly, so all eyes have time to find me. "You boys accomplish little beyond arguing. Send word to me when you are ready to think about Fraun instead of yourselves." I turn and walk out of the chamber.

In the antechamber, my steps falter. What came over me just now? They are infuriating with their ceaseless arguing, but surely I can stomach it for Fraun. My father sat in that very chair and did his best each lunar cycle. Was the council different then? Was there ever a time when they could agree? It certainly is nothing like I once pictured it would be, sitting in that room with them.

"Eselda..."

I suppose I should be grateful that Jordyn has followed me out of the room.

"Are you alright?" he asks.

"Shouldn't you be in there arguing?"

I hear his steps cross the antechamber, I feel his hand lightly on my arm. Despite my anger and frustration, I feel the heat work its way through my body at his touch. "I'm sorry for your loss, Eselda. What can I do?"

"It's not just the loss of my father. It's the loss of the ideals I thought this council stood for. Do they ever do anything other than argue?"

"It's been tough lately, that is true. They mean well."

"Do they? I'm not sure anymore. Just once, I want someone to be honest with their intentions. Not hide behind stories or one-sided arguments," I say.

"Honest?" He steps closer, closing the gap between us and placing his hands on my hips. "Here's honest."

He is whispering, the secret offered to me alone. I am suspended on a cliff, hanging onto his words for safety, holding my breath.

"I never meant this to happen, but I have fallen for you despite my better judgment on the subject. It is not best for Fraun, it is not best for you, but I cannot help myself. It is not even logical, but I cannot turn it off."

The kiss warms me to my core. I feel it attacking the sadness that has filled my soul. I wrap my arms around his neck to keep him there. In recent lunar cycles, I have had my fair share of kisses, but none compare to this. Jordyn's honest revelation, the knowledge that my feelings are reciprocated, the permission and danger to share this intimate moment with the council just beyond a door, it all adds to the heat of the moment.

When the kiss breaks I immediately long for it again. "Court me," I whisper.

"Eselda..."

I open my eyes when I feel Jordyn pulling back.

"...I cannot do that," he finishes.

Sudden cold fills my lungs. "What?"

"I just told you, it is not best for Fraun or for you." His voice wears the thick unspoken apology.

The anger rushes me without warning, hot and intense. "They why did you tell me this?" I lay my hand on his chest and push him away, harder than I meant to. He stumbles a little.

"You asked for honest," he answers.

"You are worse than the rest," I scold. "You're so..." I grapple to find the word, "...old fashioned." On my way out into the cold, I let out a wild scream.

The scream is a living embodiment of my anger. Anger at a system I no longer understand. This is it, the end of the fairy tale I thought my life would be. There will be no shining love of my life sweeping in to rescue me from responsibility and pain. There will be no following my king.

It is me. Alone.

Chapter

56

I KNOW THERE IS A SERVANT hiding in the shadows thrown by the lanterns in the dining room. I cannot even blame him. I know what I have been like lately, I've been impossible. I'm the dangerous ant charging full speed ahead at the children who are just trying to play. I see the problem, but I cannot find the strength to remedy it. This is what I have become. Deal with it.

The man rushes forward and drops into a low bow. "Your Majesty, your messengers have arrived with the daily updates," he says, handing me a stack of parchment.

"Thank you." I take the top parchment and begin to read as the man scurries out of sight again.

> *Death totals since my last update-seven (this number includes the two you are aware of)*
> *Birth totals since my last count-twelve*

Five more bodies to clothe, mouths to feed, people to train. My brain calculates this automatically. I flip to the next parchment.

Eselda,

I have given the royal painter a list of a few names I've found already. He will be coming by in the next few suns to paint them on the wall. Thank you for tasking me with this, it is good for me. I hope you are well.

Tutor

I glance to the lineage chart behind me and cannot find a change. The painter has not been here yet. I glance back to the parchment. Tutor doesn't mention my father at all. Perhaps he is unaware. I flip the parchment over, grab my quill, and jot a quick response.

Tutor,

I'm glad you find the job to your liking. I need to speak with you about changes in Enchenda as soon as possible, please. My father is no longer with us.

Eselda

Quick and simple. Perhaps he will not argue with that. I place the scroll in a new pile, to be sent out, and focus my eyes on the next parchment.

Dearest Eselda,

I remember what it was like when I was first ruling my realm, so many things to do and not always a clear idea of how to do them. I wish, at the time, someone had reached out and offered me help. Come to Sarcheda. You can ask me anything you'd like. I will help you with your new job. I'm also a great listener, we can talk about whatever you'd like.

Faithfully and Forever Yours,
Tin

I recall that during his visit to Enchenda he mentioned the same thing. A smile that has been all too rare lately graces my face. People misjudge Tin. I let people cloud my judgment of Tin. I flip the parchment over.

Tin,

> *I will come to Sarcheda, thank you for the invitation. In fact, I think I shall come tomorrow. I could use the company of a friendly face.*

Eselda

I drop this with the other, in a pile to be sent out and look to the next and last parchment.

Eselda,

> *We should talk, don't shut me out.*

Jordyn

"You said plenty," I roar. I throw the parchment to the flames and watch as they consume the material completely. "There's nothing else to say."

Chapter

57

"WELCOME BACK, YOUR MAJESTY," KING Tin calls as I disembark from the roach I have ridden. I offer him my hand to shake. Instead of merely shaking it, Tin uses it to pull me closer and wrap me in a hug. "How are you doing?" he asks into my ear.

"I am well, thank you." My stomach flutters again and I feel a blush begin on my cheeks. What is it about this man that always makes me feel like a girl again?

"You look beautiful." He smiles. "Now let's get you in out of the cold before you freeze."

Tin, dressed in black and red as he usually is, looks incredibly handsome. I cannot stop my eyes from wandering to his backside, which is snug in the pants. I look away as he holds the door to his home open for me. I tremble with nerves when he lays his hand on my lower back to guide me through the frame.

"Let's head to my dining room, it's quiet and we can relax awhile. We have some time to chat before dinner will be served."

"That sounds lovely."

In the dining room, we take two chairs by the fire, away from the table. We are angled so that our knees are pointed toward each other.

I sit up straight, trying to hold my body to the royal custom. Tin, however, slouches down comfortably in the chair and stretches his legs out in front of him. He crosses them at his ankles, throws his arms behind his head, and smiles at me. "How is being queen treating you?"

"It's fine, thank you."

Tin shakes his head and chuckles. "Why are you being so formal? There's no one around but me." His hands spread out before reverting back to hold up his head. "You can be honest here, no one will judge."

I take in the king's relaxed posture and laugh a little, letting my shoulders slump. "Oh thank goodness," I sigh.

This earns a hearty laugh from Tin.

"I didn't know if you expected me to carry myself like a...like a..."

"Like a queen?" he offers.

"Well, yes." I laugh.

"Here's something I've learned, Eselda. You are a queen now. That means you can stop trying so hard. However, you carry yourself is exactly how a queen would carry herself. Basically, you can do no wrong now because who could point out that you were mistaken?"

"I guess I never really thought of it that way before," I admit.

"Well then, you're welcome. I'm glad I could help." He winks at me and I feel myself blush again. To cover it, I glance down at my feet. If this is about comfort, I will get comfortable. I pull my feet up into the chair. "Now see, isn't that more comfortable?" Tin asks.

"It is."

"So, what can I help you with tonight? What issues have come up in Enchenda?"

"Well nothing really, I've not even been Queen for a fortnight." I chuckle. Now that I'm here and relaxing, it's hard to remember what had me so stressed. "Oh, one question I did have. Who handles your school visit here?"

"I do. Why do you ask?"

"The school teacher sent me a letter inquiring about who would handle that now that my father has passed."

"Yes, I suppose she did. They plan ahead at the school here as well." Tin smiles. "Don't let it bother you. Jordyn and I both handle our own visits. I personally enjoy it very much as ours often includes a feat of strength display." He flexes his bicep muscle and winks at me again.

I try to smile, but the mention of the king of wisdom's name makes it suddenly hard to focus. It's like black water is leaking into my eyes, clouding my vision. My head hurts again, a sharp pain throbs at the back of my skull.

"Are you that worried about the visit?" Tin asks. He is squinting at me as though trying to figure me out.

"What? No, I've handled it for many annuals, I'm sure I can take more." I fear I don't truly understand the root of his question.

"You looked suddenly distracted or upset. I had thought it was the school visit. Is something else wrong?" He sits up a little straighter in his chair, giving the impression I have his full attention.

"No. Nothing I can't handle."

"Eselda, please. Let's be honest with each other," he implores.

This time I can actually feel the anger inside me. It's like water that has been set on a low heat has finally spawned bubbles. I open my mouth and release the pressure. "Honesty can be overrated."

Beside me, Tin looks shocked. "Now where in Fraun did that come from?" he asks in a light tone.

I fix him with a confused look. "Where did what come from?" I snap. Is he making fun of me?

This time, the smile fades completely from Tin's face. Suddenly serious, he leans in closer to me, pulling his chair with him. "How old are you?"

The question catches me off guard. "Over fifteen annuals, why?"

"How long until you are twenty?" he asks.

Something about his voice is all wrong, worried or...oh no. The realization of where he is headed with this line of questioning starts to trickle in. "Oh, my...I don't know. I hadn't been counting. Do you think I'm there?" My breath is coming faster now.

Tin continues to stare at my face, cataloging my features. "Your eyes are lightening up again, back to their normal green. You are not there yet, but you approach it." He sits back in his chair again, offering me a small smile.

"What? How do you know?" I lean forward in my chair, toward the answers.

"Before my twentieth annual I had small bouts of anger often. I had trouble controlling them or even realizing what they were."

"But they weren't the real age marker?"

"No. I may have thought they were then, I don't recall. But nothing compares to how it feels when you lose yourself to the malicious age." He fixes me with a hard expression. "Nothing."

Jordyn said something similar, I remember. The thought does nothing to calm the panic threatening to drown me. "If this isn't the age marker, then can I learn to control it?" Give me answers.

"I'm not sure. Do you want to talk about what triggered it just now?" he offers.

"Jordyn." The name slips easily from my lips but I cannot look at Tin when I speak it. Instead, my eyes track to the flames dancing in the fireplace. I wish I could feed my troubles to those flames and watch them burn.

"Should we talk about it?" he asks, a sad edge to his voice.

"I'm not sure I want to."

"I'm not sure I want to hear it. But perhaps it would do you good to share some of the burdens with a friend."

The sadness in his voice draws my eyes back to him. He is staring at me, the firelight catching in his hair and making him incredibly handsome. But his face holds so much melancholy, it shocks me. "What brings you such great sadness, Tin?" I ask, always eager to put the focus on someone else.

"I saw you with Jordyn the other day, after the council," he admits. "I understand so many things now. How long have you two been secretly courting?" His eyes darken dangerously and I notice a twitch in his jaw. Signs of his age marker, perhaps?

Despite my best attempt, I cannot stop the laugh from escaping. Tin looks shocked, as though slapped by the laughter. "I'm sorry..." I say between chuckles. "I don't mean to laugh at you." I regain my composure with deep breaths. "I'm sorry. I laugh because that's what you thought this was." It comes out as a question. I rush on. "You thought I traveled here in anger to tell you that I am hiding a secret courting with the king of Renchenda?"

"Well," he thinks about it, "yes. I thought perhaps you were angry that you had to hide it from the council who surely wouldn't understand. I was afraid, perhaps, that you thought you had to hide it from me as well." He sits forward again, now using only the edge of his chair. "Is that not accurate?" he asks. Something that looks like hope lights across his chiseled features.

"Not at all, actually. I will not pretend I don't have feelings for Jordyn. But clearly, it is unreturned. He continues to tell me that he cannot court me or be with me because of the rules."

"That's not surprising at all. Jordyn has always been a stickler for the rules," Tin explains. A small version of his smile tugs at the corners of his mouth.

"Yes, well…I suppose I had always imagined someone would fall in love with me and nothing would be able to keep us apart."

"So your anger is because you wish you could be with King Jordyn?" Tin summarizes.

"No, my anger is because I'm not good enough for King Jordyn to fight for." Perhaps because I am on guard for it now, I feel the bubble of anger within. My vision begins to darken at the edges.

"Now that I understand. I can see it angers you to think of it. Perhaps we should talk of something else, take your mind off of it."

"Fine by me."

"So, if I understand you correctly, no one is courting you at this time." His eyes flash in amusement as his smile deepens.

Not this again. I don't think I can handle another person telling me that they have the best of intentions, are falling for me, but can do nothing about it. "No," I answer.

"I no longer need to ask permission from your king, as you are the highest voice in Enchenda. I know you feel as though rules, although they have their place, should not be used to stomp out emotions. So…" he leans forward and grasps my hand in his own, "…can I have your permission to court the beautiful Queen Eselda? To invite her often to dinner, to spend time with her, and to learn all the intricacies of her soul?"

I feel myself calming down as I stare into his eyes. He is pleading me to answer him. His happiness feels contagious. "I see no problem with that." I swallow hard. "Are you sure it is okay with the council you run?"

Tin leans even further off his chair, so he is standing just over me. "I dare them to try and stop me," he answers, winking.

I feel instantly calm.

That is the exact right answer.

Chapter

58

AGAIN, THERE IS GOOD FOOD and entirely too much of it. A young servant girl enters now, carrying a tray of something small and dipped in what looks like chocolate. "What is this, Tin?" I ask. "I hope you don't think I could possibly have room in my stomach for another course."

"Now my dear, are you truly going to try and convince me that you cannot make room in there for some chocolate? After how you felt about it the last time?" Tin asks.

The servant drops the plate and I take a sniff, the sweet smell of chocolate wafting into my nose. "Oh, it smells divine. What is it?" I look to the servant, but it is King Tin who answers.

"Sliced bananas covered in a chocolate that has been melted."

"You can melt it?" I ask as the servant leaves the room.

Tin laughs. "Quite easily, or so I'm told."

I lift a slice of banana in my hands and take a small nibble. A soft moan escapes my lips. "This is remarkable. I think I like it even better than the cookie from last time."

Tin chuckles. "I'll take your word for it, I don't enjoy chocolate nearly as much as you do." He gestures to his own plate and I notice for the first time that his banana slices are not covered in the melted goo.

"You don't eat it?"

"I've tried it, but I prefer the taste of my fruit plain."

"Well, I can get plain fruit anywhere." I take another large bite of my snack. "I plan to fully enjoy chocolate whenever it's offered."

Tin laughs. "I fear the way to your heart may be paved with the sweet treat."

I take another bite and shrug. "Probably." This time I join him in his laughter.

When we have both finished dessert, Tin rises and offers his hand to me. "Now, what shall we do for the remainder of our evening? Is there anything you would like to discuss?"

I allow myself to be pulled to my feet and wrap my hand delicately around Tin's elbow. "Actually, there is something I'm curious about. I have developed quite a healthy appreciation for lineage lately. Could I possibly see your family tree?"

"Sure thing. Right this way." Tin leads me down a dark and long hallway, the occasional torch lighting our path. The hall is wide enough to allow me to remain beside him. My boots clicking loudly on the stone floor, echoing our every step back to me.

At the end of the long hallway, Tin turns to the right, and we enter into a bedroom. Immediately in front of us, there is a large bed made up with a dark red blanket. The bed is easily the largest I have ever seen in my life. Likely four people could fit comfortably on it. In addition to the blanket, which looks thick and warm, there is quite an impressive mound of pillows at the top of the surface. Beside the bed on either side is a wooden table, each holding a candle. For some reason, both candles are lit although the room was empty when we entered.

"Is this your room?" I ask. I hear the admiration I feel for his lavish settings in my tone of voice.

"It is. The lineage chart is painted on this wall here." He gestures to the wall the door is on. The gold script matches that which I have seen in Renchenda and in my own realm. I drop the arm of the king and stand to look up at the wall, my eyes shining with excitement.

I begin at the top, where I note Renchenda is written as well. That matches with what I learned earlier, the ancient kings were brothers born of the same parents. My eyes trail down the tree. The names are circled and starred where necessary. This tree is considerably less complicated than mine. "Not many people in your lineage have multiple children."

"True. Is that not also true in Enchenda?"

"I suppose there are a few families that have only one, but you often see multiple children. Your line is different, I see no lines with more than one child." I trace my eyes back up the line again, having reached Tin's name, and find the observation holds up. Not one mother birthed more than one child.

My eyes stop at another spot. "What is this?" I ask, pointing to a place where three names appear in a straight line. *Twane-Tron-Sharpei.* Tron's name is circled and starred.

"Tron was the only son of Sarcheda and Alenda," Tin explains, pointing to the line showing this. "He took two wives."

I turn my head away from the wall and trap Tin with a quizzical expression. "What? I thought that ended with Second."

Tin shrugs. "My ancestors occasionally continued the practice." He gestures to another spot, further down the line, where it happened again. "They believed multiple wives helped to ensure them a male descendant to take the throne," he explains.

"Why male?"

Tin sighs. "Remember I'm explaining something other people in my lineage have believed, it doesn't mean I believe it."

I nod that I agree.

"Men are traditionally stronger than women. In a society that values strength, it's easy to see why some would want only male rulers." He shrugs. "What can I tell you? My ancestors were fools."

I turn back to the wall and feel Tin step closer to me. My eyes continue searching until I find two black circles on the far right of the wall. Here we go. "What is this covering?"

"A child born out of wedlock. The father is unknown but that covers the mother and child."

I turn to him. "So you could have royal blood outside of those marked on this wall as well?"

"It's possible, I suppose. As promised I have hired someone to look in on that. But it won't be from that source. Both mother and child died during childbirth."

"Then why go through the trouble of blacking out their names?"

"They would've been shunned upon learning she was with child before they passed."

"So if you had royal blood not tracked here, where would it come from?" I ask, steering the conversation away from the topic of death.

Tin reaches over my shoulder, touching a spot with his left hand. I turn my body to face the wall again. His finger points to the left of the wall, to a circled name. "Roberta," I read.

"This line continued to birth females. They were not needed to rule." He points to the right side of the wall, nearest his own name. "My direct lineage continued to have male blood and people to rule. After a few generations, no one bothered to check in with them anymore. I'm out of touch with this line, I'm not sure if there are more children here or not. It is where the updater I now employ was to begin his search."

"How long ago did they stop checking on that line?"

"Roberta and my father, Todd, were about the same age. That's all I know."

I turn again. As he talked Tin has stepped closer so that when I turn we are nearly face to face. "What happened to your parents?" I ask, quietly.

A dark cloud settles over the king's expression. His brown eyes literally get a shade darker. I wince. "I'm sorry, I shouldn't have asked."

"No, it's alright. It's just hard to speak of." Tin places his hands on my hips. "My parents fell into a ravine along the edge of Fraun."

"Was it hard to lose them both?" I ask. I notice my voice quavers in response to how close he stands and the hands on my hips.

"Incredibly." He leans in close to me and whispers. "Do you know what else is difficult?"

"What's that?"

"Trying to focus on a conversation with you standing this close to me in my bedroom." He kisses me almost before the sentence is finished. The kiss is hungry, deep, and full of longing. I melt like chocolate under his fingers. He greedily runs his fingers up and down my back as we kiss, keeping me pulled in close. I wrap my arms around his neck in response. I feel myself giving into the sensations, letting go of all my stress and pain.

Tin pulls away from me, physically pushing me back. "You should go."

"What? Why? Did I do something wrong?" I search Tin's eyes for answers.

His eyes are a little darker than normal, but he looks otherwise exactly the same. Perhaps a little flush from the heat of the moment.

"You did nothing wrong." He reaches out and caresses my face. "If you stay I fear we may do something we'll regret. Go home, get some sleep. I will come to Enchenda in a few days' time and we will have dinner together. I promise." The king keeps his eyes locked on my face, but steps back to put more distance between us.

Seeing no other options, I leave the room and the house.

What just happened?

Chapter

THE PATH TO THE UNUSED building is long. I gladly walk it, enjoying the break from my routine. The air on this mid-morning is crisp but much warmer than days past. I welcome the freshness into my lungs and allow it to clear my head as I walk. Two sunrises have passed since my dinner, and by extension my courtship, with Tin. The thought brings a warm smile to my face and the memories of our passionate kiss brings a blush to my cheeks.

This morning I travel to visit with the patrol, who arrived in Enchenda yesterday. When they first returned I was in the midst of showing a new servant around the home and I didn't have much time to spend with them. Instead, I directed them to the building here, which will serve as their accommodations, with instructions to settle in.

Ten men serve on the patrol and Enchenda has no place fit to house all of them together, including my own home. Instead, I was forced to offer them an old barn. I ordered some materials which could be used to fashion beds but even those were not the best quality. There is no kitchen in the building either. How do I expect them to enjoy warm meals? I will have to offer full access to my personal garden today.

As I approach I observe a young man tending to a fire in front of the building, smoke rising to the heavens. They've dug a fire pit, how creative. The man stands and waves. As I draw closer I notice the man is Danyel, the patrolman representing Enchenda.

He has changed in the lunar cycles since I last saw him. Already his shirt strains from the new muscles coming in underneath it. Tin has done well with these men. "Good morning, Danyel," I greet.

"Majesty, good morning."

"How did you fare last night? Were you terribly cold?"

"Not at all, we built a fire right in the middle of the room. It kept us warm all night. It was wise of you to offer us such meager accommodations, the boys are quickly learning humility already," Danyel says.

This boy has such strong faith in me. "It was my hope that we could provide you with something better, but you are a large group."

He laughs. "That we are. This is good, Majesty. It is a reminder to us all that the job we have undertaken is for others, not for ourselves."

"I'm proud of your humble nature, Danyel. You do Enchenda proud."

The man beams under the praise. "Thank you, Majesty. What plans have you for us today?" he asks.

"First, I believe it would be wise if you would show them around Enchenda's boundaries. They need to know where Fraun ends. Would you feel comfortable undertaking this?"

"Absolutely, Majesty."

"Good. While you are here, it goes without saying that you may come to me with anything. You all have full access to my garden, which is behind my home. Oh, and you'll want to pay careful attention to this area here," I gesture to the area behind their lodging, near the edge of Fraun, "because we had a stray ant near this area not long ago."

"We will keep that in mind, Majesty. Thank you."

"I will see you all tomorrow morning, sunrise. I'd like you to meet in front of my home for training."

"We will all be there. I'm sure they look forward to meeting you." Danyel bows low again. "Have a nice day, Majesty."

"I will, thank you. Goodbye, Danyel." I turn and head back toward my own home, a smile on my face. That went well.

I turn the corner to my garden and find Sawchett sprawled out on her stomach, a parchment in front of her eyes. Her bare feet are bent up behind her, swinging as though they hear music guiding them. "Good morning, child. What are you reading?"

"My tutor wanted me to read about age markers a little."

I freeze. "Age markers?" I try to keep my voice even. Does the girl realize her bloodline? "Which ones do you speak of?"

"My next one coming up, the tenth."

I let out a breath. "Yes, you will be full height in a few annuals. I've noticed in just the short time since you've lived here you have grown taller. I suppose your body is readying you."

"You only think that because you've stopped growing." Sawchett smiles.

"This is true."

"This says I will also have all my..." the girl consults the parchment "...reproductive parts." She turns her head and looks up at me. "What does that mean?"

I sit on the ground beside the girl and slip off my own shoes, wiggling my bare feet in the dirt. "It means, if you met someone and fell in love, you'd have all the parts needed to bring a baby into this world."

Sawchett gasps. "But I'll still be so young."

"Just because your body will be equipped for it does not mean you will have to rush to do it. Look at me, I'm past ten annuals and I have no children."

"That's true." Sawchett resumes reading her parchment. I recline back to rest, my palms flat on the ground behind me supporting my weight. "Then I'll get nice full shiny hair, like yours."

"Well, no doubt yours will continue to be the yellow it is now, not brown like my own."

"I wish mine were red."

"With luck, you will grow to love yours for the beauty it offers." I reach out and brush Sawchett's long hair with my fingers. "I wonder if your hair will cease to grow but remain straight like it is."

"I hope it doesn't. I hope I get curls like yours," Sawchett states simply, with a little pout.

"I covet your straight locks, actually. If I could find a way to keep mine equally as straight I'm sure I would do it."

"Are there other age markers, Eselda?" Sawchett asks, having reached the end of her parchment roll.

"Only for those of royal blood," I answer. Am I ready for this conversation?

"What are they?"

"Sawchett, let's go inside. I'd like to show you something." It's not right to keep a secret from the girl. I cannot allow Sawchett to be a stranger to the age markers when they arrive. I will not allow her to be blindsided by them like I was. I lead the smaller child into the dining room.

Instead of finding it empty, as planned, we find a small man standing on a ladder at the lineage chart. He is writing on the wall with a thin brush. His ladder, I note, brings him near the name of my grandfather. No time to waste. "Here child, sit," I direct the girl to the chairs nearest the fire.

"This wall here shows the history of my family. It shows where we come from and who came before us." Sawchett turns her head to look at the wall I gesture to. I continue, "This man here is responsible for tracking my family lineage, and our royal blood. Everyone on that wall experiences age markers beyond their fifteenth annual."

"What are they?" Sawchett asks, returning her eyes to my face.

"Your tutor can fill you in on that, I have something more important to share with you. What do you know of your mother's heritage?"

Sawchett wrinkles her nose as she thinks. "Nothing."

"Your mother's father, your grandfather, was actually a king."

"My mother was a princess like you used to be?" Sawchett asks, her eyes lighting up with the secret.

"In blood alone. Charlotte was never allowed to be called princess or to live in this house."

"Wow." The word comes out with adoration. "Wait, what does that make me?"

"That means that you also have royal blood flowing in your veins, yes."

"I'm a princess?" The sentence is whispered, almost as if giving it volume would make it suddenly untrue.

"I suppose you are. Would you like to be a princess?" I ask. Why can't I rule that to be so? I see no reason to deny this further.

Sawchett's eyes grow wide. "I want to be a princess more than anything."

"Then that is what you shall be. I will inform your tutor myself so your training can be adjusted accordingly. Go and fetch him for me."

Sawchett pops out of her chair. "I will. Thank you, Eselda." She runs from the room.

I allow myself a moment to wallow in the girl's joy before turning my attention to the man at the wall. "How many names do you add today, good sir?"

Never once turning from the wall or breaking in his painting the man answers. "I unearth one and add one."

"Unearth?"

"Yes, I remove the black paint from this name covered here." He taps the wall with the end of his brush.

Fascinated, I cross the room to stand by his side. Charlotte. "You can do that? It doesn't remove the gold paint?"

"I can do it."

I watch him work for a moment. "I'm quite fascinated by lineage."

This earns me a look from the man. His hand freezes as he glances at me as if noticing who I am for the first time. He smiles before turning back to his work. "I am as well," he adds once he is back to his task.

"Can you unearth those two names up there for me as well?" I point to the two toward the top of the wall.

His eyes barely grace them before he nods. "I can and I will."

"Thank you." I turn to go.

"Majesty?" he calls.

"Yes?"

"Is that girl, by any chance, Sawchett?"

I smile, I suspected he was listening to our conversation. "She is. Do you add her name today?"

"I do."

257

"Well, I would kindly ask you to keep that which you learned here today between us until I have the chance to spread it throughout the kingdom myself."

"I wouldn't dream of usurping that power, Majesty."

"Excellent. Thank you." I turn toward the door in time to hear the running feet pad down the hallway. The noise, followed by a slower set of steps, brings a smile to my face. It seems Sawchett has found her tutor and dragged him to meet with me. It's good the child is so eager.

Sure enough, the tall man enters, practically shoved through the doorframe by Sawchett's small hands. "Good day, Majesty. You wished to speak with me?"

"I did, please have a seat." I gesture to the chairs by the fire. Once he is seated I waste no time getting right to business. "I feel I mislead you when we last spoke and I'd like to correct that error of mine."

"Very well, Majesty. What seems to be the problem?"

"It's no problem with you, rest assured." I pat the man reassuringly on the arm. "It is simply that I didn't make clear the nature of the child's education."

"The nature of it, Majesty?"

I take a deep breath, hold my chin high, and muster all the no-nonsense attitude I can. "Sawchett is a princess in the house of Enchenda. She has royal blood in her veins and wishes to be groomed to one day, upon my death, accept the throne. Her education should reflect this." I worry, for a beat, that the man will argue or demand answers.

He does not. "As you wish, Majesty."

"Thank you, sir."

"My pleasure. Am I excused to continue our lesson? We have other age markers with which we must discuss in light of this new information."

"You are, thank you again." The man departs and I relax a little in the chair. A small laugh floats to my ears and I turn to look questioningly at the man painting the wall, the only other presence in the room. "Did you just laugh at me?" I ask.

"My apologies, ma'am. Did you think he would argue with you?" He laughs again. "You are the queen, after all."

"I am, that is true." Perhaps I am still underestimating the power of my title.

The man steps off his ladder and wipes his hands on his pants. "I am finished here. Would you like to look it over?"

I practically leap from my chair and walk to the board. My eyes light first upon the reflection of Charlotte's name. I allow a small payment of emotion for the girl who is recognized at last.

Then my eyes move on. Underneath Charlotte and connected by a golden thread, I see Sawchett's name. Imagine the joy the girl will feel when she sees this.

Lastly, my eyes track to the two other names that have been uncovered. I speak their names aloud to the room, "Suzette and Margarite."

"Nice names," the man says.

"They are nice names. I am glad you uncovered them for me."

"I hope I get to uncover all those that we've had to cover over the years."

At this, I turn to face him. "Do you hold the job of painting for all realms?"

"I do."

"You may be busy lately. The council has ruled all realms must update their trees."

"Yes, I had heard that as well. I suppose I owe you thanks for that?"

"You are happy about it?" I ask.

"I am, as all who appreciate lineage should be."

"Actually the idea belongs to the king of Rencheda."

"I should've guessed. He's an expert at presenting good ideas, after all. I will be sure to thank him when I am there, I have an appointment to add two names to his wall as well."

"Well good luck with that sir. Thank you for your service to Fraun."

I turn my eyes back to the lineage wall and allow happiness to fill me. "They are all recognized at last."

Chapter

HOW DID I NEVER REALIZE how busy father must have been? The sun is just beginning its trek down the sky. I am enjoying a rare moment to myself, hiding out in my room and dressing for dinner. I hear the sound of a bold knock shatter the quiet of the house. Likely that'll be some other news that needs my immediate attention.

I finish tying the simple white belt around the waist of my red dress. I allow myself the luxury of an extra glance in the reflection wall. This dress, which bells out a bit more than my usual style, is not one of my favorites but it is a nice dress. The deep red accents the little tones of red in my hair.

I pull open the bedroom door and nearly trip over Eee, who is standing in the hallway. "Your Majesty, you have a guest."

"Thank you, Eee." The roach is gone before I can even put my bare feet in the hallway. Clearly, she has more important things to do than answering the door and fetching me. With everyone else treating me different it's nice to know roaches never change. I nearly laugh at the attitude. As I draw closer to the entryway, I allow my annoyance at the intrusive visitor to creep into my features.

"You look beautiful in my colors, milady."

Tin's voice catches me off guard and melts my frown away. "I wasn't expecting you."

"You weren't? I promised to join you for dinner tonight." He crosses the space between us and kisses me firmly. "I hope it isn't too much trouble for your staff that I am here."

"I'm sure it's fine. I'm glad you're here."

"Good."

I lead Tin through the doorway into the dining room. Sawchett is already seated at the long table, in her customary chair by the fire. I smile at the girl even as anxiety begins to settle in my heart. How will I explain her? "Sawchett, this is King Tin of Sarcheda." I glance back at Tin. "This is Sawchett." How much more information should I give him?

"I'm a princess," Sawchett calls out.

Well, that answers that.

"Is that so?" Tin asks masking a different question with his tone.

"Yes. They painted my name there and everything." Sawchett points her little finger at the lineage chart on the wall.

Tin's eyes follow the path of the girl's gesture. His jaw twitches. "Well, congratulations."

"We've been hard at work updating our lineage chart," I say with a smile. I lean in closer to Tin. "Her parents are no longer with us and the girl has no one else," I pass the secret quietly, meant for him alone.

"Shall we eat?" I ask, gesturing to the table and a chair Tin should take. I open the side door which connects to the kitchen. "Excuse me."

A young woman appears. "Your Majesty?" The voice reveals confusion. "Can I help you with something?"

"I'm sorry to trouble you but we've had an extra guest to dinner. Could I please get a serving for King Tin?"

"From Sarcheda?" the girl asks, her face lighting up.

I choke back laughter at the cheery response. "Yes."

"Absolutely, Majesty. Right away."

I return to the dining room and take my seat at the head of the table. In this manner the lineage chart lies behind me, the fireplace and Sawchett to my right, and Tin to my left. I smile at them both before focusing my attention on King Tin. "Our dinners are usually very laid back so we aren't typically served. I have someone bringing another bowl, please take this one," I gesture to the bowl before me.

Tin shakes his head. "I wouldn't hear of it, I can wait."

"Do I need to wait too?" Sawchett asks. "I'm starving."

"Sawchett, don't be rude," I say.

At the same moment, Tin offers an entirely different answer, "Don't wait on my account."

I laugh. "You heard the guest, go ahead and eat."

Sawchett keeps her eyes focused on me as she grabs her spoon and takes a slurp of the soup. When she is not chastised for eating, she drops her eyes and eats more quickly.

The lady from the kitchen arrives bearing a bowl of soup and a platter of rolls. "I found some rolls in the kitchen, Majesty, that should accompany the earthworm stew nicely. I hope that is to your liking," she says, dropping the bowl of soup in front of Tin and bowing low.

I open my mouth to answer before noticing it is Tin the woman addresses. This time I have to clear my throat to stop the laughter.

Tin, however, smiles under the careful gaze of the woman. "Thank you, milady. It smells wonderful." His voice is low and somehow seductive. The woman giggles and retreats back to the kitchen.

"I think my kitchen staff fancies you, Tin," I note, chuckling a little.

"I think you're right." He gestures to his meal. "I seem to have received a larger portion than you as well."

Sure enough, the bowl in front of the king is easily twice the size of my bowl. This time we both share a hearty laugh. As our laughter dies, Tin takes a spoonful of the earthworm stew. "This is good," he says, delving in for another bite.

Sawchett grabs a roll from the tray, practically standing on her chair to be able to reach across the table. "What is this?" she asks, holding it up to her nose.

"A roll, it's bread," I answer. "Sometimes other realms send us deliveries of it as a treat."

Sawchett breaks it open, smells it, rips off a chunk, and tosses it in her mouth. "It's plain," she critiques, wrinkling her nose.

"Try using it to sop up the stew remnants in your bowl," Tin suggests.

We watch as Sawchett does just that. "Delicious." She smiles. "What a grand idea." The girl resumes eating with renewed gusto.

"Did our patrol arrive safely?" Tin questions as he also returns to eating.

"They did. I've set them up in an empty building and they have toured Enchenda's boundaries. Tomorrow they are set to meet me at sunrise to begin their formal training."

"Sounds like you have it all handled."

I inflate under his praise. This is so much easier than deciding everything alone and wondering in silence if I've done right by Fraun.

"What does training in humility entail, exactly?" Tin asks.

"I wish I knew. I've been struggling with how to bring these lessons to them. I know what I want to show them but I've never been a natural leader." I sigh. "How do I impart the wisdom of putting others before yourself? Of thinking of the greater good above thine own? Of serving others, not for compensation but because it is needed?"

"Would you like help?" Tin offers.

My face breaks out into a wide smile. "You'd be willing?"

"I'm not afraid to lead," he answers. "Besides those sound like lessons I could benefit from learning myself. I could help at least until you are comfortable."

What a wonderful gesture. Too bad I can't take him up on the offer. "I appreciate the offer, Tin. Perhaps on a day when I haven't asked the patrol to meet me at sunrise. Do you realize what time you'd have to leave Sarcheda to do that?"

Tin locks eyes with me. His hazel eyes fascinate me. The light green at the edges is consumed in the center by a brown that spreads out like flames. He raises his eyebrows in question. "I could make it in time if I do not leave Enchenda tonight."

I swallow hard, suddenly feeling very flush. "Ok," I manage to choke out.

"I'm done. May I be excused?" Sawchett calls out, already rising from her chair.

Glad for the interruption, I smile at the girl. "Yes, of course. See you in the morning." When the girl leaves the room, I sit back. My brain is desperately trying to think of another topic. I keep defaulting back to remembering the heat in my body when we kissed. I feel my face getting flush.

Tin continues to watch me. "Did I make you uncomfortable?"

"A little," I answer sheepishly. Will the truth change his opinion of me? "I've never had a man sleep in my bed." My skin flushes under the admission and my stomach leaps.

Tin reaches for my hand. "I can sleep somewhere else if you'd like. I'm not trying to rush you. I just want to be here to help tomorrow and this seems to be the easiest solution."

Oh, thank Fraun. "You're right, thank you."

Tin drops my hand and resumes eating. I follow his lead. A comfortable silence wraps around the room as we finish our meal.

Finally, Tin pushes his chair back from the table and adopts a more relaxed posture. "Are we going to talk about the little princess?" he asks. His voice takes on a small breath of indignation.

I'm caught off-guard by the onset of the attitude. "Sawchett?"

"Is there another?"

"No, no. Of course not." I push back my chair from the table as well. "My grandfather had a second child in secret with a woman who was not my grandmother," I explain.

"And you judged my family for taking multiple wives?" His eyes darken slightly with the challenge.

I open my mouth to respond, then close it again when I can think of no argument. "You make a good point," I concede. "I hadn't thought of it that way."

"At least my relatives had the decency to marry both women," Tin points out.

"I'd hardly call that decent." Tin opens his mouth to push the point, so I rush to continue. "But I agree that it wasn't decent the way my grandfather handled it either." Tin closes his mouth. "Anyway, one woman married my grandfather and gave birth to my father. The other woman married a common man from the village and birthed Charlotte, who was raised as though she belonged to the man."

"No one knew of her?" the king asks.

"Not so far as I can tell. Charlotte and her husband later had Sawchett. When Charlotte died I took the girl in."

"What is your plan for the child?" he asks, resting his chin in his palm.

I expected him to be angry. Clearly, I have misjudged him again. His interest is better than I hoped. "It is as much her right to rule someday as it was mine," I answer. "She should learn what options she has, learn the age markers that are our curse to bear, and decide for herself." Is he, perchance, questioning my decision? I bristle, ready to defend my choice.

"I agree," Tin says.

The uniformity squashes my anger. "Thank you."

"Do you intend to let her rule?" Tin asks.

"Perhaps, if she is needed and desires such a future."

"Were you given such an option?"

"No." I think on my fear of ruling, how quickly I would've given that up when my father first fell ill if I had been given the chance. Didn't I try to get out of it? I tried to convince myself letting Jordyn absorb Enchenda was best. I think how much work it is to be a good ruler now. Maybe I'm not cut out for all the pressure. "Perhaps the option would've been nice."

"I would've accepted the job even if the option to back down had been given," Tin states matter-of-factly. "It's the ultimate show of strength." He shrugs. "Do the people of Enchenda know about the princess?"

"Not yet. How should I tell them?"

"I'd just gather them all up and announce it. You keep forgetting that you are their queen, no one will argue with you." He offers me a smile. "It's nice, sitting here talking simply about life together. Somehow it makes us a real couple." He winks at me.

"It is nice." But you help more than I help you. "Is there anything going on in Sarcheda that I can offer my help with?"

265

"Can we take a walk? I think I'd like to see something out of doors in Enchenda." Tin expertly changes topics.

Though I notice the obvious derailment, I smile and push through on his chosen subject. He'll open up when he is ready. "We can. Let's go see my garden, it's my favorite place. You'll want a jacket. Did you bring one?"

"I did."

We don our jackets and traipse to the garden. The garden is a picture of beauty tonight. The ground sparkles with dew and plants are standing tall despite the cooler weather. The frost was minimal this season, Fraun snapped back to warmth quicker than in previous annuals. The change in the cycle is exciting, but that may yet mean a very warm contrasting season.

"Tell me why this is your favorite place." Tin's voice takes on an alluring edge.

"It's beautiful." I offer the simple answer first before delving into the more complex. "Life happens right here below your feet annual after annual." I reach out and caresses the leafy greens of a kale plant, which often survives winters here. "Something so perfect, something essential to life, grows from a mound of dirt and some rainwater. It's fascinating."

"You really enjoy this process."

I smile at his ability to make any conversation sound so personal. "I do love it."

"It is charming how you wear your happiness on your face."

"I do?"

"You have a face incapable of lying. It reveals your every thought and truth, even without your permission."

Something about this admission intrigues me. Rarely in life do you find an opportunity to see yourself as others see you. Somehow it seems truer than the reflection I see every day. I lean into him.

"Your green eyes and your smile tell a true story at all times." He reaches out and catches me under the chin, holding it between his thumb and forefinger. "I can read doubt, love, or truth here." He lifts my chin upward a little and my heartbeat quickens in response. He softens his tone again so that a fly would have to land on his very shoulder to hear his voice. "I can even tell you're true feelings by the blush that oft takes up its roots in your cheeks. It reveals your discomfort with the thoughts in your mind."

As if responding to his very words the coloring tiptoes up my cheekbones and settles. "There, see. Now I wonder what it is that traverses that brain and causes you to redden." He bends to brush his lips lightly on the darkening circle of heat.

My defenses lower and a soft purring sound escapes my lips like a sigh. Tin's eyes flash at the sound, a carnal response in him set off by my pleasure. "You have such an effect on me," he growls, closing his eyes.

I feel a kind of power begin in my gut. A power that can only come from igniting passion in another being. I let the power flow down my limbs, relishing it. When it reaches my fingers, I don't hesitate to trace them along the muscles under his shirt, an act I would've previously restrained. When the king's eyes fly open, I recognize deep longing in them. It acts as a stimulant. I will do anything to see that longing again. Hungrily, I kiss him, pressing my body against him and feeling the muscles in his back ripple beneath my fingers.

Electricity crackles between us, warming the air. We paw at each other, hands roaming over clothing and grabbing for some piece of the other to hold onto.

Again, as it was in his home, Tin pulls away from me. I reach for him, confused, and try to pull him back to me. I feel the cold air rush into the void he has left. "Stop," he barks. The command, altogether angry and harsh, halts all my movements.

He softens his tone, but the hard edge remains. "Please, you are going to make me go somewhere you don't want me to go." He looks me in the eye. Finding something that frustrates him, he throws his hands up. "Sometimes your innocence is so taxing." He sighs. "Eselda, we are not wed. There are things that people do when they are wed that you would stop me from doing tonight. If we don't stop now, you will have no power to stop me later."

The truth of the statement carries much weight, having just felt his muscles underneath his clothing. The king of strength would be able to get so much from me if he desired it. Do I want that? My blush deepens. "You want that?" The thought races from my lips. As quickly as it escapes, I wish I could breathe it back in. I didn't mean to speak it aloud.

"I want you. In any form which I can have you." Tin steps closer to me, but not as close as he was before. "I want all of you," he breathes.

The admission leaves us both speechless.

It is I who recovers first, "I do not want to be apart from you. Will you still sleep in Enchenda tonight?" I ask. I do not add that my heart may not survive if he leaves.

"If you find me another bed, I will. Anything else would be too tempting, I fear." He bends, kissing me again. The kiss is softer but still filled with a raw emotion.

After showing him to an empty room, I lie on my bed unable to sleep. What would the council do if they knew of the courting? Do I want to give into my base needs as Tin clearly wants to? I warm at the thought of Tin's hands roaming my body, finding places no one else has seen or touched. Tin is right about the needs inside us. If we continue in this way, I will not be able to stop myself from giving into my desires.

Chapter

61

H E PACES THE ROOM, ANGER raging inside his ribcage, beating on the bars to be free. His feet punish the floor with every step. *It was never supposed to be like this. The plan was simple, all I had to do was follow the plan.*

One ruler, like Oberian. One ruler to lead them without discord. One ruler to make all the decisions without all the incessant arguing. One ruler with royal blood in his veins.

He breathes deeply. When that doesn't calm him he crashes his fist into the thick wall. The pain has the opposite of the desired effect, it enrages the beast more.

Damn the woman for not following the plan.

His thoughts effortlessly flow to her death. Days ago he was so sure he would carry out that death. He is still sure he could do it. *But what if there is another way? What if two strong rulers of royal blood could rule together on the throne if that throne was over one United Fraun?*

Could the woman be swayed?

He drops onto the bed behind him, falling to its frame without a second thought. The mantra begins to pulse through his brain.

One Fraun. One Fraun. One Fraun.

He allows the thought to permeate the cloud of anger, sending its droplets back to whence they came.

One Fraun. One Fraun. One Fraun.

Soon, sleep visits, and in his dreams, he holds her in a way he has been denied in life.

Chapter

62

I GRAB A CUP OF TEA in each fist and drag my tired body out of the front door. The sun should be rising soon and training will begin. As I cross the dark yard, enjoying the sight of the lights trapped in the dark expanse of sky, I sip on the tea in my right hand. For the first time in a long time, I wear pants today in preparation for a day of activity. I am hoping it will show the patrol I mean business.

I lower my eyes and take in the sight of King Tin seated on the wall that marks the boundary of my family land. My heart flutters at the sight. "Good morning," I call.

Tin turns in my direction. I can feel his eyes searing my skin. "You look ready to train," he says.

"As do you." I track my own eyes down his chiseled and exposed chest. I have never before seen him without a shirt. I have never seen muscles like that on anyone. I find it hard to focus. It is better than I imagined.

"How did you sleep?" Tin asks as I perch beside him on the wall.

"Well. You?" I take a long sip of my tea and hold the other cup out to the king, which he gladly takes.

"I was a bit distracted by the thoughts of this woman I find myself falling for," he drops the comment lightly as he takes a long sip of the tea.

I blush deeper and change topics. We must remain professional in the presence of the patrol, due to arrive any minute. "Can I ask you something?"

He picks up on the business tone and copies it smoothly, "Anything."

"What benefits befall the king of the first realm during a time of war? I cannot recall the lesson and it's been occupying too much of my time lately."

I cannot see his eyes in the dark, but his lip curls up in a snarl. "I can make decisions for the safety of Fraun without consulting the council."

His age marker scares me even more now that I have experienced my own small preview. I lean back on my arms, putting distance between us. I carefully select my next words. "I only wondered what power you hold that King Mick may be coveting."

"Do you side with him?" His fists clench beside him.

"No," I answer. Suddenly all doubt is gone. I am sure this is the truth. "I do not support a renumbering at this time."

Tin breathes deeply once, twice, three times before his shoulders relax and he has some visible control. My support calmed him. This earns him a kiss on the cheek and a smile just as the patrol rounds the corner of the property.

I stand for the patrol and they form an arc facing us. If any of them are shocked to see the king of strength, they do not show it. Tin keeps his seat on the wall, but he flexes all the muscles in his upper body in an impressive display worthy of his title. The sun is just peeking over the horizon; the men are timely. "Please introduce yourselves, tell which realm you hail from, and explain how you came to be on the patrol," I order.

The first man, short and stocky but with muscles bulging under his thin black shirt, speaks. "I am Daijan from Sarcheda. I earned my place here by holding ten blocks high over my head with no sign of strain." He flexes an impressive bicep at me.

"I am Lance," the next man interrupts this show. "I was selected from Enchenda by my humble queen for being willing to serve all of Fraun above myself." I nod in recognition.

"I am Trep," the next man speaks, "also of Sarcheda. I held ten blocks over my head as well and outlasted all others, save for my counterpart here." The younger man looks to Tin as he speaks, but the king does not show signs he is listening.

My eyes track to the next in line. "Morales here from Marchenda. Selected by Carsen. Who knows why for sure?" The voice drips with disdain, which I was not expecting.

Next to him, a smaller man speaks up. "We can't exactly ask him, is what my friend here means. We can only speculate as to why we were chosen."

"And you are?" I question, turning to the new speaker.

"Vincente, Majesty. I am also from Marchenda."

"Danyel, chosen from Enchenda. I am here to bring a pride to our lovely host here," Danyel speaks up from next in line.

"Charlez here, from Farcheda. I came in second place in our footrace to see who should represent our realm on this patrol. Glad to meet you, Majesty." Another man bows to me.

"I came in first, that's why I'm here. Breth is the name." The voice comes from the far end of the line, skipping a few in between. I nod once at him before returning my eyes back to where we left off in line.

The next is significantly smaller than the others, he smiles at me with a youthful exuberance. "Carthen, Majesty. It's a pleasure to meet your acquaintance."

"Yours as well, Carthen. I assume you hail from Renchenda?" I ask.

"I do. We won a logic competition, my strength being the category of geography. It's my passion," Carthen says.

"My strength is mathematics, lady," the last man states, smiling. This one is light-haired and handsome. "The name's Garven, also Renchenda."

"Well, it's a pleasure to meet you all. I am Eselda," I hesitate before offering my title, little use of it making the word rusty on my tongue, "Queen of Enchenda. It is my job to bring you lessons on being humble." All eyes track me as I pace in front of the group, including those of King Tin who has yet to remove his eyes from my figure.

"Humility is not easy for one to learn. It literally requires you to put all others before yourself, to fight your own instincts to be proud or arrogant. We expect this patrol to be respectful of all in Fraun, to not abuse the power given to you by this position, to understand that you work for all citizens of Fraun at all times. None of you are better than anyone whom you serve." I eye the first man, Daijan, who had flexed his muscles at me. "Despite the fact that many of you won a competition to be here."

Daijan visibly scoffs, making a noise that resembles a snort. Before I can react, Tin is up off the wall and in the face of the man. "You will respect the queen, or you will deal with me. Are we clear?" Tin asks.

I have never heard Tin's voice take on this edge. It is different than when he speaks from the depths of anger. He is fully in control of this situation, commanding respect with his voice. Despite being flustered that he interrupted, I am flattered that he felt the need to protect me.

The act leaves no lingering doubts with the patrol as to why the king of strength is here. Daijan deflates under the presence of his king and bows low. "Yes, Majesty."

Tin eyes the rest of the men as he returns to his place on the wall, offering me a smile once he is seated.

"Well," I stumble, "does anyone have any questions?" Possibly because of the impressive display of anger from my partner, no one speaks. I smile at them. "Alright, then we'll proceed. The plan for today is simple. We are going to travel around Enchenda as a group. Our goal is to complete no less than ten tasks for people in the realm without being asked or forced. If you come upon someone struggling with something, you are to offer to take it or help in some way. This is not about you. Should you expect praise or ask for repayment of any kind, you will not be able to count this act. When, as a team, we have completed ten tasks we can return home for the day." I search the faces. "Are we clear on this?"

"I have one suggestion, Majesty, if I may," Danyel speaks up. I acknowledge him with a wave of my hand. Danyel continues, "I would like to propose that you not count actions you undertake as part of our total." He steps forward, turning to look at the assembled men. "I have watched this woman move about this town, she cannot help herself from stopping to help others. It is her we learn from, so I want you to observe how easily she falls into what she is asking us to do." He turns to face me again. "But I do not believe we should earn our ten acts from things we watch you complete."

"Good point." This time the voice is from the king of strength, who jumps off the wall in one motion. "But you can count anything I do. This is a skill I would like to learn as well."

"Who am I to argue with that idea? Let us away, shall we?" I say.

When we begin walking, Tin and I lead the group. The king of strength pulls a shirt from behind his back and puts it over his head as we walk. I glance over my shoulder, seeing the men all grouped together whispering. "What do you think they discuss?"

Tin turns to take in the sight as well. "I've taught them to discuss strategy in any situation. To analyze the facts they've been given and create an action plan. I'd like to hope that's what they do."

"I notice you decided to put a shirt on."

"I worried you were too distracted," he teases. I laugh. "What is the plan?" he asks, curious. "How can you be sure they will encounter ten people who require help?"

"That's not the task at all, Tin. The task is to help ten people in the midst of completing a chore who could use the help. It would be cheating to wait for someone to ask for your help. All around you on a daily basis, there are people who are completing things that you are cut out to help share the burden of. We hesitate to help them because they are complete strangers or because it is not our struggle and we have our own. A truly humble person would never pass another person who they could help." As I explain, my eyes track to the surrounding village in search of such a person.

Tin stares at me. "You truly are a remarkable person," he says, honesty flooding his every word.

"Thank you," I state. I wish there were a way to adequately express my gratitude.

Our group walks in silence for a little while longer, as the sun continues to climb the sky. I spot a small child struggling to carry a large load of what appears to be potatoes toward a house. Here is a nice easy task for the group to begin with.

We gain ground on the boy quickly, and yet no one makes contact with him. I pause in the road. As I watch, the patrol walks right by me. I clear my throat loudly, earning the head turning of the two men from Renchenda who had been at the back. The surprise moves through the group, each man stopping in his tracks as the message is received. I shake my head, point at the boy, and mouth "watch".

"Good morning, young sir. Could I help you carry those?"

"I'm not going far, Majesty. I'll be alright."

"Nonsense, I'd be honored to help you carry them and to say hello to your mother." I hold my hands out for the potatoes and the boy deposits half his load. I shoot a look of impatience at the patrol.

The look has the effect of sending Danyel and Lance to my side. "Here, Majesty, let me take some of the load," Lance offers. Danyel, for his part, merely puts out his hands and takes a few from the boy. Together the four of us traverse the road in silence carrying the root vegetable.

The patrol, unsure of what they should do and trailing the king of strength behind them, follow. When we reach a house, the little boy drops his load and runs in. "Mother, come see who is here," he says the second he is in the front door.

He returns a few seconds later followed by an older woman who smiles lazily at me before bowing low. "Your Majesty, how can we help you today?"

"We are not here for anything, milady. We simply came to help your son with his load."

"Won't you come in for a drink of water?" the woman offers with a smile.

"Thank you, milady, but we carry water with us." I gesture to the water container I carry, made of leather and strapped to my waist.

"Excuse me, milady," Tin calls, stepping from behind the group. Recognition dawns on the face of the older woman and she blushes deeply as she bows. "I notice you have a shingle there on your roof that has come loose. Might we be of some service with that?"

The woman's eyes track up to the roof the king gestures to. "My, I hadn't even noticed. I don't want to trouble all of you."

Tin turns on all his charm, smiling at the woman. "It's no trouble at all. Keeps these lads busy."

"Well, in that case, be my guest." The woman steps fully outside and sits on the ground, evidently intending to watch the patrol fix her roof. Tin snaps his fingers and the men jump into action. I stand beside the woman and watch them, a smile forming on my face.

"What are all these young men doing in Enchenda anyway?" the woman quizzes.

"They are the new patrol for Fraun, two of them represent Enchenda actually."

"Yes, I recognize young Danyel." At his name, the boy turns and waves a little. "What is this patrol for, exactly? Surely they are for a more important purpose than fixing the roof of an old widow."

I sit down beside the woman. "Actually, this is their purpose. All over Fraun, there are people in need. I am teaching this group to be humble enough to serve Fraun, and those people, above all else."

"Your parents would be proud of your humility, Majesty," the woman says.

"Thank you." We watch in silence as the sun continues to rise a little and the men fix the shingle.

Finally, job done, Daijan approaches. "You are all set, madam." He smiles. "Have a nice day."

Back in the street the men immediately turn to me, "Do we get credit for that one?"

I laugh. "I'll give you credit for the roof since King Tin came up with that on his own. You do not get credit for the potatoes since that one came from me."

"I told you it came naturally to her to find people in need," Danyel tells the group. "We need to be looking for anyone at all completing a task that is too large for them."

"Do not forget what King Tin just taught you as well," I add. "Sometimes it is as simple as finding a small job they haven't yet noticed and offering to fix it first."

"Either way, one down and nine to go," Lance notes. The group heads off toward the town square, this time Tin and I hold up the rear of the group.

"Well done, your Majesty." I smile at my handsome companion. "I am proud of the selfless act you just demonstrated."

"I learned it from you." Tin winks at me and my stomach tumbles in excitement.

By midday, the group has completed six tasks and I am growing ever confident in the patrol. They are demonstrating not only an ease with finding the tasks but also genuine excitement the likes of which can only come from putting people before themselves. There was a small incident when Breth, from Farcheda, asked for a slice of pie cooling nearby in exchange for helping. I let the boys finish the task and enjoy their pie without bursting the bubble. Once they were in the street and calling out, "three done, seven to go" I had set them straight.

"Actually," I had called from the back of the group, "you requested compensation in some form, that one does not count."

The boys had stopped dead in the middle of the road and turned on me. "Why didn't you say something then?" Breth challenged.

"What would have been the point? The gentleman you were helping didn't need to feel as though it was his mistake. I figured I would tell you as soon as I got the opportunity, which I just did."

The boys were not happy about it, but they must have learned the lesson. Now they are back in good spirits, having just helped a few boys retrieve an apple which had rolled under a fence they couldn't climb and earning their sixth task.

I take the opportunity to pull Tin aside. "Do you think you could supervise the last four tasks, Tin?" I ask. "I hardly slept last night and the fatigue catches up with me."

He smiles at me. "It would be my pleasure." He bends in and kisses me on the forehead, not wishing to be caught by the patrol in a more intimate gesture than that. "Sleep well."

In this way it came to pass that I arrive back at the house in Enchenda alone, yawning. "Your Majesty, your mail arrived," a young servant calls. I roll my eyes in frustration and hold out my hands for the parchments. The servant transfers two rolls to me. I take them to my room. Flopping on my bed I stretch the first roll out before me.

Eselda,

I looked into the man you asked me about. Tutor did live here for a while a few annuals back, although I cannot find many who remember him. I can tell you he was one of the top students at our school here. He would be about five annuals older than you, by my calculations. Kind of young to be your tutor, but not unheard of. I will keep digging.

I hope this letter finds you well.
I miss you.
Jordyn

The last sentence stings my eyes briefly. It was his choice to miss me. He had the opportunity to be with me and he has made his choice. In fact, the news about Tutor is really no news at all. This was an excuse to write to me in hopes of a response. I ball the paper up and throw it across my room. I will do no such thing.

I turn my attention to the next parchment.

E,

Thank you for the update. I am terribly sorry to hear about your father. I hope you are well. You know I believe you are ready to be queen. Likely you are doing a remarkable job; I would expect no less.

I will visit soon. I have not forgotten your expectation that I answer a few questions for you.

Respectfully,
Tutor

I drop the parchment to the floor and lay my head on the pillow. With thoughts of a visit from my friend to bring me answers, I sleep.

Chapter

63

TIME PASSES QUICKLY AND BEFORE I fully grasp how much time has passed it is the night before the next scheduled council meeting. I am in Sarcheda, we have just finished another filling meal together and are seated in a room I didn't know about until a few suns ago. The room is large and wide open like a dance hall. There are paintings of the former kings of Sarcheda hanging on the walls. The first time I saw the room I asked what purpose the paintings serve. "To remind us of where we come from," Tin told me.

Now we sit on the floor with a plate of fruit between us for dessert enjoying a comfortable silence. "Do you think they'll do it tomorrow?" Tin asks.

The question catches me off guard, I had been daydreaming about the sight of Tin shirtless as he had been days ago in Enchenda. "What?"

"Call for the renumbering. Do you think they'll do it tomorrow?" Tin repeats.

"I'm not sure. I don't think I can yell at them for fighting and distract them again." I try for a lighthearted tone, but the look on Tin's face tells me it wasn't received as such.

"I just don't know what to do about this," he admits. "I hate that they think I can't handle being the king of the first realm just because of my age. What have I done?"

He has a point. The last fortnight or so has taught me a lot about the king. His anger, when it is real, is scary and dark. But it can be helped. Even if it still scares me to try. I reach for his arm now, calmly rubbing it to let him know I am there. "You're a good king. They have no reason not to trust you. They base their accusations on fear and speculation. Do you know which way the other kings will vote?"

He groans. "Larecio votes with Mick. You vote with me. Our wildcard is your man, Jordyn." The angry eyes turn on me, sparking dangerously.

This is when he is the hardest to tame; when the anger is directed at me. I swallow the ball of fear. "My man? Nothing about him is mine," I state forcefully. I swallow again, adopt a smoother tone. "I know not which way he will vote either."

"You act as though you have no contact with him."

"I don't. I haven't spoken to him since the last council meeting. There's nothing to say." My voice, and my own anger, rise in defense.

"You don't write?"

The accusation is lobbed like a bomb, ready to throw me off my game. I see it coming for what it is and pull my hand away from the king. "He writes to me. I have not responded."

Tin stands and leans over me. "Are you lying to me?"

The anger in his eyes is at a new level, one that has me completely unhinged. "No, Tin. I am not lying." Perhaps the honesty will help to defuse him.

Seeing that attempt fail, I rise in a show of strength he will appreciate and close the remaining gap between us in two small steps. I reach for him, wrapping my hand around his neck and pulling him down toward me. He could stop me if he wanted. I would be powerless against his strength. Tin allows himself to be pulled into the kiss.

Tin wraps his arms around my waist and gives into the short kiss. When we pull apart I see the anger dying down in his expression. "I love you," he whispers, hoarsely.

I recover quickly from my shock. "I love you, too."

This time, when the kiss heats up quickly neither of us pulls away.

"Eselda..." he whispers my name against my lips even as his hands continue to roam over my back. "...come to my room."

My eyes widen with the shock of the comment. He is asking, not telling. I tell myself to think it through, but my body has already decided. I nod and allow myself to be lead to his room.

Once the door is closed we fall to the bed. I feel the weight of his strength as he balances just above me. We resume kissing with fervor. I run my fingers over the muscles that have occupied my fantasies for a fortnight. Tin slips his shirt over his head, breaking the kiss only long enough to do it.

I feel his hands reaching for the hem of my skirt. It is this act that brings me to my senses. I try to sit up. "Tin, wait." I can see the struggle on his face as he pulls himself away from me, laying on the bed beside me. "I don't know if we should..." I trail off, the point pretty clear.

Tin nods. When he says nothing else, I swing my legs toward the side of the bed. I should go.

I feel his hand wrap around my wrist, squeezing. "Stay," he commands.

"But, we shouldn't--"

"Then we won't." He meets my eyes. "Just stay."

In his eyes, I see his struggle. He has it under control. I lay beside him, my head resting on his shoulder. He wraps his arm around me and pulls me close, turning to rest his chin in my hair. I close my eyes and let myself relax. It's not long before sleep overtakes us both.

Chapter

64

Back in Enchenda, the small princess sits on her large bed alone late at night. She hasn't been sleeping well lately. Likely this is due to the large stretches of time she has been spending alone. *Eselda is often gone in Sarcheda. When she is here, he is here too.*

I wish I could explain what it is about King Tin that I don't like, Sawchett thinks. *It's nothing concrete, nothing he's done or said. It's just a feeling I get around him. He makes me uncomfortable even when he is going out of his way to be nice. I can't exactly tell Eselda how I feel. She would never understand. He seems to make her so happy.*

But the queen is awfully angry when he's not around. I caught her losing her temper with the servants. Then there was the time I left the door open and she screamed at me. Of course, she did apologize later. It's just not quite the same as I thought it would be. Perhaps it's my own fault. Who wouldn't feel the stress of another mouth to feed and another body to clothe? Eselda has always been allowed to live a careless lifestyle and worry only about herself. Maybe her anger is with me, but she is afraid to admit that.

The other thing that keeps the young girl awake tonight is the council. They meet tomorrow and Eselda intends to tell them of Sawchett.

Eselda intends to inform them that she will announce me to the realm in the near future. Tin says they will not argue with Eselda but I doubt that. Who would not argue the presence of a child that appears out of nowhere already eight annuals old? It's just strange.

Sawchett sighs and flops her blonde head around on her pillow in search of a more comfortable position.

Perhaps life would've been simpler if I'd never known I was royal blood.

Chapter

65

T HE JOURNEY TO THE COUNCIL meeting is quite a different affair today. Normally, I travel alone on the back of a roach to the center of the Fraun where the council building rests. But King Tin's home in Sarcheda is closer to the building than my own home, so we walk.

It's probably unwise to hold hands with Tin as we walk through town. People in Sarcheda could see us. But no one is outside. So we hold hands, making me hyper-aware of each finger threaded through Tin's. I haven't seen a flash of anger out of him all morning. I know he dreads the coming meeting and must be harboring some anger. Why does he shield me from it? Perhaps the more important question, how does he contain it?

He holds my hand until the building is in sight. Then, he offers it a squeeze before dropping it. "Unless you want the council to see us as a courting couple?" he asks.

Is he leaving the decision to me? I think it through. Mick will be angry. This makes me want to grab the hand again. Jordyn will be angry. This makes me want to kiss Tin right in the middle of the meeting. Larecio will be hurt. It is this thought that makes me shake my head, no. "Not today, my love. That is business for another day. Today is about you leading your council as best you can."

"Today is also about Sawchett," he says.

"True. Today Enchenda gets an heir to the throne."

Chapter

*T*HE PLAN IS SIMPLE. ESELDA will tell the council about the girl first, to soften up the old kings. *They will be pleased that there is a future for Enchenda.* Then Tin fully expects the question of renumbering to be mentioned. He has already taken the liberty to contact Mick and tell him what will happen if he brings that up, but you can never be sure if the old man received the message. Besides, Larecio may yet call for it as well. *That remains to be seen.* Either way, there are things to discuss. It would certainly work in favor of Tin's plan if the council was feeling the stress and fear of something pending. So he has an issue he wants to bring forth as well.

He looks to Eselda, she wears the customary green expected of her for the meeting and he dons threads of red. But they have conceded to wear the colors of each other's realms in a silent show of support. Eselda wears a red ribbon holding her hair back. He wears a pin of green on his lapel. *Likely no one will notice, but it keeps the woman happy.*

Tin has to admit she is beautiful. He has not lied about being in love with her, that feeling came out of nowhere and surprised even him. He has been spending every day with her, but she doesn't know everything about him. *Would she be able to love me if she knew everything?* Despite his desire to not care what she thinks, the thought bothers him. He shakes it off.

As they approach the building, Tin notices Jordyn approaching from the right. He rides a bug of some sort and moves quickly. He feels Eselda change. *Lately, that has been happening a lot. The queen is approaching twenty annuals.* Her shoulders tighten, her jaw locks, and her eyes grow dark like a field of grass suddenly cast into shadow. He reaches out and brushes the back of her hand, but earns no response.

Tin shakes his head. *I knew this was a possibility. You'd have to be an idiot not to notice Jordyn is one of her triggers. There is something there. You can try to hide it from me, Eselda, but you are a terrible liar. Stew in your anger, perhaps it will turn out good for our cause.*

Jordyn stands on the steps, apparently waiting for them as they approach. "Did you come together?" he asks. His eyes are locked on Eselda.

Eselda meets the gaze of the king of wisdom, holds them for a second, and then enters the room without a word. Tin takes in her show of strength feeling pride and the exuberance that can only come from being the one chosen. Jordyn looks to Tin, expecting an answer from him instead.

"I couldn't let the lady walk the path alone," Tin answers, stepping through the door.

Jordyn follows them into the building and takes his seat. A quick glance around the room tells him he was the last to arrive.

Tin bangs a gavel on the table. "I call this meeting of the council of kings and queens to order. Does anyone have new business to discuss?" he calls out, his voice booming with authority.

"I do," Eselda says, following the plan.

Tin watches her. The anger continues to radiate off her in dangerous waves. *For this reason, no one will challenge her in this business today.*

"The council should be aware that an underage girl has been found to have royal blood in her veins. Her parents have passed and I have decided to raise her in my home and groom her to be a princess." She looks to Mick. "I'm sure that calms your fear about the future of Enchenda?" Eselda asks.

Jordyn is first to recover from the surprise. "You are letting her live in your home?"

The look Eselda gives to Jordyn, Tin notes, *can only be described as one of contempt.* He rubs her knee, attempting to calm the obvious anger. *Should a renumbering be called today we need Jordyn on our side.*

"Yes, do you challenge that?" Eselda asks.

Chapter

67

JORDYN RECOILS FROM THE WORDS and the hatred that spews from Eselda. He has only the strength to shake his head, no. The meeting continues on around him but Jordyn cannot focus on it. Fear clenches his throat, constricting his breathing. *Tin and Eselda arrived together, which cannot be good news. Is it a coincidence that Tin wears a green lapel pin?*

Eselda turns to look at Tin, offering him a smile for something he has said. Jordyn notes a red ribbon affixed at the base of her braid. *Not a good omen.* Jordyn's anger bubbles. *So it wasn't a coincidence then that the words Eselda offered me just now echoed the words of Tin after the last council meeting.* The monster rages and Jordyn allows it to consume him.

Chapter

68

O N EITHER SIDE OF HIM, the anger pours out. For a second, although he would not admit it to anyone, Tin is actually scared. He looks from one to the other, in awe of the communications passing between the two of them although they are not speaking. He decides to take this opportunity to broach a new topic, perhaps his young companions will calm themselves before any renumbering is brought up.

"I would like to propose a capacity law to the council," Tin says.

"For what purpose?" Larecio questions. The man is unrecognizable from his former self. His hair has turned a deeper shade of gray since their last meeting, he is gaunt, and his face clearly shows that he is out of cares for these decisions.

Why does he even bother to interject into this conversation? "There are more births than deaths every time I am updated. I grow nervous for the time when our food runs out," Tin says.

"Are you running low on food in Sarcheda?" challenges Mick. "We have the same problem with births to deaths but our food remains intact."

Tin looks beside him to the one person who could answer this question as well as he could. She continues to fume in her own anger.

He turns his attention back to Mick "I do have a shortage. We are having trouble feeding everyone." The lie slips into the room undetected.

Fear crosses the old man's face. "Truly?"

"Did you doubt this would happen? We feed ten more people every time I turn around. The numbers grow in leaps and bounds," Tin says.

"What would this capacity law entail, exactly?" Mick asks, entertaining the thought.

"One child per family."

"What of the families, like my own, who already have more than one?" Mick challenges.

"This will be a new law. I'm not a monster, Mick. Anyone already with a child can proceed to have their infant. This will affect only those who are not yet bringing infants into this world."

"See here, it's not the business of this council to tell people how many babies they should have," Larecio booms. "Jordyn, surely you see this for the foolishness it is."

Tin looks to his right noticing the king of wisdom is deep in the throes of agony now. His hands grip the table as though it is parchment he can tear in half. His dark eyes continue to stare down Eselda. *Jordyn cannot answer you right now, I'm afraid.*

"It's not illogical, Larecio." Tin keeps his voice even and calm. "I'm merely afraid that without such a law we will likely run out of food soon. Imagine if this isn't followed, where would that put us in ten annuals of growth like we've seen? Do you have the food for that many? Do you have the housing for that many?" Tin sees the fear register in Mick's face and has to bite his cheek to keep the smile from showing.

"Maybe it's not such a bad idea, Larecio," Mick says in a lower voice, head turned toward the old man. "Perhaps it's an issue we can side with the young king on."

"Fine. Call the vote, Tin," Larecio yells, shaking his head.

Tin pinches the leg of both royals on either side of him as he calls out. "Those in favor of the capacity law, limiting all to one child per household except in cases where more than one already exists, say aye."

Chapter

69

I COME TO ATTENTION AT THE pinch and give Tin a strange look. What is going on? I listen as Tin calls for a vote. Oh no, what are we voting on? I notice the almost imperceptible nod of his head. He is helping me. My heart soars with gratitude. "Aye," I call, fishing under the table for his hand and squeezing it.

Chapter

70

JORDYN WANTS TO SMACK THAT smug smile off Tin's face. He hears the law called out for a vote, he hears all four of the other royals vote in favor. *I refuse to vote.*

"Let it be known that Renchenda doesn't vote in favor but will still adhere to the law," Tin says.

Jordyn grinds his teeth. "So be it," he mumbles.

Chapter

71

"ANY OTHER NEW BUSINESS TO discuss?" Tin asks. When no one says anything, Tin offers a small smile to Eselda. *They heeded my warnings,* Tin thinks. "Then I call this meeting adjourned. See you all in another lunar cycle."

Eselda immediately leaves her seat and jogs out of the building. Larecio is not far behind her. Mick takes his time gathering his things and heading to the antechamber. Before following, Tin steals a quick glance to be sure Jordyn is still locked in anger.

Chapter

72

MANY MINUTES PASS IN THE silent room. Jordyn fears he will not get the beast under control again, ever. He tries to think of Eselda, which has always calmed him before, but he can only call up images of her with Tin. He shakes his head.

No, no. I will not lose control.

He slams his hands down on the table, the anger burning his lungs.

Control. Control.

A capacity law? What is his game? Intending to catch the king and ask him, Jordyn finally rises from the chair and heads to the antechamber. He is almost to the door when he hears voices. He slows to decipher who they belong to.

"I didn't call it, calm yourself."

That voice is Mick. Jordyn leans closer to the doorframe.

"I just wanted to be sure that you knew I was serious about what I wrote in that letter," says Tin.

The anger flares again. Jordyn has to stop himself from bursting through the door and starting a fight he surely couldn't win.

"I got the message," Mick says.

"Good. You just be sure you don't forget. If you should change your mind and decide to threaten my seat with a renumbering, I'll just use the army you've provided me with and call for a war."

"I didn't give you that army, I gave Fraun a patrol." Mick tries to sound confident. It falls flat.

"Yet I'm the only one who has trained them, aren't I?" Tin laughs and the sound sends chills up Jordyn's spine.

"Hasn't Eselda had her time with them?" Mick asks.

Tin laughs harder. "I've offered to help her train them. The army is loyal to me and me alone."

Jordyn hears footsteps moving away from the doorway. He risks a glance and sees Tin heading for the door. When Tin suddenly turns on his heel Jordyn barely has time to pull his head back in the door.

"Oh, and Mick..." Tin calls out, obviously not noticing Jordyn, "...If you get it in your head to tell the council about this meeting I'll kill you just like I killed that damn prince." The laughter follows Tin outside and leaves Jordyn frozen in place.

The anger fades completely until Jordyn is consumed by his fear. He drops to the floor and puts his head on his knees. His hands shake and his mind rolls.

Tin controls the council, Tin controls the patrol.

Does Tin control Eselda?